THERE'S NO PLACE
LIKE HOME

JANE LOVERING

Boldwood

First published in Great Britain in 2023 by Boldwood Books Ltd.

Copyright © Jane Lovering, 2023

Cover Design by Debbie Clement Design

Cover Photography: Shutterstock

A CIP catalogue record for this book is available from the British Library.

Paperback ISBN 978-1-80415-242-3

Large Print ISBN 978-1-80415-243-0

Hardback ISBN 978-1-80415-241-6

Ebook ISBN 978-1-80415-244-7

Kindle ISBN 978-1-80415-245-4

Audio CD ISBN 978-1-80415-236-2

MP3 CD ISBN 978-1-80415-238-6

Digital audio download ISBN 978-1-80415-240-9

Boldwood Books Ltd
23 Bowerdean Street
London SW6 3TN
www.boldwoodbooks.com

This book is dedicated to Lin Chadwick (Hawkins) 1960–2022. We grew up one road apart and used to joke about being one another's 'oldest' friends. She was a great supporter of my writing and books and had the best laugh of anyone I've ever known. We didn't see one another much latterly, but when we did it was as though we'd never been apart. She is much missed.

This Week's TV – Channel Listings Magazine
Tonight: UK Wildlife Channel 9.30pm
New Series *Hunting the Hidden*

Four teams of members of the public, each with a Celebrity Tracker, searching for mysterious giant cats around the UK. Each team is living wild in the surrounding countryside and filming themselves as they search for evidence, which will be evaluated by experts back in the studio.
With £50,000 prize money for scientific proof, and £250,000 for a captured animal to be won, expect competitive sightings and mistaken identities galore!

1

The rain dripped through the tent roof and plopped disconsolately onto the nylon beneath. We were all already so wet that nobody paid it any attention, but we shifted occasionally to keep out of the rapidly forming puddle in the middle of the groundsheet. At last, the girl who'd complained really loudly during the five-mile walk across the moors and whose make-up was beginning to come off in patches, leaving her with uneven eyebrows, said, 'I thought it would be like *Love Island*.'

She sounded on the verge of tears. The man sitting next to her patted her arm briefly. 'If it's any consolation,' he said, 'I didn't really read the description either. I'd envisaged sitting in a comfortable hide somewhere. With coffee.'

I looked around at the assorted collection of soggy humanity in the tent with me. We were three women and two men; all of us wearing almost all the clothes we possessed under the provided 'waterproofs', which weren't, huge boots covered in mud and expressions ranging from the 'mildly cheated' to 'about to sue'.

'I wish this so-called celebrity would show up.' Another man. He'd turned off his body-cam and microphone, I noticed. We were supposed to keep them on 24/7, unless asleep or going to the toilet, although there was very little to choose between this tent and lavatorial activities, when I looked at it. Damp trousers either way. 'Then maybe we could get something to eat.'

'I hope we get Bear Grylls.' Odd-eyebrow girl produced a mirror and began repairing her face. Her accent was so sharply upper-class that she could have used it to cut her way out of the tent. 'It would be the only thing that could make this worthwhile.'

'That and the quarter of a mill we win.' This was 'Coffee in a Hide' Man.

'Should...' I began cautiously, and everyone turned to look at me, rain-soaked hair flicking so that the inside of the tent pattered with more water. 'Should we introduce ourselves? If we're going to be stuck together in tents for the next few weeks on these moors, we should at least know the names of our fellow captives.' I smiled, trying for a weak joke to lighten the atmosphere. 'I'm Izzy, short for Isabel. I'm from York and I saw the ad for the new reality show and wrote in. I didn't really care what happened from there on.'

I looked expectantly at the man to my left, the one who'd turned his comms off. He gave me a slightly dirty look as though I'd put him on an unexpected spot, but unless he wanted to be known as Camera-Off Man for the next month, he didn't have much of a choice. 'My name's McKinley,' he muttered. 'From Glasgow.' He didn't tell us what he'd expected from the chirpy ad, but he did look as though fame and fortune were not his primary goal.

Eyebrow-woman was called Kanga, although I very much doubted that was her real name. We already knew about the *Love Island* expectations, and a very great deal more about life in a big house in Notting Hill with a million handbags and large disposable income than we could ever want to know. On my other side, a quiet and very young-looking girl who'd said nearly nothing so far introduced herself as Ruth. 'I just wrote in asking if they had anything I could be on,' she said sadly. 'I didn't really think it through, did I?'

This left the remaining man. He'd been talkative during our hike, and had put himself in charge of the map-reading which had got us here to these ready-pitched tents on this wind-flapped stretch of the North York Moors. He seemed capable and practical, and his face, under his

Sherpa-style hat, was weather-beaten and brown. He looked slightly older than the rest of us. 'I'm Sebastian,' he said. 'I'm a farmer from Sussex and, as I said, I didn't quite realise what this was going to involve.' He glanced around the group. 'I think we're all wondering what has hit us, aren't we?'

We all went quiet again. I remembered the email that had come as a reply to my request for information on the show.

Hi Izzy!
We're starting out filming a new game slash reality show next autumn – adventure and exploration and the chance to win a massive cash prize! If you'd be interested, please get in contact, sending your name, age, a little bit about yourself and a head and shoulders picture to ABCAdventures@gmail.com
Dax Williams

Yes, they'd actually written 'game slash reality' instead of punctuating it. That should have tipped me off to the type of thing I was dealing with. But then, I was desperate.

I looked around again. From their expressions, backs hunched against the wet fabric of the tent, the others were also recalling that they'd been promised adventure and exploration and that, on the evidence so far, those particular elements had been oversold to us. The likely trench-foot, dysentery and the opportunity to be knifed to death by one of our fellow participants had, by the looks of it, been *undersold* to an almost criminal degree.

'I don't suppose...' Ruth said cautiously, 'that there's any chance that we could just go back and say we've changed our minds?'

Another silence, into which the rain plopped and the outside of the tent shivered as a breeze ran past on its way to somewhere more salubrious.

'We signed something, I think,' I said, when nobody else had anything to contribute. 'To say we accepted their conditions?'

At this point, everyone started to talk at once.

'...didn't know it was going to be like *this*!'

'...will be fine once the rain stops and we settle down.'

'The money will come in useful, I mean, at least they're paying us to *be* here...'

'Bear Grylls better turn up soon, they wouldn't let me bring my make-up case and I've only got a spoonful of cover-up left! I've got a *lovely* place in Notting Hill and I wouldn't have come, only my agent told me this would be the quickest way into a presenting job!'

McKinley from Glasgow, I noticed, didn't say anything. He'd got his knees under his chin in an attempt to keep his boots out of the rapidly increasing puddle in the centre of the tent, and he looked disgruntled to the point that his gruntle might be waving farewell forever.

I smiled at him. 'Nothing to add?' I asked.

He turned a look on me that was so sour I could feel my tongue dry out. 'You're the cheerleader then, are you?' he said. 'There's always one Pollyanna. Going to tell us it's not as bad as it could be?'

'Izzy's only being pleasant.' This was Sebastian, who'd taken off his Sherpa hat now to reveal blond hair standing in points. 'She's right, we're going to have to exist together and rely on one another to get through this. There's no point in being rude for the sake of it.'

McKinley averted his gaze. 'Yeah,' he said. 'Sorry.' But he wasn't looking at me and he didn't sound as though he really meant it.

My heart had dropped. Yes, actually, I *had* been about to point out that at least we had tents and we'd be heading to our permanent camp site tomorrow, where we'd been promised food and a proper toilet; it might be raining but at least it wasn't snow or frost and we were being paid to be here, to say nothing of the putative prize money if we managed to find evidence of some kind of what Dax had called 'an anomalous creature'. Quite frankly, it *could* have been worse, and I didn't think that made me a twinkly starshine girl, just realistic.

At that moment, there was the sound of a vehicle outside and we all leaped to our feet and started trying to look like a bunch of reality TV contestants rather than wet, cold and tired campers.

Kanga consulted her mirror again, then snapped it away. 'Do you really think we'll get Bear Grylls?' I asked her, as we filed our way out through the tent flap.

'How many trackers who are celebrities *are* there?' She pulled down the zip at the front of her jacket. At a guess, she was used to doing this to flash her cleavage; all she was showing was a down-filled gilet, but the thought was there.

Outside the tent there was still a lot of rain. The sky was leaden and didn't seem filled with the promise of sunny frolics, and beyond the camp was a Jeep. In the Jeep was Dax, who was the man behind the show. He leapt out, all legs and expensive waterproofs. With him were a cameraman, who'd been briefly introduced to us back in Leeds as Callum, and a sound man who seemed to go by Steve. I was beginning to realise why the introductions had been brief, presumably Dax hadn't wanted them to let any details slip in case we ran away en masse.

'Oh, good, you're all here!' he trilled. I wasn't sure whether he'd expected us to have walked off or hidden from him, but given the conditions, it would have been a fair assumption. 'Any questions so far?'

Ruth put her hand up, cautiously. 'Um. Dax, is... well... is this *it*?'

'It?' Dax looked baffled inside his enormously fluffy down-filled hood, from which his face protruded past the tightly fastened toggle. He was wearing big, round-framed glasses, so the effect was that of being addressed by an owl in an anorak. 'Well, yes. The premise of the show, as I think we've gone over, is that you're all out here looking for evidence of anomalous creatures, big cats, that sort of thing.' He looked around our spartan site once more. 'You have to carry all your things, you see. Move from place' – he indicated with his hands, as though we were all unfamiliar with the concept of motion – 'to place. D'you see? Carrying your things? Whilst tracking?'

Another grim silence resulted. Whilst the premise of the show hadn't exactly indicated five-star hotel rooms and spa treatments, the element of deprivation conjured by the tent, the rain and the gear hadn't, I was fairly sure, been covered in sufficient detail. The five of us huddled closer together. Darkness was beginning to crayon its way around the edges of the moor, and the early November wind was sharp. We were wet, cold, hungry and tired and I hoped that Dax wasn't readying a pep talk because we were likely to rush him and steal the keys to the Jeep.

Callum shouldered his camera nervously. He was young, and looked as though this might be his first real job that didn't involve burgers.

'Anyway. I've brought you your tracker,' Dax carried on, a little uncertainly. 'Everyone, I'd like you to meet Bo "Junior" Acassi!'

Another man peeled himself out of the Jeep. He was enormously tall, wearing only a T-shirt which showed off tattoos a little darker than his skin, and army trousers tucked into calf-high laced-up boots. His head was shaved to a shiny baldness and he looked as though he'd have been more at home gunning down insurgents with an AK-47 than camping out in the moors of North Yorkshire.

'Hi,' we all chorused. Except McKinley, who was still silent.

'Junior is a very well-known tracker in the US,' Dax was talking quickly, 'where he hosts a show tracking Bigfoot for one of the cable channels.'

I wondered if he was talking fast to try to distract us from thinking about what made a celebrity. I had certainly never watched any 'cable channel Bigfoot programmes' and, from the expressions on my fellow captives' faces, neither had they.

Junior raised a hand in greeting. I watched Kanga stare at his muscles. They were improbably large; he looked as though someone had taken an ordinary man and inflated him with a bike pump in strategic areas. 'Hi,' he said, his voice so deep as to be practically infrasound. 'I'm looking forward to tracking this here big cat of yours.'

'Yes, well, we don't *actually* know that there's a big cat,' Dax, looking flustered, went on, still speaking fast. 'That's the point of the show, you see. We've got groups all over the country trying to find proof; there's a group on Bodmin Moor, looking for the Beast of Bodmin, and one up in the Highlands of Scotland, and another in Cannock Chase – all places where out of place animals have been sighted recently. The show revolves around you all *finding* that evidence.' He sounded as though he'd been pitching that idea in the same combination of words for so long that he was parroting it without really thinking about what it meant.

For us, out here in on the moors, it evidently meant wet, mud and misery. We shuffled about in a discontented way like a herd of cows seeing the vet on the horizon, but nobody actually *said*, 'Who's going to watch a bunch of people getting rained on and arguing and not finding anything?'

Compared to some of the game shows currently on TV, this was practically genius-level viewing.

'Plus, there's the whole social element.' Dax loosened a toggle and reached a hand inside his enormously insulated coat to push hair back under the hood. 'This is why we've asked you to keep your cameras and microphones on at all times. People will be *fascinated* watching a group of such disparate people trying to cooperate and establish their positions within the group. I'm seeing it as a sort of *Big Brother* meets *Love Island*.' He did the 'choppy thing' with his hands again. 'With elements of *Survival of the Fittest*. You see,' he finished, now sounding slightly desperate.

Steve coughed and adjusted the boom mic.

'With enormous overtones of *Lord of the Flies*.' This was McKinley, speaking for practically the first time without being spoken to first. His gruntle was still not in evidence.

'Yes, well, that's up to you, isn't it?' Dax said, waspishly. 'And, Mac, turn your camera back on for the love of god, we can all see that your live feed isn't enabled.'

Looking as though he would happily club Dax to death with a tent peg, Mac grumpily groped about inside his jacket and the little light showing he was recording blinked on his shoulder.

'Right, I'll leave you all to get to know one another then.' Dax began shuffling towards the Jeep, without turning his back on us. Perhaps he assumed that Mac really *would* attempt murder if he didn't keep an eye on him. 'And then tomorrow you can start out over the moors. We're setting up the camp site now and we'll send the coordinates tomorrow morning, unless, of course, Junior picks up the track of an animal in the meantime.'

'Tomorrow?' Sebastian's head came up. 'What do we eat tonight then?'

Dax's retreat got faster. 'Er. I think there may be basic supplies in your packs?'

We all looked towards the rucksacks we'd been given. They lay in a damp pile outside the tent and were not giving off 'four-course dinner' vibes. By the time we all looked up again, Dax, Callum and Steve were speeding away in the Jeep, only visible because the lights were bouncing their way across the moor. It was almost completely dark, and raining again.

'Well, that's a bit of a bugger,' Sebastian said. 'I was at least hoping that they'd send us in someone to cook.'

Everyone chimed in here with their own expectations and it became evident that we'd all been fed different stories about what the living environment would be whilst we were tracking the, probably mythical, animals. Kanga had been told there would be 'accommodation provided', from which she had deduced that there would be guest houses, hot showers and comfortable beds. Ruth and Sebastian thought that 'all needs catered for' meant that we'd be bussed to a nearby town when filming finished, to hotels. Mac, once again, didn't say anything and I had to admit that I hadn't really thought about it. Someone had mentioned paying us £100 per day whilst we were out here and then they'd dangled the prize money, and I would have agreed to sleep in a cave wrapped in leaves for a chance at that.

'We'd better eat,' rumbled Junior. 'Gonna be a long day tomorrow.'

Nobody asked how he knew this. I think we'd had all our ability to question anything squashed under the insistent rain and the amount of mud that clung to our boots and doubled our bodyweight.

Happy campers we were not.

After a few moments wrangling the baggage, Sebastian, who seemed to have become our de facto leader, in his own head if nowhere else, wrenched out a small primus stove and some packets of what looked horribly like dehydrated animal feed. He sent Kanga and Ruth to fetch some water from the stream we could hear rushing its ominous way past the campsite, whilst he and Junior assembled the food and Mac and I were designated In Charge of The Primus and told to light the stove and get it going somewhere out of the wind. 'But not inside the tent,' Sebastian said sternly. 'People can die from carbon monoxide inhalation that way.'

Mutinously and showing all the team-working ability of a bunch of cats, we each set off on our allocated tasks. Mac and I dragged the primus round the back of the tent, where the wind was slightly less omnipresent and a small tree kept the worst of the rain off.

'So, how do you come to be out here with us?' I asked him, holding up one of the provided torches so he could see to set the stove up. In deference to having been accused of 'cheerleading', I tried not to sound as though I cared about his reply.

Which was just as well, because there wasn't one. Mac ignored me totally, other than grabbing the torch to direct the beam more closely in while he fiddled with a knob. There was a hiss of gas, a spark as he lit a match, and the primus flamed into feeble life.

'It's hardly going to make riveting viewing if we don't find anything to track, though, is it?' I continued, talking to his back now as he rummaged around to find the frame to stand the food containers on over the flame. 'A bunch of people blundering around the moors?'

I might as well not have been there for all the notice he took. He turned a few more knobs and the height of the flame went up and down, then, evidently satisfied, he set the frame over the apparatus and sat back on his heels, holding his hands out to the warmth of the fire. His absorption in the task annoyed me.

'Look, we don't have to like each other, but if we're going to be stuck out here, the least you can do is be vaguely polite,' I snapped. 'I don't know if you're trying to cast yourself as the mean and moody one of the group, but I've seen enough reality TV to know that making yourself unpopular does not go down well with the audience.'

There was another moment's silence, broken only by the hiss and rush of the flame and the distant sounds of Kanga and Ruth getting wet down in the stream. Then, to my surprise, Mac turned around and stood up. He did it quickly too, with a grace that was unexpected in someone wearing so many clothes that their arms stuck out sideways.

'Yeah,' he said, still sounding fed up. 'You're right. Sorry. I'm just hugely pissed off at being here at all.'

I stared at what I could see of him. The low gas flame didn't illuminate much more than his boots. 'Well, fine, but I don't think any of us are composing a song and dance routine about it. And surely you signed yourself up for this?'

Mac sighed. 'No. No, I didn't.' He took off the beanie hat that covered most of his head, and ran a hand through his hair. 'I got co-opted. Dax is my brother, you see. One of the men that was meant to be part of your team suddenly had to drop out and it was too late to put someone else through the vetting procedures and Dax – well, let's say he brought family pressure to bear on me. Hence...' He shrugged and pulled the hat back on. 'This is *not* my idea of a great holiday,' he said dismally.

'I don't think it's *anyone's* idea of any kind of holiday,' I said, reasonably.

'There you go again, with the cheerful.' But he sounded as if he was smiling as he said it this time. 'So why are you here? What made Mrs Upbeat decide to fester away in this mud-soaked hellhole?'

The flame flickered and spat. Somewhere behind us, Sebastian and Junior were muttering about the food. Well, Sebastian was, Junior was probably talking but his deep bass was just uprooting trees and diverting river courses.

'I need the money,' I said, deciding that prevarication wouldn't do me any favours. 'I want to rent somewhere to live and there's no family money for a deposit and I don't earn enough to ever save up what's needed. I want...' I tailed off. My camera and microphone were still on and I didn't want to go into gut-wrenching detail for the viewers. Enough of them would, hopefully, empathise with the basic desire for somewhere to live. 'There's nothing lost if we don't find any evidence, though.' I tried for 'cheerful within reasonable and comprehensible boundaries'.

At that point, Ruth and Kanga arrived with a container of water. 'I had to go *into the stream* for this,' Kanga said, in the same tones as one might announce that they had had to fly to Vancouver.

'It was too muddy nearer the edges.' Ruth sounded a lot more practical. I thought I probably liked her, but the jury was still out on Kanga. 'We used to go camping with the church youth group. I remembered that you're supposed to take the water from where it's flowing fastest.'

'Oh, thank god,' said Sebastian. 'Someone who knows about camping.'

'Amen,' Ruth said, and it sounded as though she meant it.

'I don't think you understand.' Kanga shook a booted foot at us. 'I am *wet*.'

Mac looked around. We were now all grouped tightly around the feeble warmth of the primus flame, clearly not being filled with gastronomic delight at the sight of the foil dishes of grit-and-turnip which appeared to comprise our supper. 'Wet seems to be fitted as standard,' he said, rather grimly. 'I don't think your feet are special.'

'Well, I'm going to change.' And with that, Kanga stomped off towards the tiny sleeping tent that was meant to be occupied by the three of us women, but was only going to work if none of us snored or stretched beyond a foetal position.

For the first time, I seriously began to wonder what I'd got myself involved in. I needed money, but I was beginning to think that even pole dancing in the local topless bar would have been better than this. I didn't know any of these people, yet here I was looking down the barrel of spending a month in their company, whilst soaked, cold and with mud drying my skin to prickly irritation. I had thought all reality shows were full of people in swimwear and Botox, prancing around in picturesque places and I'd never seriously considered I'd be a contender, but it had seemed like a gamble worth taking. Any swimwear out here would be swiftly followed by hypothermia and a trip to the local hospital. Where, I had to concede, at least it would be warm, indoors and the food would be edible.

'Here.' Sebastian poked a foil container my way. 'I'm not sure what it is, but it's warm and – well, actually, it isn't anything else. But eat it anyway, all right?'

In a sullen little huddle, we all sat on a groundsheet under the branches of the overhanging tree, which dripped its cheerless plops of water around us, as we ate in silence. Over at the tents, an occasional bulge of canvas or muffled swear word told us that Kanga was still getting changed. What she was changing *into*, bearing in mind we'd been told to wear as many of our clothes as possible to save carrying them, I didn't like to think. It probably wasn't going to be 'a charming and helpful person'.

The food tasted mostly of dehydrated boiled swede, but I'd lived with cold chips and leftovers for long enough to wolf it down without smelling it or letting it touch my tongue. The true horror of my situation was beginning to dawn on me. *This is it. For a month.*

To distract myself, I turned to Junior, who was squatting next to me, efficiently scooping the inedible meal into his mouth. 'So, you're a Bigfoot hunter? That must be interesting.' Oh, good grief. Cheerleader had been bad enough, now I'd come over all gracious and royal as though only the crumpled foil container in my hand was preventing me from waving.

'I guess,' Junior said, and the tree shook more water down on us. He went back to eating, clearly a man of few words, and I didn't bother trying to squeeze any more out of him. I didn't really feel like conversation either, to be fair. I was tired and disorientated and all the other things that came with being dumped on a moorland in the rain. Even my usual optimism had vanished. It had probably dissolved.

Ruth took a container of food over to the tent and poked it through the flap. 'Here's some food for you, Kanga,' she said, averting her eyes to the extent that I wondered if Kanga was naked in there.

A muttered reply and then a long bare arm came out, took the food, and retreated back inside the tent.

'She says she's going to bed,' Ruth reported, returning to us. 'And doesn't want to be woken.'

'Unless we teleport in, I think she is very much going to be woken,' I said, slightly bitterly, and I heard Mac make a sound like a muffled laugh, which he covered by scrunching up his foil dish and putting it in the bag we'd designated for the rubbish.

'Cheerfulness beginning to wear off, is it?' he muttered to me, as I collected the dropped forks to put in the bag as well. 'That didn't take long.'

'No, I'm still cheerful,' I whispered back. 'I'm just realistic.'

'So, you're realistic, and yet you're on a show where we're hunting for panthers in the countryside of Yorkshire? Bit of hypocrisy going on there?'

His tone of amused condescension scratched against nerves already stripped of the trappings of solid meals, rest, bodily comfort and any pretence of privacy, and I had the brief urge to clock him one with the side of the stove, which wasn't at all like me. 'Whether we find any evidence or not,' I hissed, now without any semblance of cheer, 'I'm getting £100 a day, and that's looking pretty good right now.'

He didn't reply. There was barely any acknowledgement of my having spoken, apart from a sideways inclination of his head which, with any luck, had sent a trickle of water off his hat down the back of his neck.

'We all ought to turn in.' Sebastian turned off the primus. The dying of the little blue flame was, I thought, probably a reflection of the dying of any hope of a decent night's sleep in all of us. 'Tomorrow could be worse.'

I opened my mouth to suggest that it couldn't possibly be worse than this, and then the possibility of storm-force winds, more rain and less food thundered in and I shut it again. Beside me, Mac snorted. I wasn't sure what had provoked the snort, but I didn't want to do anything to cause another reaction, so I said nothing.

'That's a good idea,' Ruth said. 'Kanga shouldn't be asleep yet, so we won't disturb her if we get to bed now.'

'Oh, and there was me looking forward to a game of gin rummy round the campfire,' Mac said, and the sarcasm dripped more than the rain did. 'But I shall manage my disappointment.'

'Hell, yeah,' Junior put in, apropos of I wasn't sure what.

'Come on then, Ruth.' I headed toward the tent, where a dim light showed faintly through the flap. I was pretty sure that Kanga wasn't lying in her sleeping bag reading *The Decline and Fall of the Roman Empire*, so maybe she'd left the light on for us?

'Just a moment, Izzy. I would like to pray first.'

'I'll leave you and God to have a chat, then.'

She smiled at me, which made her look even younger, and I wondered how old she was. It was almost impossible to tell what anyone looked like now, what with the hats and immense amount of clothing and the mud, and I'd barely noticed her before we'd got kitted out, but I wouldn't have put her at much over eighteen. Only Junior was fully visible, in his T-shirt and army boots, but I couldn't make a guess at his age either.

'I'll be in in a minute.' She wandered off behind the tents. The men were packing up the groundsheet we'd sat on and arguing about the best place to put the primus to cool down, with Sebastian clearly winning out through force of bossiness, but I ignored them and slid inside the tent flat, to find that Kanga was sprawled in her sleeping bag in the middle of the floorspace. She was asleep, or pretending to be, surrounded by the tissued-off remains of her make-up, which littered the floor disconcertingly like tiny bits of skin. Nothing of her was visible, she'd crawled right down inside the bag and was only a tuft of hair and a lot of orange nylon, but she was snoring in a realistic way, so I tiptoed around her, peeled off a couple of layers of the wettest of my clothing, and got into my own sleeping bag.

I'd got a sleeping mat underneath me, but the ground was still hard. Kanga's sprawl had me almost up against the tent wall and I could feel a draught snaking its way down the side of the tent. Clearly, the first one to bed had had the best chance of a comfortable night, I thought, and decided that a month of early nights wouldn't do me any harm. Earlier than Kanga, anyway, who twitched and muttered in her sleep as I shifted and shuffled about, trying to get comfortable. But I must have fallen into a sleep born of hunger and exhaustion, because I didn't even hear Ruth come into the tent.

2

I woke in a fug of bodies that hadn't washed recently and a suspicion of fart. Today looked better. Today looked, in fact, like a 300 per cent improvement on yesterday, with the sun streaming in through the walls of the tent and a cheering lack of wind noise.

Around me, Ruth and Kanga lay inert in their bags, glowing slightly orange. I hoped this was because of the light coming through the tent walls and not because last night's dinner had been radioactive and, at the thought of food, my stomach gave a groan that I worried might wake them. Scrambling out of my bag and trying not to stand on anyone, I pulled my big jacket on, wincing at the moist cold of the lining, and crept out through the tent flap to meet the morning.

I didn't have to make much effort, because the morning rose up to meet me, with some force. The air was very cold and shaded blue where the sun wasn't quite getting into all the hollows and dips. Where the sun *did* reach, mainly the tips of the spindly trees and a slice of ground near the tents, the light had a brittle look, as though it was frozen in nitrogen and might shatter at a touch. When I looked up, the sky was clear and felt very close.

Nobody else was about. There was no sound, no movement. Only me and this azure air, shadows and cold. I took a deep breath and the bottom of my lungs almost clanged with the impact.

A flicker to the side of my vision made me turn. A fox, russet against the blue and dappled among the snatchy growth of heather, stopped for a moment and turned its head my way. We eyeballed one another for a second, then it went back about its foxy business, high trotting down the dale without a backward look and I watched it go for lack of anything else to stare at. The damp inside my jacket had made its way through another layer of clothing and was pressing the back of my neck in a slither of wet nylon, like being licked by my own coat.

I took another breath. Only a month. I only had to stand this for a month. Even if we never found anything, even if it was a month of trying not to kill one another, I'd still be three grand nearer safety. I could use it as a deposit on a rental property. I let myself imagine a tiny flat, a kitchen I could cook in and a bedroom with a door that locked. *Only a month.*

A voice rose from the tent I'd left, in a high crystal note of complaint. It sounded as though Kanga was awake and not happy, and a couple of moments later, she burst out through the flap wearing what I'd learned yesterday whilst being kitted out by Dax and two 'directorial assistants' was a 'base layer'. Calling them long johns would probably not have gone down well.

'Urgh! There's an *earwig* in there! That's disgusting!'

She was flapping about and brushing herself off as though she thought she might be covered in them, and instantly the frail peace of the early morning was in tatters. The other tent opened and the men emerged one after another, popping through the flap like a cartoon.

'What's the matter?' Sebastian, wearing a big coat over his base layer, started towards Kanga and her waving arms. 'Are you hurt?'

'Insects! Insects *everywhere!*' she overstated, still brushing away at herself.

Mac didn't say anything. He turned around and went straight back into the tent again, letting Junior squeeze past him in the entrance.

'Better make a start. Now we're all awake.' Junior was fully dressed, I noticed. Well, fully dressed for him, which seemed to be a thin cotton shirt over those combat trousers. I couldn't imagine Junior in a base layer.

Well, no, more precisely I couldn't imagine a base layer that would *fit* Junior. He'd have to have inserts to allow for all the muscles. Plus, he really didn't seem to feel the cold.

'Is there breakfast?' Ruth asked hopefully, poking her head from our tent. 'Before we go?'

Junior was already out, scouting around the campsite, looking at the ground. 'We have to head to the camp site,' he said, eyes trained on the heather. 'Before we eat.'

'Is it likely to be far?' Sebastian was getting dressed out in the open, pulling random layers of clothing on whilst hopping about. 'Because we really must eat something, if it's a long march.'

Kanga had stopped flailing, I noticed, and was doing something that involved a lot of bending over, presumably to reveal how slim she was and how pert she looked in her minimal clothing. She seemed to have forgotten about the earwig. I wondered if it had been real or whether it had been her attempt at Being Noticed. Everyone's camera-on lights were flashing away.

'Something's been here.' Junior bent low. 'Undergrowth's all mussed up.'

'Just a fox,' I said, without thinking, and he straightened up.

'Hey. *I'm* the tracker here, bud,' he said, and I couldn't help but take a step back. His muscles were flexing as though he'd got toddlers moving under his skin. 'But yeah. Looks like a fox,' he added, grudgingly, eyeballing me again as though he suspected me of having concealed a vulpine about my person solely to make tracks. 'You know about tracks, huh?'

'Well, not really, I...'

'We should get moving.' Mac had appeared again, fully dressed now and with his hat pulled hard down over his hair. 'We've got the map coordinates for the site and we need to eat.' His camera light was off again, I noticed.

Kanga was still doing her stretch and bend routine. I thought she was pretending to check the tent ropes, but what she was mostly doing was flaunting her buttocks. Then I caught myself thinking 'flaunting' and bit the inside of my lip.

'Kanga, stick some clothes on,' I called across. 'It's not as warm as it looks out here.'

Kanga gave me a narrow-eyed look from between her legs, where she was in a cross between a yoga pose and a beachwear modelling shoot, but she didn't say anything. I did see her glance across towards the men, though, to see if they'd noticed her, but only Sebastian was looking, and he was holding out a jacket in her direction.

'Izzy's right,' he said. 'We need to get moving to warm up.'

'And get to the food,' Ruth added. 'I've prayed for bacon. Do you think there will be bacon? Only I'm really hungry now.'

We'd been told, during our briefing, that we'd be based at a permanent camp site, and these tents would be removed later, which at least saved us the humiliation of having to work out how they went up and down. That was probably an entire series on its own, I thought, as we picked up our rucksacks and shouldered them. Mine was heavier than yesterday, I was sure. It dug into my collarbone and settled along my spine in a press of damp cold. My boots were still wet when I tied them on, despite the fact I'd dug out a pair of dry socks and I was pretty hungry too.

Junior went on ahead, eyes trained on the earth like a hound trying to pick up the trail of a tasty morsel. Mmmm, bacon... My mind wandered off in search of food to obsess about as we set out tramping over the moor, Sebastian in charge of the map and the coordinates as seemingly the only one who'd ever seen a map before. The rest of us moved in a cluster as though we feared physical separation, with our rucksacks bumping against one another. Kanga was monologuing about how unlike Knightsbridge this was, and how she ought to be sorting her vast collection of designer bags into alphabetical order or something. I wasn't, to be honest, really listening.

'We're like snails, aren't we?' Ruth said eventually.

'Slimy and mostly feet?' I asked.

'Carrying everything we need on our backs. Making us realise how little we really do need for day-to-day living. That we burden ourselves with "stuff" when all we need, when it comes down to it, is what we can carry.' She stopped for a second and took off her hat, shaking dark curls out so that the wind spread them over her shoulders. I wondered, cynically for a moment, whether this was a performance for the camera, then stopped that train of thought. Kanga would have done that. Ruth was doing it to let the breeze get to her head.

'Except that we've got no food or tents, and I'm pretty sure we need those too.' Mac drew up alongside us. 'I don't think our clothes and wet weather gear really constitutes "everything we need", does it?'

His pragmatism annoyed me. I wasn't really sure why, but it probably had a lot to do with the fact that I hadn't had nearly enough sleep or much to eat. 'Well, we could hunt for our food and build our own shelters,' I put in. 'So clothes are basically what we *need*.'

Ruth gave me a big smile and Mac huffed and walked on past us to catch up with Sebastian and Junior, who were having a minor conference where the heather gave way onto a sandy path.

'The Lord will provide,' Ruth said cheerfully.

'I hope He provides soon then,' I muttered. My stomach muttered an agreement. 'Where's Kanga got to?'

'Behind us. Over there.' Ruth pointed. Kanga was a hundred metres or so in the rear, tramping along almost bent double under her rucksack. 'I'll go and see if she needs any help.'

'She'll probably want a piggyback.' I was still muttering. The constant wind was scraping my nerve endings, the light was too bright and too clear, and my digestive system was, by the feel of it, working on breaking my internal organs down. I was tired and I was cold and none of this... *none of this* was in my life plan. I had a quick memory of what my vision for my life *had* been – comfortable relationship, comfortable flat, and bumbling along through life, perhaps acquiring a couple of children and a dog. I'd had to rewrite that expectation. Even the new version hadn't been so bad, though, it had still held possibilities and a degree of certainty. It had been what came after, when everything had been screwed up and thrown into the air to land in a mess of awful insecurity and shame that had led me to this muddy moor. I *still* couldn't believe I was out here, with the cold air making my lungs contract and the weight of my rucksack digging into my collarbone.

'You don't look so cheerful now.' Mac had waited for me to catch up with him. 'Reality getting to you, is it?'

I thought about being defensive and snapping that reality was doing fine for me, thanks, it was the people inhabiting it that were annoying me, but I didn't. There was something understanding in his tone, and something about the way his brown eyes, which were practically the only part of him visible between the brim of his tugged-down hat and the zipped-up collar of his coat, seemed sympathetic.

'A bit.' Having to admit to some human frailty nearly killed me, but I didn't have the energy for prevarication.

Mac sighed. 'Yeah. Do you get the feeling that everything is being invented behind the scenes on a day-to-day basis?'

I turned to face him. It was a staccato move, because my rucksack kept catching the wind and trying to revolve me in the opposite direction. 'Is that likely?'

'Knowing my brother, it's *more* than likely, it's practically inevitable.'

'Does that mean...' I began, hesitant because I wasn't quite sure I wanted to know, '...that there might not *be* any bacon? When we get to the camp site?'

Mac grinned. It made the skin around his eyes crease in a way that made him look more approachable and less of a misery-guts. 'I'm putting my faith in his assistants understanding that we're going to need more than military iron rations to stop us from rioting and walking out,' he said, and the grumpiness was a lot less in evidence now. He sounded almost cheerful.

'Hey!' It was Sebastian calling us. 'Over here, everybody. Gather round. Junior's found something.'

Mac and I exchanged another look, then began hauling ourselves over the leg-breaking terrain towards the track. Behind us, Kanga and Ruth were making their way slowly over the moorland, Ruth half-supporting the weight of Kanga's pack. We could hear Kanga's voice, raised in complaint, even though we'd got our own bodyweight in wool pulled over our ears.

'This is *ridiculous*! I mean, why do we have to walk? Why can't we go to a hotel, set up some bait and the cameras, and wait for the big cats to come to us? We could record what comes and, there! Proof and job done, while we get a massage and swim.'

Ruth, wisely, said nothing.

'I mean, all this walking and mud and these awful clothes! Is it really *necessary*, Ruth? *Is it*?' Kanga rambled on, but only in the verbal sense. Physically she had stopped walking altogether, presumably to add emphasis to her dislike of the activity. 'And now what are they doing?'

'Junior's found a print!' Sebastian yelled over. Junior was bent over the sandy path, his nose almost touching the ground. He seemed to be sniffing the soil.

'Yep. Could be,' he said laconically. 'Looks feline. Big, too.'

I, who had previously held no particular views on large cats and their existence in the British countryside, suddenly found a well of disbelief under my muddy surface. 'Oh, come on! Really? On our first day? I reckon the production team planted this to give us something to find.'

Everyone turned to look at me. There was a silence that seemed to be outlined by the blinking of their camera-on lights, the distant barking of a far-away dog, and an almost palpable hostility. Even Mac, who'd seemed friendly a moment or two ago, was regarding me with a degree of antagonism. He was the first to speak. 'So, you're accusing my brother of fixing things?' His words were cold.

I thought of Dax and his somewhat random, 'Let's drop a bunch of people on the moors, make them walk about, and film what happens.'

'Er, no,' I said, trying not to sound placatory, because I didn't want to give away that it was *exactly* what I'd been thinking. 'Not as such.'

'So you think I don't know what I'm doing?' Junior had straightened up. 'You saying that?'

'No.' I really hadn't thought this through. 'No, of course not.'

I had, apparently, become the bad guy member of the team without even trying. God, I hope they cut this bit out in the edits.

'So, what *are* you saying, Izzy?' Kanga put her hands on her hips. 'Are you trying, perhaps, to sabotage this mission?'

'So it's a mission now, is it?' I asked, stung. 'A minute ago, you thought we could hang up half a sheep, set up the cameras and go and lie by a pool somewhere!'

Sebastian stepped in between us, hand held up. 'All right, all right. Izzy, maybe we got lucky, how about that?'

Junior rumbled something below hearing frequency. Kanga continued to keep her hands on her hips, and with the width of her rucksack, it made her look as though she was attempting to catch enough updraught to lift off. Everyone else dropped their eyes and muttered.

'I think,' Mac said at last, slowly, 'that we have to consider this as a genuine sighting. Whether or not it's been faked up for us to find – and even with my brother being a total idiot and having got the only good name in the family, I can't believe he'd do something that stupid – we have to follow the tracks if we can.'

'What about the bacon?' Ruth asked, which was the first sensible question I'd heard for a while.

'We're still on target for the new camp and breakfast,' Sebastian consulted the map. 'This footprint—'

Junior boomed inaudibly.

'Sorry, this *paw* print could well be here because this is the first place where the soil is capable of holding a proper identifiable mark,' Sebastian finished.

I looked back at the couple of miles of soggy moorland we'd just crossed. There was mud out there that would have shown if someone had whispered in the last decade. But, what with not wanting to become the Nasty Nick of the team, I tried to keep my look as unsarcastic as I could.

'Izzy? What do you think?' Sebastian asked. 'If you really think it's a fake then we can declare this whole thing pointless and ask to be taken home.'

Oh, now that wasn't fair, making me responsible. And, I thought, cynically, if the production team *were* planting evidence, then maybe they were aiming on us actually winning the £250,000? But any plan that could possibly end in me being a quarter of a million pounds richer had to be worth working through, surely...

'No, I'm sorry,' I said. 'I didn't really mean it. It seemed very – coincidental, that's all, but coincidences happen all the time, don't they? No reason this should be sinister.'

Mac hugged his arms around his body. 'Agreed then, we go on? Before we all freeze to the ground and have to be chipped out of the mud like a really unsuccessful polar mission!'

It may have been my imagination, but it did look as though he gave me a tiny wink, but that could have been the tassels from his hat blowing in his eye.

'Must we?' Kanga had started to unshoulder her rucksack, presumably in preparation for rescue.

'Group consensus.' Sebastian had refolded the map. 'We agreed when we set out up here that the group would take priority over individual decisions. Unless you want us to leave you here to wait, in case the cat comes back this way?'

Kanga shivered, dramatically. 'Absolutely not. I do *not* intend to end my life as a pile of bones mauled by a mythical beast. That is the way to become a side piece in the *Daily Mirror* or something.' With the aid of Ruth, she began to struggle her pack up again. 'And *nobody* wants that.'

Slowly we began our trek over the hills again. It was easier now we'd hit a proper path. We didn't have to lift our knees like a group of chorus girls over the deep growth of heather, which was reduced by the early winter winds to tripwire stalks and horribly stunted twigs, waving up from damp ground like thousands of drowning arms. We were going more steadily now too. Junior kept stopping and checking the ground, so even Kanga could keep up.

I did have to admit that it wasn't so bad, really. We were sheltered from the wind by a ridge of hill that rose to the sky and lurked along the horizon, leaving us on the lip of a shallow bowl which ran down to a river in its base. The sky was very blue and sported only the occasional cloud, and, whilst the sun wasn't doing much in the heat department, having to struggle along under weighty packs was keeping us warm. Partridges whirred into the air ahead of us, with the sound of particularly irritating children's toy, and somewhere off to our left in the belly of the basin, a dog was still barking.

Apart from us, the regularly spooked partridges and the barking dog, there was no evidence of life. No casual walkers, no sheep, no buildings.

'This is a particularly isolated part of the moor,' Sebastian said, as though he was also wondering where everyone was. He'd got the map out again. 'No settlements for miles, no roads, just these old trackways. I'd guess that's why we're going to be based out here – it's the most likely location for a big cat to be living.'

Kanga snorted. 'If you could call this living.' She swiped an arm out to indicate the general paucity of sentience. 'It's hardly Notting Hill, is it?'

Nobody answered her. We kept our heads down, trudging like a particularly unsuccessful army in full, downtrodden, retreat. I could hear my boots creaking and feel the pinch of them around my heel. We'd been advised to break in our walking gear before we'd been brought out here to begin filming, but I hadn't anticipated this much walking, so hadn't bothered. The production company had made it sound as though we would only be strolling out from our tents for a bit of a look around, rather than route-marching over what felt like most of Yorkshire. I really should learn to read the small print, I decided, trying to rearrange my rucksack so that there was less pressure on my shoulders. Read the small print, don't agree to anything that's offered just for the money, and definitely, *definitely* never apply to be on any TV show ever again. Ever.

'Is that the camp over there?' Ruth pointed and we all stopped again to look.

Our home for the rest of the month was tucked in under a boulder outcrop. Tents slightly larger and more firmly anchored than the ones we'd spent the last night in, a fire already established, and a Jeep parked next to the whole thing, presumably so that Dax and his team could film our arrival from a distance at which we would look attractively dishevelled and communal. Definitely not close enough to smell us coming or hear the arguing.

Kanga removed her hat. The wind stripped her blonde hair out behind her and she did a 'shampoo ad' toss of the head.

'I think they'll wait for us to get closer,' Mac said. 'We could be any bunch of walkers at the moment.'

'Oh, right, because this place is *stuffed* with masochists and idiots,' she snapped back, but put her hat back on again anyway.

'Well, there's six idiotic masochists here already,' I said, unable to help myself. 'We wouldn't want competition.'

Mac stifled a laugh and it made my heart rise a little from its position lurking somewhere below my stomach. Maybe I wasn't the Miss Nasty member of the team. Maybe I was the realist, telling it as it was? Maybe viewers would identify with me?

I hoped not.

Junior bent low to the trackway again. 'Could be a print,' he rumbled. 'It's something, anyways.'

I wondered why he wasn't cold. The rest of us were bundled up in layers of knitwear and waterproofing and he was still wearing a loose shirt over a vest and no jacket. Maybe he was too macho for insulation? Or maybe they hadn't found anything that would fit over his biceps, which waggled about as though they had a thrilling internal life of their own.

We clustered around, but a little half-heartedly because the lure of camp and food was making us restlessly keen to round the head of the dale and get to our new base.

'You think that's a print?' Sebastian and Mac had bent down next to Junior. 'Just looks like a mark in the dust to me.'

Junior straightened. 'Ah am an *expert*,' he announced to the valley, his Southern drawl loud and noticeable in the bright air. 'You wanna challenge my decisions?'

Personally, taking in the fact that he was about six feet ten and built like a tractor, I wouldn't have challenged him if he'd announced that he and Bigfoot were on first-name terms.

'Well, yes, but you're a Sasquatch expert surely, not a big cat specialist?' Mac spoke very reasonably, I thought, for a man taking his life in his hands. 'I mean, there has to be a difference.'

Junior rumbled a few subsonic imprecations then said, 'Tracking is tracking,' rather succinctly and meaninglessly.

'Will we be safe, camping so close to where something has been?' Ruth had clearly cast herself as peacemaker. 'Won't we get attacked if we're outside in the night?'

The attention of the group instantly swivelled on to her. Junior stayed crouching, I noticed. Touching the surface of the ground with a flat hand, as though he could sense the animal that had made the mark. Or, cynicism reared its head again, trying to scrub out what he'd seen so nobody else could examine it too closely?

'We'd need to camp close to a lair, though, surely, to stand any chance of finding the creature.' Sebastian took a step towards Ruth. 'So, I'd guess that the people running this thing will have done their research. No point in setting us up miles from the last sighting.'

'Well, I won't be going out after dark.' Kanga looked defiant. 'I'd rather pee in a bucket than run the risk of getting eaten.'

'I think you've already established that.' Mac's tone was chilly. 'Although quite how you think you'll be in with a shout of winning the quarter mill when you don't seem to want to have any contact with anything that's not above room temperature and totally inert, I fail to see.'

'Let's get to camp.' Sebastian rivalled Ruth in the peacemaker stakes. 'We'll eat, change our clothes, make ourselves feel a bit more human, and then we can plan out a strategy.' His tone held a level of finality that was not going to allow for arguments. I wondered why he had taken on this role of our leader so easily. Maybe *he* was behind an attempt to plant tracks out here?

Nobody, clearly, was going to argue, though. I was almost sure that I saw the word 'bacon' flash behind everyone's eyes and I felt my mouth start to water in preparation. If there wasn't any bacon, then Dax and his crew had better have a good turn of escape speed, I thought, starting the oppressed trudge again, that would bring us along the track around the top of the valley and over to the camp, where the cameras, Dax and hopefully a large fried breakfast were waiting.

3

Dax briefed us as we ate. He'd tried to talk to us when we arrived, sweaty, itchy, overloaded and cross, but nobody would listen and he seemed to know when he was beaten. The crew had waited, Callum sitting swinging his legs and Steve filling in a crossword in pencil in the Jeep whilst we ignored the tents and pummelled our way through the food supplies until we found bacon, bread, eggs and milk, with little cries of joy. We'd been out of civilisation for about twenty-four hours, and we were already behaving as though the epitome of decadence was the smell of food frying and very strong tea.

There were camping chairs, so we sat and ate. Even Kanga, who I didn't think had eaten outside a restaurant since 2015, enthusiastically dug into the greasy, carbohydrate-laden meal. Dax and Callum were setting up equipment over on the rock outcrop that sheltered the camp when Mac shuffled his chair over to me.

'Do you want me to ask my brother?' he said in a half-whisper that was only just audible over the sounds of vigorous plate-clearing. 'If this is really legit?'

'Do you think he'd tell you, though? If they'd planted footprints, if this whole thing is a set up? Wouldn't that ruin the show?' I kept my voice low too.

Mac nodded at my chest. I frowned at him. He nodded again, head on one side as though it was meaningful and I tried to work out how my boobs, securely covered in several layers of clothing and encased in a guaranteed non-bounce sports bra, were relevant in any way to the conversation.

Eventually he hissed, 'Turn your camera off,' and I felt myself get hot with embarrassment. Why the hell had my mind gone there? I fumbled the switch and the little blinking light that I'd already become so accustomed to that I'd forgotten its presence went off.

'I reckon I can use a little good old family blackmail.' Mac put his now empty plate on the ground. We were perched on our chairs side by side, a little way apart from the others, who were gathered much closer to the fire. 'If you want me to.'

I looked up on the rocks above us. Dax, looking frozen in trendy jeans and a coat more suited to shoplifting from supermarkets than moorland walks, was directing the camera and sound. I shook my head and explained the reasoning that I'd come to earlier.

'If it's a set-up, we might win. If it's not, we still might win. If we let them know that we *think* it's a set-up, they'll double down and remove all evidence. We could be stuck up here for a month with absolutely nothing going on, apart from Kanga bitching and Junior trying to cause avalanches.'

'Not exactly riveting television,' Mac observed drily.

'Unless they manufacture some kind of drama for us. Let's stay quiet for now. At least we're earning money.'

Mac gave me a look. 'Not *that* much.'

'Enough. And maybe—' I looked out across the dale. Miles and miles of nothing meant sound from invisible settlements carried up to our ears on the sharpening wind. A tiny copse of trees down at the bottom of the dale shook its branches, and the river ran its white-noise way down the hilly slope and out of sight. 'Maybe there really *is* a puma or a leopard living out here.' The possibility, which had seemed outlandishly ridiculous when it had been put to us back in a warehouse studio in Leeds, suddenly seemed far more realistic. *Anything* could be out here in this wilderness. Ghosts, goblins and poltergeists had stopped sounding impossible now we were surrounded by rippling heather and black mud. Once you stripped away the lights, roads and crowds that formed civilisation, it felt as though we stood on the edge of a fairy tale. And not one of the nice ones that ended in marriage to a prince, either. There were echoes of wolves and monsters out here.

'Okay.' Mac shuffled his stool a little further back. 'Don't say I didn't offer, though.'

A thought struck me. 'How come you've got such unusual names? Dax and MacKinley? It sounds as though your parents thought they were having Labradors.'

Mac sighed. 'Family names. They're a curse. Dax is really D-A-C-H-S; Dad's mum's maiden name, she was a war bride from Germany. MacKinley is my mother's name.' He sighed again. 'I'm only glad there weren't any more of us. Her mother's maiden name was Pobblebury, and that is not a moniker that any child wants to carry through life.'

'Oh.' It was all I could think of to say. But this conversation, banal as it was, made me feel a little bit closer to Mac and that was comforting. As though we needed to forge bonds to get us through this, and our little moment of superficial intimacy was going to make things easier to bear.

'And what about you?' Mac asked. 'While the cameras are off, anything you'd like to share?'

I thought then about the reason I was here. The *real* reason I'd applied to a TV show, the desire to get away. Sofa-surfing between any friends that would have me, sleeping on floors and in back rooms, waitressing and bartending to earn a pittance, the desire to have somewhere I belonged.

'No,' I said, giving him a cheery smile. 'I'm boring, me.'

Mac looked at me out of those deep eyes which, now he'd removed the hat and undone his jacket a little, were no longer quite as much the focus of his face but were still steady enough to make me feel a bit embarrassed. 'I am sure that's not the case,' he said. 'But I'd guess we all have our reasons for being here.'

I looked over at the rest of the group. Now they'd stripped off some of the layers of walking clothing, everyone looked a little more individual and less like a homogenous mass of outdoor humanity. Sebastian, with his spiky-cut hair and blue eyes in his tanned and pleasant face and his outdoor-work honed body. Ruth, whose dark hair had been confined to a ponytail which made her look as though she was fresh from a Sixth Form PE class. Kanga we'd already seen quite enough of during her earlier stretch routine, and Junior's well-muscled sparsely clad shape that looked as though he'd been assembled in an Action Man factory and dressed in 'All Purpose Tracking Gear (Warm Weather)'. I wondered if his boots actually came off or if they'd been moulded onto his legs. And then I found myself wondering if he'd been included to make our group more diverse, as the rest of us were relentlessly WASPish.

'Right, I'd like each one of you to do a little piece to camera, if you will.' Dax bounded down from his perch atop the rocks. 'A little individual snippet of how things are going so far, what you expect to find, how you're managing, that kind of thing.'

Mac rolled his eyes at me and combed his hair back with both hands. Without the striped beany he'd been wearing, his hair was an unruly twisting of half-curly lengths that reached his chin, where stubble was beginning to darken his cheeks. 'Shall I go first then, Dax?'

While Mac was away filming, I helped to clear up the pots and pans. Ruth had clearly taken on the domestic role, because she'd pumped water from the bowser set up at the side of the camp and was preparing to wash the dishes, rolling up her sleeves and searching through the supplies for washing up liquid.

'We should set up a rota for cleaning,' I said, stacking the plates. 'Otherwise I'm afraid it's going to fall along traditional lines and we females will end up housekeeping all the time.'

Ruth glanced at me over her shoulder. 'I don't see Kanga going along with that,' she said, her voice tactfully lowered. 'She's apparently been told to sit like that for an hour after meals, to help her digestion.' She jerked her head to where Kanga had taken up a complicated yoga pose, eyes closed and hands on thighs. Purely coincidentally, it was within shot of Callum filming Mac's interview.

'She's really determined to make this into as close an approximation of *Love Island* as you can get on the Yorkshire Moors, isn't she?' I muttered back, drying the plates as they came through the bowl and restacking them.

'I don't blame her.' Ruth carried on washing. 'She wants to get noticed. It's her big hope for her future, to set up her own brand and become a media star.' She glanced over at Kanga, who, I was almost sure, had one eye slightly open, making sure that the camera didn't refocus elsewhere. I didn't want to know what she'd got planned if it did.

'I suppose it would beat working for a living.' I sounded a bit sour and I knew it. I'd turned my camera and mic back on again after my little tête-à-tête with Mac. Mostly I forgot it was on, but now I remembered and hoped that I didn't come over as bitchy.

'I'm sure God has a plan for her too,' Ruth said, rinsing suds. 'He has a plan for all of us.'

'Maybe He'd be good enough to give me a sneak peek at mine?' She smiled at me and I found I was grinning back. 'So, what made you decide to stick with this? Once you found out what was actually involved?'

Ruth gave a small sigh, and much attention to the dishes. 'I need to grow up,' she said softly. 'My parents and I, we're members of a church. They like to keep to the Lord's words, so I've had a sheltered life so far. I just felt it was time—' She stopped, as though the weight of thought was dragging the words back inside. 'If we find any evidence, I want to give the money to my church,' she went on, eventually. She dried her hands and tipped the water onto the earth, where we watched the bubbles from the eco-safe detergent sparkle and pop on the grassy surface like tiny miracles. 'We're all encouraged to raise money for church works.'

Hm, I thought. I really hoped that Ruth wasn't part of some cultish religion that forces its members to raise money in preference to earning their own incomes. She seemed very young and rather naïve, and it was worrying that she thought living in a tent and pursuing an imaginary animal might be a good way to 'grow up'. But then maybe this was the only way her parents would let her leave home? Supervised by cameras and spied on by strangers?

'Your turn.' Mac touched my shoulder. 'Five minutes of first impressions, that's all he wants. Oh, and to hear all the gossip and back-biting that's gone on, obviously.'

'There hasn't really been any, though, has there?' I prepared to clamber around the back of the camp, where the slope ran up, cutting into the rocky outcrop.

'I'd make some up if I were you,' was Mac's parting shot. 'I did.'

I could see Dax, Callum and Steve, wrapped like parcels against the wind, waiting for me at the top of the hill, but on the way up, I stopped and turned around to admire the sheer wild beauty of our location, even though most of it was trying to occupy my clothing alongside me. I wondered, for a moment, whether Dax was on a sponsorship deal from the North Yorkshire Tourist Board because the moor was spread out before us in a series of curved hills and steep dales under the morning sun, like a poster illustrating the joys of holidaying in Yorkshire. Then I reasoned that, if he were, he'd have been filming during a season when there were flowers and birds and less of the bleak windswept thing going on. Dark rises of land were counterpointed by plunges into unlit valleys like a solid and tormented seascape. Feeble attempts at woodland huddled in the more sheltered spots, where the spindly trees had the arboreal equivalent of comb-overs – a few sparse leaves grimly hanging on to upper branches as though to persuade us that the tree was, in fact, still fully covered.

A movement caught my eye. Down at the bottom of the dale, where the river ran and the trees crouched, I was sure something had appeared briefly between the shadows of boulders and branches. A flicker of darkness. I tried to force my eyes to focus, but whatever it was had moved into shade and was invisible now. It may not even have been a solid object, clouds were skittishly tracing their way across the sun, randomly obscuring the light in patches that made the carved ridges look momentarily diseased and blotchy. There was nothing there now.

'So, if you could tell us how things have gone, so far?' Dax was jiggling about inside his coat. 'Just a quick vox pop, nothing too detailed.' His eyes pleaded with me not to complain about the cold, the wet, the lack of decent food, the miles of walking, the too-small tents and every other aspect of 'The Show – So Far'. 'How everyone's coming across, whether you've seen anything yet?'

There was a desperation in his voice that told me this was Dax's first time helming an actual production; that he was hoping for a gritty reality

show that would set the viewing figures alight. Whether or not we actually found any evidence of a big cat was probably beside the point –
people would be watching to see sleep-deprived grubby people fighting
over the last chocolate bar and arguing about... well, arguing about
anything at all. From my memory of the few reality shows I'd watched, the
arguing had been the most addictive viewing.

I tried to make our hike so far sound vaguely interesting, but there
wasn't much to say. Ruth praying, Kanga bitching and Junior's inaudible,
subsonic pronouncements didn't make it sound fascinating, but I did my
best.

'And have you seen any evidence of anomalous life forms yet?' Dax
asked, with an almost indecent urgency. The camera got right into my face
and I could see Callum's grin behind it. He clearly didn't believe in any of
this any more than we did.

'We've... there's been... we're not really sure,' I said honestly, and then,
as Dax's face fell, 'Junior thinks there may be tracks out there.'

Dax brightened and the camera pulled back a bit. I found myself
staring at Dax, trying to work out whether he was the kind to want definite results, even if he had to make sure that they happened, or whether
filming us all getting filthy and exhausted would be enough. Real attempt
to find a big cat, or a social experiment? What the hell *was* this, anyway?

Mac didn't seem to think his brother would fake things, but I wasn't so
sure. TV production companies are tough places to work, I guessed.
Results would be everything. I had the horrible feeling that one of us
being mauled and eaten would be less of a tragedy and more of a viewing-
figure triumph, as far as Dax was concerned, and I didn't want to be the
one who lost a limb in the search for media stardom, even if it would,
briefly, get me my own TikTok meme.

Sebastian went off for his talking head piece, and the rest of us began
to investigate the camp more thoroughly. We'd been more concerned with
eating than exploring when we'd arrived, but it did appear that the
production company had thought our permanent campsite through a
little better than our first night's temporary accommodation. There was a
small Portaloo tucked away inconspicuously and screened from the camp
by a stand of gorse bushes. We had a tent each, and the tents were laid out

in a semi-circle, surrounding the fire pit and overlooking the dale. Storage boxes held food and other supplies, there was the water bowser – all in all, it was a lot more luxurious than some of the places I'd been finding myself sleeping lately, so I was happy.

Kanga, predictably enough, wasn't. 'Where do we shower?' she asked, once she'd got up from her meditation pose. 'How do we heat the water?'

'We don't.' Mac seemed philosophical. 'We wash the best we can. No one's going to judge you for being a bit muddy, you know. Not out here.'

'But my *skin*!' As though to illustrate her distress, she pointed at her face. 'I've got a regime, you know. Cleansing is *so important*.'

'I thought mud was good for the skin,' I observed mildly. 'Mud packs, and so forth.'

'Well,' Kanga narrowed her eyes. 'You would think that, wouldn't you?'

'Cold water is fine,' Ruth said. 'It's all I use.'

Kanga opened her mouth, presumably to come out with a pithy riposte, but as Ruth's skin was as smooth and clear as the chilly sky currently above us, even she couldn't gainsay the power of pure water. 'You're still so young,' was what she came up with. 'When you get a little older, you'll find it harder to maintain a complexion.' Then, seeming to realise that she'd aged herself, 'Or so I'm told, apparently. I can still be a bit lackadaisical about my routine and get away with it.'

Mac caught my eye and shook his head slightly, which made me smile. 'Where's Junior? Is he doing his bit with Dax?' I asked him, trying to block out Kanga's blow-by-blow account of her cleansing products.

'I think he went off to secure the perimeter.' Mac looked around. 'Yep, he's down there.'

'Do we need a secure perimeter? We're tracking an animal that's so elusive it may not even exist, not trying to keep zombies at bay.'

Mac shrugged. 'It's what he said. I think it's an excuse to be out of camp, myself. Have you thought, he's the one brought in by Dax, he's the one finding all this evidence?'

'He would, though, being the professional.' I watched Junior, who was creeping through the frost-withered bracken halfway down the slope between us and the water. 'And I thought you were saying that this is all above board? Did Dax tell you something just now that's changed your mind?' I turned to look at Mac now. He was actually quite nice-looking, for a man who'd not washed in a couple of days. It crossed my mind now that maybe Dax was trying to pair us up and had told Mac to pay me attention. It would make great television if we all started snogging and shagging – like *Big Brother* meets *Love Island* and you could cut out all of that Lord of the Flies stuff. Basically, it would be like *EastEnders*, without the pub.

Mac had clearly noticed me giving him the once over because he smiled again. 'We're all getting less and less telegenic by the day, aren't we?' He ran a hand over his stubble. 'Apart from Kanga, obviously.'

'And even she won't survive a month of this without having to let her standards drop a bit.' I lowered my voice. 'She smuggled make-up through, did you notice?'

'I did.'

We smiled together now, a smile of complicity. Dax needn't imagine that I'd be getting off with Mac, however Machiavellian his behind-the-scenes plotting might be, but it would be nice to have someone friendly in the camp. Someone who knew about my suspicions that the whole thing was a set-up. And he hadn't answered my question about whether Dax had let something slip in that regard, I noticed.

4

As soon as the sun had dipped beyond the furthest hills, the cold re-intensified its grip on the air, like a miser tightening its fist around the last gold coins of daylight.

I'd bagged the tent that stood with its back to the rock wall with Sebastian's tent on one side and Mac's on the other. I hated, with every fibre of my being, to admit it, but I felt slightly safer knowing that those two stood between me and the open side of the camp. As the dark came in, the dale felt more and more bleak, more and more threatening.

'Don't be stupid,' I told my camera, which was heaped with my clothes over my rucksack, its blinking light the only illumination in the tent. We'd been given solar-powered chargers to put the cameras on at night to keep them working, but, bearing in mind how little sun we'd seen so far, I gave them about a week. 'I'm pretty sure being nervous out here at night is all psychological. The place is exactly the same in the dark as it is in the light, the only added danger will be breaking an ankle tripping over something.'

The light winked on at me, as though provoking me to say more. But what was there to say? I turned it off and huddled deeper into my sleeping bag. I'd changed into a dry base layer and very thick socks, and there was a surprising amount of comfort in clean clothes and the warmth of the insulated bag. I wondered if I was going native.

Beyond my tent, the men were setting up various equipment; Dax had given us a motion-sensitive light and camera and Junior was insisting on patrolling the perimeter again, as though he half-expected the wildlife to have tooled up and be coming for us in the dead of night. I lay and listened to them arguing about the mechanics of the camera and where to put it, interspersed with Kanga's occasional high-pitched interjections about putting all the equipment a long way from the camp so she wouldn't be woken by the light going on and off during the night. 'I need *at least* eight unbroken hours,' she said. 'I can't have my skin collapsing and going all dry, or getting bags under my eyes, like Izzy's.'

One of the men must have said something to that, because she notched up the whine a little. 'I'm thinking of my future *career* here. Izzy isn't looking to establish herself as a media star, is she? She can look however she likes. I've got my *image* to think of. *Presence.*'

A voice, that I was fairly sure was Mac's, said, 'Izzy doesn't look so bad.'

'But why is she even *here*?' Kanga had lowered her voice a bit now and I had to strain my ears and shuffle my sleeping bag closer to the entrance of the tent. 'I can see Ruth's point, she's like the *ingenue*, she's here to show how worldly and sophisticated the rest of us are. I'm here to add some glamour; as a reason for the men to watch. Izzy – really, what is the *point* of her? What's her role?'

There was a rumble, presumably a pronouncement from Junior, and a burst of general laughter. I didn't catch the words, and, as they were followed by Kanga's 'Oh, you!' I gathered she hadn't either. I wondered why she was out there, with the men, while Ruth and I were in bed – showing off? Enjoying the male attention? She certainly wasn't helping with the equipment, I'd heard nothing but her attempts to get Sebastian to explain what each piece did, no offers to help install it, because that would have meant moving away from the fire.

I shuffled back onto my sleeping mat and closed my eyes.

'I think we should get some sleep.' Sebastian was, from the sounds of it, banking up the fire. 'Don't forget to turn your cameras off. Save the batteries and all.'

It felt oddly comforting, lying in my tent and knowing that there were people outside, banking the fire and preventing any huge cats from slicing their way into my tent and dragging my inert body out for a good chew. I felt myself drifting off to sleep listening to the occasional voices and the sounds of the others getting the camp ready for night.

I was woken by lightning. One brief flash that broke into a restless sleep and made me sit upright suddenly, forgetting where I was for a second. I'd learned the knack of being able to sleep almost anywhere, however uncomfortable, so the hardness of the earth beneath me didn't give me the clue it ought to have done, until my head brushed the nylon of the tent amid the last vestiges of a nightmare about being trapped, and I nearly hyperventilated myself out of the flap.

There was no storm. The night air was clear and empty, except for the swaddling band of stars which wrapped around the earth as far as the eye could see. The moon lay on its back on the horizon, illuminating the hills with a pale, cut-out sort of light, but a steady beam, no clouds to cause flashing of any kind.

I stood, breathing carefully, not only to manage the panic that resulted from being woken in the middle of a bad dream, but also because the air was so cold that deep breathing was like drowning in sorbet. I reached back through the tent flap and grabbed my big jacket, which had taken on a layer of mud that made it keep my shape even when I wasn't wearing it, and pulled it on, then tottered out across the sandy circle of the camp towards the edge of the moor.

The fire was out, and the ashes were cold. It was late then. So what had the flash been?

'It was the camera,' said a voice right beside me, and I squeaked, stepped back suddenly and found the jacket taking on a pugilistic stance entirely by itself.

'What?' I asked in a quiet voice, not just because I didn't want to wake anyone, but mostly because my vocal cords had frozen in terror.

'The flash. It was the camera we set up earlier. It woke me too.' The whisperer was Mac, at my elbow, wearing a fleecy suit that explained why

I hadn't heard him coming and made him look like one of Santa's little helpers. 'It's set to flash when it photographs something moving within its sensor field.'

'What's wrong with night vision?' I hissed. 'Why do we have to be woken up to know that something is moving out there?' Then a thought struck me. 'Unless it's to give us time to get away.'

Mac bent towards me. He'd still got his beanie hat on, sensibly enough I supposed, but it squashed all his hair downwards so that ends protruded beneath it and made him look like a children's cartoon character. 'It's so we can go and check,' he whispered back. 'There's not much point us being out here trying to get evidence of something that we don't actually want to *see*, is there?'

'Suppose not.' We stood for a few moments more. 'So, should we go and look?' I finally asked, when it became evident that neither of us were about to take the initiative.

Mac hesitated. 'What if it's dangerous?'

'If it's dangerous and also not scared off by a big flashing light, then we're probably already in trouble.' I tugged at his fleecy sleeve. 'Come on.'

'You're very brave.' He came along but I could feel his reluctance when the fabric of his suit stretched in my hand for quite a while first. 'And also, awake. How come nobody else woke up?'

'I'm used to sleeping with one eye open,' I said grimly. 'And there's more danger out on the streets than out here, unless you twist an ankle, so come on. You know where you put the camera and I've got no idea.'

Cautiously, lit only by the long-shadowed light from the moon, we tiptoed out away from the campsite and a little way down the valley. At the bottom, the river hushed and gurgled, and the trees of the sparse wood swung in an unfelt breeze.

'It's here.' Mac stopped me with a hand. 'We should check for prints first, shouldn't we?'

'Should we?'

'I don't know.'

We looked at one another.

'Have you got your camera on you?' I asked at last.

'No. It's still inside my coat back in the tent. What about you?'

I tapped at my jacket, but I'd left the camera propped in the tent where I'd put it to do my monologue last night. 'No! So we'd better hope that there's nothing out there.'

'In case we vanish and the rest of them never discover what happened to us?'

I gave him a stern look. 'I was thinking more of the fact that we could be face to face with a big cat out here and not getting any evidence that's going to win us the cash, actually.'

'Oh. Right.'

The camera was on a stand, jutting above the twiggy heather. I picked it up and turned it over. 'What do we do with it?'

'It's set to capture thirty seconds of video when the trip goes off. It's got night vision; the flash is to let us know it's filming.' Mac took the camera from me and fiddled with it. 'Yes. It's recorded something. Shall we look?'

I looked dubiously at the little box. 'Shouldn't we take it back and show the others? If it *has* filmed something?'

Mac glanced ostentatiously around the night-black dale. 'We could re-set it, leave it until the morning and then *tell* them we think it recorded something,' he said. 'Not a lot of point in waking everyone now, there's nothing to see out here.'

'True.'

He pressed a couple of buttons and the screen on the camera sprang to blue-toned life. A few sprigs of whin moved at one side of the frame, then a black leg came into focus. It moved away, came back and then the creature walked in front of the lens, pausing only to sniff at the box in a terrifying nasal close up. The thirty-second film ended with a large striped bottom shuffling away into grumpy solitude.

'Badger,' said Mac and I in unison and slightly relieved tones.

There was a pause. 'Did you think it might be a cat?' I asked, eventually.

'No. Not really.' Mac sighed. 'But there's something about the middle of the night out here.' He puffed out a steamy breath. 'It feels... *odd*, somehow.'

'A bit like there could be dragons?' I hated to admit it, but it gave me the same feeling. As though the land was so old that it could have been hiding anything. As though, out here in the small hours, folklore was law. 'It's spooky. Makes me feel as though I'm being watched all the time.'

We turned our backs on the moorland spread and headed back to the camp, which had begun to feel like the security of home.

'*Do* you think there's anything out there? Apart from badgers, that is?' Mac said conversationally, as we reached the ashy cold of the firepit. 'Seriously?'

'For the fifty grand, I'll take my chances,' I replied, stirring a socked toe in the sandy ground. 'Do you know what kind of evidence we have to get for that?'

Mac stuck his hands under his armpits. 'Yeah. It's got to be lab-verified. So actual physical traces that can be tested and proved to be big cat in origin. Pictures won't count as evidence, it's too easy to misidentify a big domestic moggy, apparently. Unless it's actually dragging one of us off to its lair, when we'd have someone in shot, for scale.'

My heart sank a notch or two. I didn't know why, really. Fifty thousand pounds each was a lot of money, they were hardly going to pay out on the say-so of a bunch of sleep-deprived randoms or a blurry photograph of a tail moving out of shot. 'Oh.'

'Yep. Advertisers are putting up the prize money so they want big answers. Definites make headlines. A local farm cat walking through camp and stealing the milk would make them look a bit daft. And pawprints are too easy to misidentify or fake. So it's got to be the real thing.'

'What the hell do we have to do to win the quarter of a million, then, sleep with it?' I was feeling a bit tetchy now. Whilst I'd never *really seriously* contemplated the possibility of there being large cats living out here on the moor, I now realised that I'd been half-hoping that we might have managed some out-of-focus shots of a moving *something* on a hillside, and been paid for our trouble.

Mac grinned.

'I'm going back to bed.' I shoved my tent flap aside and bent down.

'Yes. Goodnight.' Mac moved on to his tent. 'I'm sorry it was just a badger, by the way.'

'Why? You don't need the money, do you?' I snapped, and forced my way through the flapping nylon to throw my jacket off into a corner and crawl back into the sleeping bag. *A hundred pounds a day, Izzy. Concentrate on that. For a month, that's all. Then you've got enough money to at least find yourself somewhere to rent. Just stick it out for a month.*

The sleeping bag was still warm and I fell asleep quickly.

5

I woke up late the next morning. Everyone else was clustered around the fire whilst Mac showed them the film from the overnight camera. Apart from the badger's brief starring appearance, there had been no other activity, which I'd already gathered from the fact that the flash hadn't woken me again.

I crawled out of the tent.

'How on *earth* can you sleep so late?' Kanga, cross-legged on the ground, asked me. 'It's so uncomfortable.'

'Practice.' I stretched and pulled my jacket on. My outer layer of clothing was beginning to feel like my second skin already. My first skin was a bit itchy underneath it. 'Did I miss anything?' I slid my camera over my jacket and tapped it on.

'Mac's told us about last night.' Ruth settled a big kettle over the fire. 'And I'm making tea.'

'Junior's out on patrol.' Sebastian straightened up from where he'd been rummaging in the food store. 'I've asked him to look for somewhere we can put the camera where the flash won't wake half the camp at night. And I think we ate all the bacon yesterday. I've found some sausages, though.'

We all made noises of pleasure and encouragement, except,

predictably, Kanga. 'All these processed products are playing havoc with my digestion,' she said. 'Aren't there any wholefoods in there?'

'No. And I'll eat yours if you don't want them.' Sebastian sounded a bit abrupt, which wasn't like him. During our, admittedly brief, acquaintance, he'd always been upbeat and cheery, if rather fond of the sound of his own voice telling us what to do. Maybe Kanga was beginning to get to him. She'd already got so far to me that she'd passed clean through and was out the other side, but perhaps it took longer with the men.

Kanga shot him a hurt look. 'I need to keep my strength up,' she said, wounded innocence dripping from every syllable. 'I've far less... physical resilience than Izzy.' She made 'physical resilience' such an obvious stand-in for 'fat insulation' that I was tempted to poke her with the sausages, but I restrained myself.

'Ruth's smaller than you and she seems to be managing,' Mac said innocently, but as he turned to deal with the now steaming kettle, he gave me a most definite wink and I saw Sebastian smile too, which made me feel warmly grateful towards the pair of them. It was a nice feeling, less like being an outcast.

'Ruth has smaller bones,' snapped Kanga. 'I need to meditate.' And, unfolding herself from the ground, she stalked off into her tent, leaving the rest of us basking in a slight point-scoring glow.

I went over to help Sebastian disentangle the sausages. 'Are you all right?' I asked him quietly.

He glanced over at Ruth and Mac, whose camera lights were flashing on, and grimaced towards mine. I slapped it off. 'She tried to come into my tent last night,' he half-whispered.

I pulled a face. 'Ah.'

'She was actually quite insistent,' he carried on. 'But I'm married and my wife is putting her all into running the farm while I'm away; I'm really not here for dallying with someone, least of all Kanga.'

'Why *are* you here?'

Sebastian gave me a half-smile. 'I don't know if you know much about farming,' he said ruefully. 'But we're flat broke, and it was worth the gamble. Plus—' He stopped talking and began concentrating on portioning up the sausages into a pan.

I tried to look silently encouraging, which wasn't easy. Particularly with sausages as competition.

'I thought I saw something.' Sebastian threw me a look that challenged me to give a pantomime reply of 'Oh, no, you didn't!' 'Last year, out on the farm. I was up on the Downs, checking the sheep early one morning and I saw – I *thought* I saw – something.'

He kept up the challenging look. 'What was it?' I finally asked, when it became obvious that he didn't want to say anything unless I explicitly wanted to know.

'I don't know. It looked like... oh, it sounds really stupid, but I guess, given why we're here... it looked like a puma. Sandy coat, really big. I only caught a glimpse but – well. I suppose I'm here to convince myself that they really *are* out there and I wasn't mad to think I saw a big cat that day on the Downs.' He raised his eyebrows and gave me a shame-faced smile. 'So, now you know. I'm one of the bonkers "I want to believe" crowd.'

I remembered that feeling I'd had, looking over the dark vale in the small hours of the morning, with Mac. That sensation that *anything* could be out there. 'I don't think that's bonkers at all,' I said softly.

'Thank you. I didn't realise that it was going to mean fending Kanga off quite so vigorously.' He rubbed his arms. 'I love my wife and I'm not here for any of that. I want answers, if I can get them, and the money, obviously, and a bit of an experience.'

'I'm sure sex with Kanga would be an experience.' I sounded slightly acerbic and Sebastian grinned.

'Probably. But she'd almost certainly keep her camera running, and I don't need that kind of notoriety among the Sussex sheep fraternity.'

'We're ready for the sausages,' Mac called from where he was making the tea. 'Junior's back too. Apparently he's seen signs of something further down the dale and he thinks we should split up and spend the day looking for prints along the track.'

So that's what we did. We were each given a section of the sandy track to examine and what I thought would be the work of minutes took a whole day. First we moved the motion-sensitive camera further out onto the moor to try to photograph anything that moved along the trackway. Then Junior wanted us to go over the track in such minute detail, looking for hairs, partial prints, any strange marks, that my eyes were prickling and my nose itched by the time we broke for lunch. Every slightly disturbed grain of mica, any pebble that lay at an angle, Junior wanted us to call him over to examine. I became an extreme expert in identifying sheep poo, by the end of the day I could practically tell you which sheep each lump had come from, and I could only imagine how much editing this footage would take in order to make it look interesting to the viewing public.

'Gotta know the area,' Junior rumbled. 'Gotta know what's normal, so you can see what's *not* normal, you get me?'

From the expressions on our faces as we all looked at one another, we all wanted to 'get' him, but in a completely different way, particularly after the cold, *detailed* morning we'd had.

'Are... are you *sure* that Bigfoot is like tracking big cats?' Ruth asked timidly, from behind Sebastian. 'I mean... transferrable skills?'

Junior narrowed his eyes and we collectively braced ourselves. 'Trackin' is trackin',' he said finally, and then turned around to head into the heather, in something that in someone less enormous could only have been called a flounce.

What was *not* normal, I mused on his earlier words, on my hands and knees on the track again, was a bunch of adults crawling about like toddlers, seizing on sticks and feathers and shoving our hands in random dips and bumps. If it went on much longer, we were going to start jumping off 'big rocks' and demanding an ice cream. Surely, as we were looking for *big* cats, our work should be more on the macro end of the scale? Or at least involve staring into the picturesque distance of the moody blue-tinted rise and fall of the hills, if, as I suspected, Dax was obtaining some of his funding from the Yorkshire Tourist Board.

Or did Junior know that there was something to find?

'Junior?' It was Ruth, scanning the area of the track farthest from the campsite, right at the end of the chain of crawling people. She was practically in the valley bottom, where the path devolved into a peaty mudslide towards the river which looked as though only deer were ever likely to use it. Oh, yes, we could now all identify deer hoofprints too; more pointed in the toe and narrower slotted than sheep, knowledge that would probably only stand us in good stead in future if we wanted to feature on *Countryfile* or take Junior's job.

Junior stopped patting down his patch of the track and slithered down over the heather to Ruth. I straightened up and eased my back, watching her pointing and then Junior getting down on all fours, face to the earth. I sidled over to Mac.

'What's she found?'

'No idea.' He stood up too and squinted. 'I am going to kill Dax for this. Well, I'm going to make him eat sprouts, and that's pretty much the same thing.' A sigh. 'I should have been in Croatia now.'

'If you feed him sprouts, Croatia probably won't be far enough.' I shaded my eyes to watch Ruth angling her camera downwards. 'Why Croatia?'

Mac sighed again. 'I write and film for a travel programme,' he said and named a YouTube channel and website that even *I* had heard of. 'I was meant to be filming out in Croatia and Hungary this winter, but then Dax had to pull in a family favour.'

'Sounds exciting,' I said, slightly enviously. 'I've always wanted to travel and see the world.'

'What about you? What do you do for a day job? When you're not grovelling in the dirt for £100 a day, that is.' He smiled at me, and it was a nice smile, brown eyes crinkling under the pulled-down hat and the line of hair which flicked out sideways and made his face look a bit like a sunflower middle peeping out from between the petals.

'I'm... I've...' I groped. 'I have an Etsy site,' I decided on.

'Very creative. You work from home?'

I felt my teeth begin to clench and seized on Junior's standing back up again as the perfect excuse. 'Shall we go and see what Ruth's found?'

I saw the quick frown that made his hat draw down over his eyebrows, but it was fine. Only a month. I only had to be with these people for a month, they didn't need to know my entire life story to help establish that big cats didn't exist in the wild on the moors and earn three grand for the privilege, did they? I trotted off at a brisk pace, giving Mac no real choice but to follow behind, his question unanswered.

'Could be a print.' Junior sounded animated. Over his shoulder, Ruth gave me a little smile and a wave and I wondered whether this was her attempt to reingratiate herself with the big man. After all, she had questioned his tracking, maybe she'd faked up a print to make him feel wanted? I shook my head at my own cynicism. This was Ruth, after all. 'Looks like the same animal that left those prints we saw on the way down.'

'How can you tell?' Ruth was definitely trying to build bridges.

Junior grunted. 'See here? Steps slightly to the left. Same size, too.'

'So it's the pawprint of a big cat?' I angled my camera down at the shape in the dust. It looked like a blob to me, a random scuff in the sandy path, but maybe you had to have years of experience of tracking to tell what it was. 'Evidence?' I bent down so my camera could get a close up of the blob, in the faint hope that it might be a £50,000-winning mark in the earth.

'Could be.' Junior straightened up again. 'Or it could be another creature. We need more evidence. This could be a fake.' He looked around at us, everyone's faces showing a level of expectancy that almost supposed he was going to whip a puma out from behind his back and say, 'Just kidding. Here it is.'

'But why...?' Ruth's baffled expression almost made me laugh.

'Fifty thousand pounds,' I said. 'It's an awful lot of money.'

'But a footprint isn't enough.' Mac bent down to look at the print. 'It has to be lab-proof, to eliminate any possibility of cheating.'

I was *almost* sure that Sebastian slumped a couple of centimetres. Kanga, who'd been quietly fidgeting whilst admiring Junior's muscles at work, said, 'Then why are we bothering to *look* for prints and do all this grovelling around in the dirt?'

'Because where there's prints, there's a trail.' Junior, probably unconsciously, flexed his biceps. 'If you can track the beast, you can find it. And if you want the big prize, then you gotta find it.'

Well, I *did* want quarter of a million pounds. As, evidently, did everyone else in the group, from the shrugs and deprecating nods. 'When you say *find it*,' I said carefully, 'what exactly do you mean?'

Junior reached a hand inside his trousers. For a couple of seconds, I wondered where the hell this was going, and then he withdrew his hand. Holding a pistol. 'For quarter of a mill, they need a body.'

'I never thought we'd have to *kill* anything,' Ruth said eventually, and the edge of tears cut through her words. 'I'm not sure God put me on this earth to kill anything.'

'Oh, this is no gun.' Junior patted the shiny barrel. 'It's a tranquiliser. We don't kill the beast, we drop it and bring it in.'

A moment of quiet as we all mentally rehearsed the practicalities of 'bringing in' an animal which might suddenly revive and maul us all.

'And then what happens?' I asked,

'They gotta do experiments. Find out where it came from, DNA sorta thing.' Junior shrugged, carelessly. 'Then, I guess, a zoo?'

There was a collective indrawing of breath that made the clouds move towards us a fraction. Then Junior, clearly having exhausted his vocabulary, stomped back off up towards the campsite, leaving the rest of us huddled in our own individual pods of thoughtfulness.

I looked out over the wild expanse in front of us, where little sand devils were being whipped by the wind to scour the dry earth. Thousands of acres of bracken-padded wilderness, where the only sound was the hiss and gurgle of the river and the occasional emergency croak of a grouse getting airborne.

'I don't think I like that,' Ruth said eventually. 'Taking a wild animal and putting it in a zoo.'

'It... it doesn't seem right, does it?' I looked at the others. All of them, except Mac, were staring at the rise and fall of the horizon. It seemed we were all imagining the same thing, bars, wire. Noise. 'Making something live in captivity, just because it had the misfortune to come across us.'

'For a quarter of a million pounds, I think it's a great trade-off,' Kanga said, but even her voice was a little less strident than usual. 'Zoos aren't so bad. Regular meals.'

'But it wouldn't be able to roam!' Ruth was suddenly animated. 'All this space, Kanga! All this sky and being able to hunt its own food and sleep where it wants to and eat what it wants!'

'Which could be us,' Kanga responded.

I turned on Mac. 'You knew, though, didn't you? That the only way to win the money was to capture the animal?'

Mac shrugged. 'There's nothing out here *to* capture,' he said, reasonably. 'Except those bloody birds that make that squeaking sound in the middle of the night, and those I would cheerfully see put in very small, and most of all soundproof, boxes.'

The newly rising wind skirled around our legs. The air of disappointment was almost solid, everyone had slumped a bit more and, as we'd been bent double all day without any noticeable elevation, that meant most of us were almost horizontal. 'Oh, shit,' said Kanga, and it was probably the first time in this entire venture that I'd agreed with her.

'Also,' I sounded peevish, I knew it, 'I'm not sure how happy I am about one of us running around the place *with a gun*.'

'Why? Because he's American? You think he might go postal and shoot us all in our sleep?' Mac's voice was dry and the only warmth came from the sarcasm. And there I'd been, thinking he was on my side in all this. 'And it's not even a real gun.'

'No!' I wasn't entirely sure how I could voice my objection to the over-muscled and subsonic Junior being armed. I wasn't even entirely sure what my objection *was*. 'But – we all had to hand in our phones and stuff, didn't we?' I looked around, desperately hoping that the others weren't going to burst out with 'What, they made you hand over your *phone*? We've all got ours...' Nobody did. 'And anything could happen out here. What if... what if Sebastian goes insane and steals the gun and holds us all hostage?'

'Hey,' observed Sebastian, mildly. 'Why me?'

'Proximity,' I snapped. He was standing on the other side of me. 'All right, what if God sends Ruth a message saying we're all evil and have to be eliminated? And she tranquilises us all and then suffocates us while we're unconscious?'

'Um. He doesn't work like that. Actually.' Ruth sounded diffident, but slightly offended.

Kanga curled a lip. 'I'd like to see her try.'

'I don't like the idea of there being a gun in the camp, that's all,' I finished rapidly. 'It's not Junior having it that's the problem, it's that *any* of us could get it.'

'You want to take on Junior and wrestle away a gun, you go ahead.' Mac's tone still sounded dry. 'He wouldn't go down easy. Don't you think that, of all of us, he's probably the *best* person to be armed? He's trained to use it, he's got experience in the wild, he knows how to handle a gun – I hope you're not objecting because he's black?'

The idea that Mac could have thought that I was being racist by objecting to there being a weapon kicking around made me suck in my breath so hard that my tongue almost went down my throat. I toyed with various forms of words that would convey my lack of caring whether Junior was black, white or any permutation of colours thereof, but all I could come up with was, 'Don't be so bloody stupid.'

'I don't like guns either.' Ruth waded in and I could have kissed her. 'And I understand what Izzy is saying. It's not Junior, it's the gun. And anything that could tranquilise a panther probably wouldn't be good if a human got shot with it.'

'Well.' Sebastian, in his role as general boss, made a movement that dispelled the stasis we'd been standing in. 'Maybe we could work something out. We could ask Junior if he'd agree to letting us lock the weapon away in the medicine container, unless it's needed?'

We exchanged a look. 'Who's going to be the one to ask him, though?' I said. 'It does sound as though we suspect him of murderous intent. I don't think he's going to get the whole "us being British and not used to guns being waved around".'

Kanga sighed. 'I'll do it.' She sighed again. 'I've got a rapport with Junior, and he'll take it better coming from a woman.' She looked at me sternly. 'As long as you're *sure* you're not being racist?'

'No.' I fought not to roll my eyes. 'I'm being gunnist. I would feel exactly the same if it was one of you lot that was armed.'

In fact, given the way Mac was looking at me right now, I'd feel even worse if it was him that was armed. Between the new beard that was making its way up his cheeks, and the hair that protruded from beneath the hat in curls, like a seventeenth-century wig, his expression was decidedly hostile.

'And then there's the fact that someone has to have the key,' Mac said. 'Who do you declare to be mentally stable enough to keep the key to the container that has the gun in, Izzy? In your infinite wisdom?'

'Oh, I say, there's no need for that!' Sebastian stepped between us. 'I actually think Izzy has a good and sensible point. None of us know how being out here is going to affect us, mentally, do we? *Any* one of us may experience a psychotic break and being unwell whilst armed – well, it could be a recipe for disaster. I'm only sorry that I didn't think of it first.' He turned to me and smiled. 'Sorry, Izzy. It shouldn't have had to be you that raised the issue.'

I smiled back, and, to my relief, Mac's grim expression lightened up a touch. 'That's all I meant,' I said, slightly weakly. 'Honestly.'

'How about' – Ruth came in cautiously, as though slightly afraid we might all team up and drag her down like lions with a gazelle – 'we take it in turns? If someone different has the key every couple of days, it lessens the risk of that person being the one who may... er... may have any issues?'

'Look.' Kanga put her hands on her hips. 'I've got to get him to agree to give the gun up first. He might decide that he doesn't want a bunch of utter fuckwits anywhere near his weapon, so let's not get ahead of ourselves here, okay? Anyway. No time like the present.' She loosened her jacket zip a few notches and I switched from feeling sorry for myself for being misunderstood, to feeling sorry for Junior, who was about to be hit by Storm Kanga, and hadn't had chance to tie everything down yet.

We watched her confidently striding her way across the heather, as the sun began to sink over the opposite hill, making her shadow stretch long and lean before her. There was a moment of awkward silence, then Mac said, 'Sorry, Izzy. I didn't mean to imply... er.' He stopped and I saw him look to Sebastian for help.

'And I didn't mean to imply that I thought any of you might be teetering on the edge of insanity,' I said, slightly emboldened by his apology. 'I think I was more taken aback to realise that a gun was involved anywhere in this.'

'I didn't know we'd have to *shoot* it,' Ruth chipped in, her voice small. 'I don't think the Lord would approve of that. Or putting a wild animal in a cage just so that people can come and look at it, not after all this.' She waved an arm to indicate the wild, spreading moorland.

'How about...' Sebastian's tone was cautious. 'How about if one of us was under attack from the beast, how would we feel about shooting it then?'

We all went quiet, sunk, presumably, in our own individual battles with morality. 'I suppose...' Ruth, still sounding timid, put in, 'that would be all right.'

'But then what would we do?' I asked. 'Leave it unconscious and try to run away really, really quickly, before it came round with a panther-sized headache and a grudge? Because we couldn't keep it under until Dax got here, and even if we did, then he'd crate the creature up and take it away. So it would be us, a really cross and – and I have to stress this – bloody enormous – cat, and no chance of escape.' I knew I sounded sarcastic, but I didn't really like the way this was going.

'Just the principle, Izzy.' Sebastian still looked thoughtful.

'You're all crackers.' Mac suddenly burst out laughing. 'You're planning escape from an animal that probably doesn't even *exist*, let alone might be hanging around up here! And discussing the ethics of putting an imaginary beast in a zoo is pretty high up there on the list of "totally bananas things I have heard", I have to say.'

Another silence descended, preceded by the dimness of twilight drawing down around us as the sun finally slithered down over the horizon to the west, leaving the sky streaked with the red of its passing. The air instantly felt colder.

'Well. It's good to be prepared, even if only hypothetically,' Sebastian said briskly at last, and I remembered what he'd told me about his possible sighting. Sebastian believed that there might be a big cat out here, even if the only evidence currently was some blurry prints that could have been anything. 'Anyway, who's on cooking duty tonight?'

'You, I think,' I said jovially, trying to pick up his change of subject and run with it to cover my sheer embarrassment at the way all this had gone. 'Any plans?'

'Not really. We're getting a bit low on the fresh fruit and veg, so it might be some kind of stew which doesn't bear close examination. The swede is starting to look like a scrotum.' Sebastian glanced at Ruth. 'Sorry.'

'Dax has promised us another drop of fresh food in a couple of days,' Mac said unexpectedly. 'He's coming to do another talking-heads, so we can report on what we've seen and how we're getting on.'

There was a moment of quiet. Ruth, Sebastian and I looked at him.

'Okay,' I finally said, when it was apparent that nobody else was going to react. 'Are you telling us that you are in contact with your brother? Like, on a daily basis? As in, you have a mobile or other communication device somewhere, despite what we were all told?'

'Shit.' Mac slapped off his camera, turned around and stormed, in as much as anyone *could* storm over that uneven surface in flappy waterproof trousers, off towards the camp without a backwards glance.

The remaining three of us watched him go. In the end, Sebastian sighed into the gathering dark. 'We were doing so well, I thought,' he said, taking his stripy knitted hat off and running a hand through his hair. 'Izzy, can you go and have a word with him?'

'Why *me*?'

'You and Mac seem to have more of a bond. Besides, *I'm* cooking, Kanga is seducing Junior and Ruth—' We looked around. Ruth had vanished. 'Where *is* Ruth?'

'I'm down here.' Ruth's voice came from knee level. 'I'm praying for guidance.'

'Ruth is praying for guidance,' Sebastian went on smoothly. 'So it's down to you, Izzy, to find out whether he really is hiding some kind of communication device.'

'I don't have to strip search him, do I?' I asked, rather nastily.

Sebastian beamed at me. 'I think asking will do,' he said, and then waved at me in the manner of a head teacher dismissing a pupil who's been reported for smoking in the toilets. 'I've got to go and use up three packs of mince that go out of date tomorrow, some floppy veg and a scrotal swede, so I am actually half-hoping that Mac is telling the truth about a fresh food drop-off.'

I was tempted to pray for guidance myself, but settled for trailing Mac up the hill back to camp, and then following him all the way to his tent.

He'd zipped the flap shut, which we'd collectively agreed was the symbol for 'leave me alone'. 'Knock knock,' I said, trying for that non-confrontational tone again.

There was no answer. But, as I knew he was definitely in there, I pressed my case. 'Look, we need to know, all right? I mean, it's only sensible, if you think about it, having some way of contacting the outside world; what if one of us fell off a cliff? Or Kanga sprained one of her boobs?' I added, in a lower voice, because the lack of response was getting to me. 'We'd absolutely *have* to be able to make an emergency call, and with you being Dax's brother, it makes perfect sense for you to be the one with the means of calling for help. I think everyone's just a bit upset that we didn't know about it, so it came out of the blue.'

'Are you going to pause for breath now?' Mac's voice waspishly came through the nylon.

'I don't know. Are you going to explain, or are you going to leave me to fill in the gaps by myself?' His tone had made me feel less than agreeable.

'Oh, for fuck's sake.' The zip opened and Mac's face poked out. 'Look, come in here. I can't face Sebastian and his fucking self-righteous expression at the moment.'

'He's cooking,' I pointed out reasonably, but I still bent down and crawled inside the tent. Mac's tent was slightly smaller than mine and I had to stand like a sycophant, head angled towards the floor and my hands clasped together, once I got in. 'So you can't see it. He's full of mince and bollock-swede.'

Mac was sitting on his sleeping bag. 'For god's sake, sit down,' he snapped. 'You're making the tent bulge.'

I sat. 'Whilst you,' I said, avoiding his eye by arranging a fleecy jacket underneath me to give me some padding, 'are hiding quite a lot of stuff from us, aren't you?'

'Turn your camera off,' he said suddenly.

'What?' Once again, I'd genuinely forgotten that our cameras were recording everything. It was so natural now to see the blinking lights from everyone's shoulder that it had become a part of us all. We remembered them only sufficiently to turn them off when we went for a wee or to bed.

Mac leaned forward. It was sudden and I didn't have time to pull back,

so all I saw was the flash of approaching beanie, and then I felt the poke
on my shoulder. 'That's better.'

'You aren't allowed to do that!'

Mac sighed. 'Might as well be hung for a sheep as a lamb,' he said and
sounded slightly bitter. 'Look. Yes, I've got a phone. One person in each
party has to have one, for emergencies. They were going to give it to you,
but once Dax had to draft me in, he decided to make me the person in
charge of reporting in, to save you from being compromised. We're told
not to reveal it unless it's absolutely necessary.'

I stared at him. He was cross-legged, quite relaxed, and he'd taken his
boots off. My eyes were drawn to the Tweetie-Pie socks. 'Why?'

'Oh, my sweet summer child.' He almost laughed then, the dark eyes
sparked with humour and I stopped noticing his socks, because his face
was more attractive. 'Everyone would suddenly have an emergency that
meant they absolutely *had* to phone home, right this minute. Or text, or
send some other form of message. And the whole concept of this show,
the whole *point*, is groups of people isolated from the rest of humanity.
Not,' he added with the smile broadening, 'being able to send daily
reports to newspapers or online sites. We'd have the *Mirror* doing photo-
shoots from the opposite hill and we'd be on the front page of *TV Weekly*
before we knew what hit us.'

I rearranged my legs. 'Oh,' I said, inadequately. I hadn't really considered any of this.

'And, as we're supposed to be tracking a notoriously solitary, cautious
and probably non-existent, creature, having half of the country coming
along to see what we're doing, how we're getting on and whether anyone
is naked yet, would rather bugger up the operation, don't you think?' He
smiled at me more broadly now. 'So. Now you know. I feel pretty stupid
for slipping up and giving it away, but, well. Here we are.'

This spirit of honesty made him feel more approachable, so I asked
the question that was really burning away in my head. 'And you're really
not planting evidence for us to find, to keep the show running?'

'No, Izzy.' The smile had wilted a bit now. 'I am not.'

We sat quietly for a moment. From outside, we could hear Ruth
helping Sebastian to sort the ingredients for what sounded as though it

was going to be a borderline-edible stew. There was no sound from Junior or Kanga, and no lights coming from any of the other tents.

'Does that mean...' I couldn't look at him. He looked like a man who made his living from flitting from country to country with all his possessions in one small bag. Very contained, very observant, and owning almost nothing. 'That the marks that Junior found today could actually *be real*?'

Mac shrugged. 'You tell me.'

'You think *I'm* planting them?' I found myself on my feet. 'Oh, that's not fair!'

'Well, *someone* is,' Mac pointed out reasonably. 'And sit down. You'll go through the roof if you don't, and as this is my tent and barely weather-proof as it is...'

I subsided back onto the jacket and Mac and I regarded one another levelly for a moment. I had a sudden moment of wondering what he saw when he looked at me. I hadn't taken my hat off for three days, and I felt urgently in need of a wash that took in more than just my face, and a reapplication of deodorant.

'You're the only one of us who hasn't complained about the sleeping arrangements,' Mac said eventually. 'You don't seem bothered about the no showers, or the rather random meals. Kanga's been kicking off like a princess and even Ruth has muttered once or twice about how uncomfortable it is sleeping on the ground. Sebastian's a farmer, he'll take more or less anything, and I'm used to roughing it a bit when we're filming. But you—' He stopped and tipped his head on one side. 'We don't know much about you, do we, Izzy?'

There was a tone in his voice that I couldn't decipher. It could have been concern or it could have been suspicion. Was he seriously suspecting *me* of mocking up paw prints? Was *that* what was behind this?

'There's nothing *to* know,' I said stiffly.

'So you absolutely promise, with your hand on the Bible that Ruth has probably got as her bedside book, that you haven't been parachuted in by the production company to be the *agent provocateur* in this operation?' Mac's expression was as indecipherable as his tone now. Steady and level but I could see him chewing at his lower lip, among the incipient beard growth, as though my answer was really important.

'Wouldn't you know if I were? Is your brother that good at keeping secrets from you?' I felt itchily embarrassed by that level stare, even though I knew I had nothing to hide. Well, nearly nothing.

He dropped his eyes at last. 'I don't know.' His voice had lost that undertone now. 'Dax and I don't exactly communicate...' He shook his head and raised both hands to tweak at the ends of his hair, which was springing from under his hat in curls and random growths in a 1980s rock star sort of way. 'Sorry. I think the lack of sleep is getting to my operational systems.'

I saw him flash me a look. Well, if he thought that him not being able to sleep was going to draw any confessions from me, he had another think coming. 'Someone could be doing it without Dax knowing,' I said slowly.

'Who, though?' The beanie hat came off now and his hair sprang free, like a prisoner released from a long confinement. 'We've established it's not you or me. I don't see Ruth compromising her principles by faking stuff, and Sebastian's too straightforward.'

'Which leaves Kanga.'

We looked at one another.

'She was nowhere near where Ruth found that print, though,' I said, eventually, despite the fact that Kanga was clearly leading the 'fake for money' rankings. 'I know she's the one of us most likely to, but she had no chance this afternoon. I was keeping my eye on her.' I didn't want to confess that I'd been making sure that she kept well away from Sebastian. After his confession to me this morning, I felt slightly protective towards him, so I'd been checking that Kanga wasn't sizing him up for another go.

Mac drew his knees up under his chin and looked thoughtful. 'So, we're left with the possibility that there's something out there,' he said. 'Again.'

'But it might not be a big cat. For all his confidence, Junior's not used to tracking in the English countryside.' I could smell dinner cooking now, wafting in through the thin walls of the tent, and it was making my mouth water. 'I don't really know what there could be making prints like that – a big dog, maybe?'

'There's a dog down the valley,' Mac said slowly. 'It was barking its head off last night.'

I felt the probability drop down around me, with the noise of a quarter of a million pounds going down the drain. 'Of course.'

'The farmer probably lets it out at night for a run round.'

Oh, well. Three thousand pounds, for the month. 'And I bet it's bloody huge.'

'And probably comes up here for a sniff around to see if we've left any food out,' Mac finished, and looked smug. 'So, do we tell them?'

Our eyes met. I didn't know what he could see in mine, but there was a soft look in his, almost a kind of sympathy. It made me want to tell him things, made me want to confess. But that voice in my head that whispered that it was all my own fault meant that I couldn't. 'I don't think so. Why would we? Your brother might call all this off, and at least it's giving us something to find, to stop this being the most boring TV in the world.'

He nodded an acknowledgement and stopped looking at me. 'Okay. So, this is social drama, we're not going to find anything, and we stand no chance of winning any money.' Now the gaze was back on me again. 'How does that make you feel?'

I closed my eyes to stop my face giving me away. 'Little bit cheated, but it's okay.' I took a deep breath. 'Even if it *had* been real, what were the chances we'd find any evidence worth £50,000, anyway? And I think we all agreed back there that we weren't up for shooting it and putting it in a zoo, not even for £250,000.'

'Izzy, look...' he began, but there was a sudden commotion at the doorway to the tent, and a shadowed presence loomed.

'Food's ready.' It was Sebastian. 'I think. It looks cooked anyway, and Ruth says it's probably fine. I don't really cook much at home, to be honest, so I'm learning as we go.'

Mac and I got slowly to our feet. My body complained about standing, after all the bending, and let me know that sleeping on the ground wasn't doing it any favours. 'We're coming,' I said, and let Mac unzip the tent flap.

I didn't miss that thoughtful look he gave me, though, as we passed through and on out into the night air.

6

In the morning, Dax came over in the Jeep, filmed a few bits of us each in our tents, and left more food. I did notice that he spent more time in Junior's tent than with the rest of us. I didn't think Kanga was still in there with him, there wouldn't really have been enough space for three people, and I could only hear Dax's voice and the occasional deep reply from Junior. She must have left, quietly, in the middle of the night. That in itself was surprising, it didn't seem to be in Kanga's nature to do things without a degree of theatrical shrieking. I wondered why she'd felt the need to return to her own tent without alerting the entire postcode to her movements.

I sat at my tent flap with the zip slightly down, staring out at the rain-obscured valley and wondered what Dax and Junior were talking about in there. Planning? *Or plotting?* Was Dax giving Junior his instructions for Phase Two of our adventure? I watched Dax leave, tiptoeing his soggy way back to the Jeep with the equipment on his shoulder. Even Callum and Steve hadn't wanted to turn out in this weather, so he'd been a one-man crew – had that given him the opportunity to set up more false trails? Just how real *was* any of this?

We didn't even try to track anything all day, the rain was washing down over the pathway and forming little rivulets through the heather as it made its way down to the beck at the bottom of the valley. When I braved the outdoors to make my way to the Portaloo, the rocks were streaked and shiny with wet, the ankle-level bushes flapped and flicked water and the constant hiss of rain on the nylon tents sounded like everyone was talking at once, just under the level of hearing.

We ate cold food, in solitary confinement. I didn't want to talk to anyone anyway, I wanted the whole 'gun' business to die down first, and we hadn't seen or heard from either Kanga or Junior yet. I stayed in my tent, listening to the rain and occasionally unzipping my tent flap to a haze of drizzle and a cold wind. I read a book and then lay on my sleeping bag and thought.

Mac had been right. This *wasn't* as bad for me as it was for the others. I had space of my own, regular meals; I didn't care about the quality of the accommodation or the food, the fact it was *there* was enough. I hadn't come from the luxury of my own house, my own flat, as the others evidently had, so being able to lie down in the middle of the day and not worry where my next meal was coming from was really quite pleasant.

I was woken from a dreamy doze by Mac, clearing his throat outside.

'Izzy? I've got something to report. We're all gathering in Sebastian's tent in ten minutes.' I waited a moment. There was no sound of him leaving, just a rustling and then his voice lower down, as though he were bending very close to the tent. 'Are you all right?'

Such soft concern. Nothing that should be considered out of the ordinary, just a question in a gentle tone, but the unexpectedness of it made me choke for a moment.

'Yes. Yes, I'm fine. Sebastian's tent in ten. I'll be there.'

'Are you *sure* you're okay? After that shit with the gun... and you've not been about much today.'

I managed a half-laugh. 'Have you *seen* today? Bigfoot and the giant cat could be waltzing together down in that valley and we wouldn't be able to tell.'

'Fair enough.' More rustling, then Mac's voice over at Ruth's tent, telling her the same thing, only without questioning her welfare.

I really needed to pull myself together if a query about my well-being was going to make me come over all teary-eyed. I needed to be tougher than this. I *was* tougher than this. But the rain had kept me awake last night, so I was sleep-deprived and cold; this whole thing was making me wonder what the hell I was doing here, and it was eating its way into my reserves of not-caring.

I emerged, somewhat cautiously, into the damp day. The light was leaching from the sky, pressed by the weight of clouds, and the far side of the valley was nothing but a hazy smear when I glanced up and around. The rain was hushing and glugging, tapping on the top of my waterproofs insistently, and making little mud slides of the paths we'd examined so carefully yesterday.

The flap of Sebastian's tent was invitingly open and a gleam of lamp-light sliced its way out into the gloom. I followed Ruth in and we paused to take off our boots in the nylon porch.

'This weather is horrible, isn't it?' I made conversation as we fiddled with laces. 'We're never going to see anything out there if it stays like this.'

'I'm sure it's part of God's plan for us,' she said equably. She was wearing fluffy pink socks, I noticed, with little furry cuffs around the ankle. I wondered why I thought them incongruous, and then realised that I somehow suspected that Ruth led the life of a nun, denying herself comforts or anything that might count as frivolous, and I didn't really know why.

'You said you want to give any money we may win to your church?' My laces were tangled and had become tight with the damp. 'Is that God's plan for you?'

'We all do what we can to raise money to help those less fortunate.' Her voice was gentle. 'There's no need to be sarcastic, Izzy.'

I hadn't been aware that I *was* being sarcastic. 'I meant – does your church – I mean, is it one of those where you have to give them money all the time?'

Ruth gave me a level look. 'It's not a cult,' she said, and it was disconcerting, being schooled by someone a good ten years younger than me. 'I don't know what you're imagining, but we don't *have* to give money, we *choose* to, because it's the Christian thing to do, to give to those who need help.'

She went past me into the main body of the tent and I sat back against the damp canvas. I'd got it wrong again. There I had been, imagining Ruth to be some poor innocent, taking part in this horror of a show to try to get money to keep some overweight pastor in white Rolls-Royces. But it turned out that she was doing it for the right reasons; to help others. Now I felt stupid and angry at myself for what I'd thought – of *course* Ruth wasn't a member of some money-grabbing obscure sect, she was a good church-going girl who really believed in what she was doing. The pink socks should have given me a heads-up on that front.

So, she, Sebastian and Kanga all had perfectly good reasons for being here. Which left Mac and me as the outsiders as the only suspects for planting evidence. I was fairly sure that it wasn't me planting fake pawprints in the dirt, unless I was sleepwalking. And even my dreams hadn't involved mysterious walks across moorland; they had been a lot more prosaic. I'd woken in a sweat a couple of times, only to realise that I was safer, more secure here under a nylon sheet, than I had been in any house.

I hated to admit it too, but somehow, I'd grown to trust Mac. He'd come clean about the phone, he'd got stroppy first, of course, but he could have lied his way out of it. He'd seemed honestly relieved when we'd decided the prints had probably come from the dog, which I could hear again now, barking crazily into the weather from a distant farm some-where behind the curtain of rain. Mac seemed genuinely annoyed at being here; co-opted by his brother.

So that meant the only outlier was me. So maybe it was natural that I should come under suspicion. Of course, there was also Junior, but, as the tracker and presumably on the payroll, he wouldn't have any investment other than professional in finding anything that might be living out here. Or would he? I remembered how long Dax had spent in his tent earlier. Had they just been filming a longer segment, more in depth than the five minutes of 'how is everything going' that Dax had got from the rest of us?

Everyone else was already in the tent, which had fugged up with the smell of unwashed skin, mud and too many people breathing in too small a space. Kanga and Junior were there, sitting side by side but seeming a little awkward. He'd put a shirt on, tight over his biceps and shoulders, which looked as though it had been stitched onto his body. Kanga was a bit rumpled and was keeping her eyes strictly to the front, almost as though ashamed of herself. This struck me as odd, as she'd been the one to volunteer to persuade Junior to give up the gun. I wondered how that had gone, whether he was still armed, but when Kanga caught my eye and gave me a straight-mouthed smile, I assumed she'd succeeded in her mission.

Ruth and Sebastian were scrunched up together at the far end of the tent, making room for the rest of us. Mac had taken up a position in the centre, legs tucked under him as though he was about to swing into a yoga routine. I hunched myself into the only available space, inside the door, with the payment of a trickle of water damping my socks as it blew through the entrance flap every now and then.

'Okay.' Mac looked at us all. 'Bad news. You all know by now that I've got a phone, so that Dax and I can message one another – he's sent me a message today.' Mac held out the phone, but the steamy mass of bodies meant that I couldn't read what the screen said and I doubted anyone else could either.

'Right.' Sebastian heeled himself closer to Mac. 'Looks like a weather forecast.'

'The Met Office are forecasting blizzards with extremely cold wind.' Mac tucked the phone away again. 'And because we're on high ground, it's going to hit us worst, overnight.'

We all looked at one another. My scalp prickled. 'So, snow,' I said, when nobody else spoke. 'And that's worse than what we've currently got, because?'

'Well, cold.' Mac frowned at me. 'And wind. The tents might blow away and leave us without shelter. But mostly the cold. Dax has asked what we want to do. We can abort if we want to, they'll come and take us down off the moor this evening and cut our entire contribution from the programme. Apparently,' he added, with a slight tone of bitterness, 'the Cannock Chase team reckon they're on the trail of something, and the

Bodmin guys have got some hair samples. They can lose our section without any real loss to the programme.'

We all looked at one another. 'So everything so far would be wiped?' Ruth sounded unusually dismal.

'And pointless,' Sebastian added.

'And we wouldn't be on TV at *all*?' Kanga looked horrified. 'Oh, no, I'm not having that.'

'Even if all you *do* get famous for is being a frozen corpse?' Mac asked her.

'Fame is fame.' Kanga tossed her head. She'd still got her hat on, so it didn't really have the desired hair-whippy effect, but her bobble swayed about and conveyed the general emotion.

We'd been out here for nearly a week. I was doing mental calculations. At £100 a day... no, it still wasn't enough. I needed over a thousand to have a decent deposit, even for a room in a shared house. And that was only the start of it. 'I vote we stay too,' I said, trying to inject a tone of 'I want to get to the bottom of the mystery' into my voice. 'We're in the shelter of the rocks and we've got plenty of food.'

'But... cold?' Sebastian looked dubious. 'I mean, I'll go with the majority, I need the money, but is it wise to try to front it out? Could we not ask Dax to bring us off the moor for the duration of the storm and edit that bit out?'

Mac shook his head. 'If we leave the moor, it's all over. The show's supposed to be as authentic as possible, and I get the feeling that us being snowed off would add a bit more spice to those who carry on. A sort of "this is why these cats remain unfound, because they live where it's hard for people to find evidence" subtext.'

'Fuck subtext,' Kanga said succinctly. 'I've got a presenting career to think about.'

Junior subsonic-ed something about evidence being easier to see in the snow, and Mac nodded. 'Ruth?'

Ruth stopped fiddling with the toes of her socks and looked up brightly. 'I put my life in God's hands when I came out here,' she said, and I was sure I heard Kanga give an impatient little sigh, 'and I trust Him to keep us all safe. I'll stay.'

'Right.' Sebastian seemed to remember that he was our sort-of leader. 'Then we make arrangements to protect against the weather. I've been snowed up on the farm a couple of times, we need to make sure we've got warmth, food and protection from the weather.' He looked around us all, crowded into the tent, most of us unable to stretch our legs out. 'We can't all stay in here, but I'd recommend pairing up; two people can keep one another warm and watch for signs of hypothermia. It's also safer, if one of the tents goes down, we'll have empty tents for immediate occupation.'

There was a moment of silence. I knew we were all mentally pairing ourselves up and not really liking the results. I felt sorry for whoever got to be sealed in a tent in a snowstorm with Kanga and her pneumatic chest, it would be like being shut in a cupboard with a bunch of party balloons.

'Kanga and Junior can take one,' Mac said, carefully not referring to whatever activities they might choose to undertake to keep warm. 'Ruth and Sebastian in here and Izzy and I can take my tent. Dax suggested we pair up too.'

'Shouldn't Ruth and I be together and you and Sebastian?' I offered. 'To avoid any... well... anything...?'

Mac shook the phone at me. 'Dax wants the frisson. He's advised girls share with boys. Better viewing, apparently.'

'Nobody is viewing my frisson,' I said tartly. 'Are you absolutely sure that there's snow forecast and we're not being manipulated into – well, a Situation?'

'Nothing going on my end, promise,' Sebastian said. 'Ruth is perfectly safe with me.'

'And I'm saving myself for the right man,' Ruth said.

'My wife will be delighted to hear that,' Sebastian said and raised his eyebrows. 'So, Kanga and Junior, are you two all right to share?'

There was a momentary pause, during which Kanga and Junior gave one another sideways glances, and then both nodded.

'Right,' Sebastian went on. 'I'm spoken for, and Ruth is happy to stay with me. That's just you and Izzy to agree then.'

Reluctantly, as though the air had become thick, I looked up and met Mac's gaze. 'I don't know,' I said.

'Keep your camera on if you don't feel safe,' he said, not sounding as embarrassed by my evident lack of keenness to be shut in a small tent with him overnight as I might have expected. 'But I honestly think we need to regard the weather as the biggest danger here.'

'Or you can come in with us.' Ruth waved an arm to indicate Sebastian's tent, piled with bodies. 'If you'd rather.'

'That would leave Mac on his own. There's no room for four to sleep in here, and we really shouldn't have one person alone. Hypothermia can kill.' Sebastian was evidently not reading the atmosphere. Never mind hypothermia, I was going to kill him armed only with my expression.

'And I'm not going in with Kanga and Junior.' Mac winked at Junior, who looked away. Although Kanga was half-cuddled up against him, he didn't put his arm around her, I noticed. But then, in this confined space, she couldn't really help but be snuggled up into him. I was practically sitting on Ruth's lap, and there *definitely* wasn't anything going on between us.

'I'll stay with Mac,' I said and saw him make some movement out of the corner of my eye. I wasn't sure what it was, whether it was surprise or a twitch towards me. 'It's only tonight, right? We're not expecting a fortnight of raging arctic weather?'

'Just a blast coming through,' Mac said. I was determinedly not looking at him. 'Cold, wind and snow. Not sure what comes after that, plague of frogs, possibly.'

There was a momentary silence, into which the renewed flapping of the tent fabric acted as a kind of punctuation. The wind was certainly rising, as though it wanted to make a point.

'When do we start?' Kanga bumped herself towards the entrance. 'Because if I'm going to move into Junior's, I need to bring stuff.'

Junior frowned. 'What stuff? You know it's a small tent, right?'

'Well, yes, but there are things a girl needs for an overnight stay.' She grabbed her hair and looked ruefully at the gritty ends. 'My leave-in conditioner and my make-up remover and things.'

'Well, let's get ourselves sorted before dark, shall we?' Sebastian intervened. 'Body heat will be the thing that gets us through, so we need to be established by the time the temperature starts to drop. Everyone who's moving, get what you need, and those of us whose tents are being moved into need to check their ropes and fixings, we don't want anything blowing away.'

He left a pause, into which I supposed one of us was meant to insert a 'blowing' joke, but we were all too damp and tired to bother.

'Right. Let's get moving,' Sebastian finished, when it became evident that nobody could force themselves to insert so much as the tip of an entendre.

As if in answer, the tent gave a shudder and there was a peculiar noise, a kind of rising wail. Presumably the gale was getting trapped under the rocks that protected our backs, and not liking it very much.

We all left. I went into my tent and rolled up my sleeping bag and mat to take with me. As an added precaution, I put extra socks in my pocket and, as I did so, I noticed that my camera light was blinking away. It took me by surprise. It was such second nature now to slap at your chest to turn off the camera before sleep and when entering the Portaloo that the presence of the tiny winking blue light mostly went unnoticed. But, as Mac said, it was my security. Everything was being recorded. And his awareness of my uncertainty also meant that he'd noticed things I would rather he hadn't. I hoped he wasn't going to try to quiz me about my life again, because the only weapon I had to hand was this rather crusty pile of socks.

The wind wheezed through my tent like an asthmatic in search of an inhaler. Any doubts I'd had about the weather forecast – including suspecting Dax of trying to force us to cohabit in order to stir up sexual tension – died away under the force of it. Whilst the day had been mostly soggy, there was now the suspicion of something colder and more destructive on the edge of the rain and the wind was practically solid when I made my way out of my tent and over to Mac's tent next door.

I stood for a second on the threshold and looked up. The sky, invisible all day behind a duvet of fog, now stood pin-sharp above me. The first faint stars were emerging and seemed almost to move with the force of the wind, until I realised that it was me, pummelled into swaying, that made them wobble. I had to step and brace to stay upright. Further down the valley, the dog which was our Suspect Number One for the pawprints howled into the dark. I hoped he had some shelter to crawl into when the weather really hit.

'Are you coming in then?' Mac's face had appeared at the tent flap. 'I've finished double-pegging the top bit, hopefully that's enough to hold us down.'

'I was just looking at the sky.' The rain had stopped too now, it was just the wind cutting grooves into the landscape with its sharp edges.

Mac crawled out of the tent and gathered himself to his feet beside me. We both looked upwards. 'Are you suspecting Dax of lying about the forecast?' Mac asked. He didn't sound as accusatory as might have been expected.

'Why, are you?' Surprised, I looked at him, but he was staring out across the dale, to where the pale night sky was outlining the hills, haloing them with stars.

'Little bit.' Still he didn't look at me, but he jerked his head, hopefully an acceptance that I'd *also* suspected his brother of manipulation. 'But I double checked and, yes, gales and blizzards for tonight. Come on, let's get inside, if "inside" is the proper word.'

He held the flap aside gallantly for me to crawl in first. For what it was worth, the tent was warmer than outside, and scrupulously tidy. 'Sling your bag down over there.' He pointed to a corner. 'I doubt we'll get much sleeping done, but we need to keep an eye on each other in case the cold gets too much.'

I put my bag down and then sat on it. There was a moment of uncomfortable silence.

'Turn your camera off a sec,' Mac said suddenly.

'What!'

'I want to ask you something and it's a bit... sensitive.' Mac slapped his own camera off. In the next-door tent, I could hear Ruth and Sebastian sorting belongings out, noisy and mundane. I turned my camera off too.

Mac looked at me seriously for a moment. 'Were you raped?' he asked, eventually, when our camera lights had both stopped blinking.

'No.'

My blunt denial seemed to surprise him. His eyebrows rose to vanish under the flat fringe that persistent hat-wearing had forced on us all. 'Oh. I thought...'

'It never got as far as that. But he used to try to force his way into my bedroom.'

I'd spent long enough trying to tell myself that it wasn't my fault that I should have been able to come out with the whole story by now. Just trot it out, upfront, straightforward. *It wasn't my fault.* And yet, and yet – that inborn sense of shame, that feeling that somehow, *somehow*, I should have been able to stop it, still made me reticent about saying any more.

Mac blinked. After a moment, he said, 'I had a friend who was raped. I didn't handle it well – I didn't know how to. Since then, I've learned a lot, including seeing the signs. And you are giving off a lot of them, so I wanted to make sure that I didn't do anything...' he glanced around the tent, 'to make you uncomfortable,' he finished.

I looked around the tent too. 'I think this entire venture is "uncomfortable" by its very definition,' I said, not sure if I was trying to change the subject or not. 'If we were living in luxury yurts, I suppose the viewing public wouldn't be regarding this as "must-see TV"?'

He didn't answer. Instead, he sat back against his bedroll and cocked his head at the sound of the wind, which was gusting down the valley so that backwashes of squall caused the tent to bulge and flex like a circus strongman. We were mostly sheltered by the rock overhang, although I didn't want to think about landslips.

'So, no,' I went on. 'I don't know what it is that you see in me, but it's not rape.'

'Okay. Okay.' Mac rubbed a hand through his hair. 'I'm sorry. I've obviously got the wrong end of the stick. Sorry.' He began unlacing his boots now, concentrating so ferociously on the task that I could see his embarrassment oozing through the three layers of coat, jacket and undershirt that he'd got on. 'Sorry,' he said again, sounding so abject that I wanted... I *needed* to set the record straight.

'I'm homeless,' I said. 'That's the real reason I'm here. It seemed like an easy way to raise the money to get myself a deposit for somewhere to live.'

One boot half-off, he looked at me. 'Ah.' A Tweetie-Pie sock slowly slithered into visibility. I wondered how long he'd had those on. 'That can't be easy. What happened?'

And it was that simple. Just a sympathetic question. I'd always thought it would be harder to talk about than this, that bringing up the subject would be enough to silence people into their own wonderings and imaginings. But Mac really, genuinely seemed to want to know.

'My relationship broke up and neither of us could afford to keep the flat, so I moved home to live with my mum. She was on her own, the two of us sharing expenses made sense, she had a spare room I could sleep in and use for crafting. I made book rooms for bookshelves.' I couldn't help the note of pride slipping into my voice there. I'd been *good*. 'They're book-sized ornament things that are 3D, you put them in between your books and they look like little rooms, all lit up. I did personalised ones to people's own designs, and it takes quite a bit of equipment and space.'

I stopped talking. There was such a huge gap between what-had-been and what-was-now and I wasn't sure I had the words to describe it.

Mac nodded. 'Sounds cool. So, you argued with your mum?'

'No, we had a great relationship. Until she met Paul.' Once the name was out there in the open, everything else followed along behind, as though his name dragged the following events heavily and reluctantly like a tired dray horse. 'He moved in and got a bit of a "thing" about me.'

'A bit of a thing' hardly even covered the surface of the obsessive levels of watching, of following, of listening in to my phone calls – all done under the guise of 'caring about me'. The trying to come into my room at all hours of the day and night, to 'check I was all right'. Paying for Mum to go out on spa days and mini-breaks, so he'd be alone with me. The gradual, gradual creep of the sinister, dropped in so infrequently that it looked like concern; concern that I only rejected because I was 'difficult' or 'having a bit of a breakdown'.

'It got – well, it got really bad. And then he told me that, if I didn't have sex with him, he'd tell Mum that I was trying to seduce him.'

Mac drew in a breath so sudden and sharp that I wondered if he'd injured himself on something for a moment.

'I, of course, didn't, so he did, and Mum threw me out,' I finished. 'She gave me five minutes to put some clothes in a bag, and then I was out, on the street. No chance to explain, and I'm not sure she would have listened if I had. Paul was... he's a master manipulator.'

'Oh, Izzy.' Mac's eyes were huge in this flashlight-illuminated space. I had the awful feeling that this was like telling ghost stories around the campfire. A vicarious chill, to be felt by those who knew they were safe and warm and there was no greater danger to their persons than eating some unwise hotdogs.

'Yeah, well.' I tried to lose the feeling in pedantry. 'Nothing you could pin on sexual assault, no rape. Some inappropriate touching, if I wasn't quick enough. I'm here because I hadn't managed to save enough money to move out, and, without my equipment, I can't make any more book rooms. I've been sleeping where I could and waitressing to try to get somewhere, but it's a long job saving on minimum wage, and I kind of ran out of friends to circulate round...' I tailed off. The word 'homeless' should tell him all he needed to know. He could fill in the details of sleeping wherever there was space for a blanket; in backrooms of shops, in unsecured basements, anywhere there was cover and nobody trying to mug you for whatever you had. 'It's that good old story of accommodation being expensive, and if you don't have a steady job and money behind you things are tough.'

He shook his head slowly, but not in denial. More as though he was trying to rid himself of whatever he was seeing. 'So this...?'

'This is "home" for however long we are filming. It's a roof, of sorts, over my head, regular meals and I'm earning money. If we can run it right to the end, then I'm hoping for enough money to be able to rent somewhere on my own. Sharing is a bit – well, after Paul, I'm wary, put it that way, and I still need a deposit to put down, even for a shoebox in a house of fifteen. I'd really and truly like us to find some evidence so that I've got real money behind me, so I can buy the equipment and start crafting again, but I'll take what I can get.'

Mac eased off his other boot. Tweetie-Pie, somewhat less than radiant, emerged soggily. 'It all makes sense now,' he said. 'You, your attitude...'

From somewhere under a bag, something beeped. He hunted around for a second and then came up with a phone. 'Dax. Telling us – and I quote – to "turn your fucking cameras back on". Charming.'

Reluctantly, but not sure why I *was* reluctant, I slapped my camera back on. 'Are they watching us all the time?' I asked.

'Think Dax is monitoring the footage. He's got to build a watchable TV programme out of all this, you can't really blame him. And the advertisers are being shown some, to convince them it's watchable TV.'

I looked at him. Big brown eyes, a smooth area of cheekbone slowly subsumed under stubble that was definitely becoming beard and hair that shuffled across his forehead in the draught. 'You and Dax,' I said. 'Sibling rivalry?'

A smile. 'He's an idiot. But he's an idiot with drive and ambition, while I'm an idiot who floats around writing and filming destinations. He's hardly Harold Pinter, but then I'm not exactly Michael Palin either, so, you know. We do what we can.'

From the tent beside us, I heard Ruth give a high laugh, and Sebastian say something. Outside, the dog howled again, a desolate, lonely sound down the valley. 'Do you regret coming along on this expedition then?' I asked. The flashlight illuminating our tent flickered and Mac picked it up.

'Not really. I'll put my trip off for a couple of months, go after Christmas. It's only me; I do my own filming and sound, so it doesn't matter. Besides,' he looked at me, the torch beam putting me in a spotlight and him in the dark, 'I got to meet you. So it's not been a complete waste of time.'

I didn't know what to say to that. The beam flickered again and Mac shook the flashlight.

'Great. All we need is for the batteries to fail. The spares are out there with the stores.' We both looked towards the tent flap, which was being pushed inwards by the pressure of the wind. 'And I'd rather sit in the dark than go out there right now.'

The dog howled again, and then began barking. 'Pretty sure this is how most horror films start,' I said. 'Lights go out, howling dog. I think one of us becomes possessed by a demon in a minute.'

Telling Mac about my life had made me feel – lighter, somehow. As though I'd confessed to something I'd thought of as a strange perversion that turned out to be completely normal, something everyone did. His acceptance, the way he was still treating me as a functional human being, was reassuring. My life may have been utter crap, but it was just 'stuff', just a background for me to exist against, and Mac wasn't holding any of it against me. Any residual guilt that I felt at some of those accusations that my mother had shouted as she'd slammed the door in my face and left me with nothing but a Sainsbury's carrier with slowly tearing handles was my own problem. The weight of shame about being homeless, about having a title that pigeonholed me in with those that society had let down in the worst ways – well. That was something I lived with so constantly that it stopped my breath and made me hunch and scuttle through the world. There was no lightening that weight.

'If your head rotates, I promise to kill you quickly and efficiently.' He waggled both Tweetie-Pie'd feet. 'I would actually kill for a shower about now.'

'It gets a bit itchy, doesn't it?' I looked down at where part of my forearm was protruding from the sleeve of my several jackets. 'I've learned to wash the visible bits and some of the smellier concealed ones. You do it really quickly with a little bit of water.'

'I thought you looked a bit less sweaty than the rest of us.' Mac grinned at me, and then seemed to realise *why* I'd learned the art of concealed washing. 'Oh. You've...'

'I've had plenty of practice, yes. Six months of no bathroom to call your own will give you that advantage. Swimming is good too.' I lapsed into silence as an advance party of the building gale came sneaking into the tent and whirled through our belongings as though searching for something.

'Yeah, think I'll put a hold on the swimming for now.' Mac leaned over towards the loose bit of tent that had allowed the wind to get in, and weighed it down with a boot. 'Even the thought of taking my trousers off is making my skin shrivel.'

We sat in the flickering silence as the torch beam tried to decide whether or not to keep going. Outside the tent, all we could hear were the faint voices of our teammates as everyone settled down, and the persistent whine of the wind scuffing its way through the gorse and heather. The distant dog had stopped howling now. I hoped someone had let it indoors.

'We should get some sleep,' Mac said eventually. 'I mean, interesting as it is sitting here, we may need to do some digging tomorrow, and I expect Junior will be wanting to get out and – I dunno, track, whatever it is he does – while the snow is lying.'

Whatever he does, I thought. This was not the time nor the place to raise my suspicions again.

'True.'

We continued to sit.

'I'm... going to get into my sleeping bag.' He inched himself back. 'Do not be alarmed.'

I started to laugh, and it felt good. 'Me too. It would be pretty stupid if we sat here and froze to death to form a tableau of British Politeness and Good Manners, wouldn't it? I mean, it's not even as if we're going to take any clothes *off* to go to bed, is it?'

Mac grinned again. I was beginning to notice his smiles in a way that made me feel warm, but only deep inside. Most of my extremities were anything but. It had been so long since my last relationship broke up, and then there had been the period of general disgust with all men that Paul and his creepy fixations had engendered in me, that I had forgotten I could actually enjoy the company of a man. That I could find one attractive, especially when he was keeping a distance and being so all round decent. There had to be a drawback, apart from his inclination towards cartoon socks and hats that made him look like a yak.

'Right. Shout if you start to feel weird in the night, or ill or anything.' He dragged his sleeping roll open and clambered inside, with a neat economy of movement that showed how used he was to living in a tent. Then he winked at me, said, 'Turn the torch off, will you?' and closed his eyes, looking like a gigantic blue nylon sausage roll.

I turned the torch off, slithered into my own sleeping bag and lay down, listening to Mac breathing quietly. The entire camp was silent and I couldn't see the glow that would indicate anyone else being still awake. It was ridiculously early in reality to be in bed, but, in the absence of TV or parties or, indeed, any kind of life outside of tracking and arguing, we'd all taken to going to bed pretty much as soon as it got dark anyway.

The tent actually felt quite warm, despite being a nylon skin that was leaching our body heat straight out into the night. I shivered as a finger of breeze found my neck, and pulled my collar up to my ears. It didn't only feel warm, it felt oddly safe too. As though the presence of another body in here would stop any of the evils of the dark moors from creeping in; as though having Mac here would stop the nightmares.

It didn't, apparently, because I was shaken awake to a thready light in my eyes and a hand on my shoulder. I fought it for a moment because the dream was stronger than reality, then sat up, heart pounding and sweat running down my spine, despite the almost solid cold.

'Izzy? Wake up, come on now. You're here in a tent, you're all right, it's me, Mac.' The hand dropped away from my shoulder and a shape moved in the shadows. I was still trying to get my breathing under control. 'You were having a bad dream, I think,' he went on, his voice a steadying monotone. 'You were starting to scream and, flattering as the thought may be, I didn't want the entire camp to wake up and think we were having really noisy sex.'

My breathing slowed. His words started making sense as the dream world dropped away from memory and I properly woke up. The tattered half-memories that draped me in shame and regret slithered completely from my shoulders, and I shook my head.

'Sorry, Mac! I'm so sorry, I didn't mean to wake...'

'Ssssssh.'

At first, I thought his peremptory hushing was to stop me apologising, but then I saw the way he was focused towards the front of the tent. I ssshed. 'What is it?' I whispered, my breath clouding in front of my face in the cold.

'I thought I heard something,' he breathed back. 'Outside the tent.'

I held my breath now, which was difficult as my heart was still pounding from the dream. I couldn't remember the details, but it was the kind of dream that doesn't really *have* details, more a mood that follows you. An atmosphere of building tension; a doorhandle slowly turning, footsteps on stairs...

'There! Did you hear that?' Mac crept to the tent flap. 'It sounds like something moving about out there.'

All I could hear was an ominous silence. If I concentrated, I could pick out the sound of the river's sullen gurgle, swollen by a day of downpour, and the faintest of crunching sounds.

A shadow brushed the tent. Just a darker outline moving quickly between the orange nylon and the sky, the merest hint of a shape. It could have been a cloud, except that it made the fabric bulge inwards a fraction, as though *something* had leaned in for a second. The shape was impossible to make out, it was long and lean but too indistinct to establish any detail.

'Do you think it's that dog?' I half-hissed back.

'Could be. I'm going to have a look.'

'Should you? It could be dangerous.' I put my hand on his arm, and he smiled.

'It hasn't caused any damage yet. It might even be one of the others breaking out for a midnight wee.' Cautiously and carefully, he began inching down the zip that kept the flap closed. When the zip reached halfway, he moved the flap and instantly about a metre of snow fell into the tent, spilling onto the groundsheet and my hat. 'Ah.'

We sat and regarded the heap. 'Looks like a snowman fainted,' I said eventually. 'Are we completely covered, can you see?'

Mac seemed to have forgotten about the mysterious shape. He began tapping the tent. 'Not completely. I think it's drifted against the front, so we're going to have to dig ourselves out, but the back is sheltered by the rock.' He cocked his head. 'It's gone now. Whatever it was that was moving about out there.'

'There will be tracks, though. In the morning.'

'Maybe.' He sat down again. 'Does that happen often? The bad dreams, I mean, not the animal prowling at night outside a snowbound tent, because I should think that only happens under a very particular set of circumstances.'

He wasn't looking at me. Almost as though he were trying *not* to look at me, in fact. He began pushing snow off the groundsheet and piling it up inside the flap. It was so cold that the snow wasn't even attempting to melt.

'I'm not really sure,' I said. 'There isn't usually anyone to tell me, and I've forgotten what I was dreaming about by the time I wake up. Once or twice, if I've been sleeping on someone's sofa, they've mentioned that they heard me shout, but...' I finished on a shrug. I hoped that the shrug encompassed nights of sleep too shallow for dreams, always wary, always listening for that creak of the door or the shadowy figure trying to slide through a gap formed by a wedged chair.

'It sounds tough.'

Moonlight must have been bouncing off the snow because, even without the torch, there was enough light in the tent to show Mac's expression. Eyes wrinkled with concern and his mouth pulled down at one side. The careful, non-questioning tone of his disquiet and the distance he was keeping between us was comforting. He was so cautious, so wary of intruding on my personal space that it made me feel oddly secure in his presence, even though the tiny nature of the tent meant that he was almost having to press himself up against the wall in order not to touch me.

'To be honest, when you have to sleep wherever you can, there's not too much room for PTSD about a man trying to come into your room,' I said honestly. 'I've slept in places where literally *anyone* could have stepped over me. You sort of learn to sleep with one eye open when you're homeless, but I'd already learned that lesson from having Paul trying to get into my room every night.'

'That can't be very restful.'

'Which is why a tent, and company you can more or less trust, although I'm still not quite sure that Kanga won't try to murder me in my sleep with a mascara brush, is so fabulous.' It was flippant, it was superficial, but I couldn't go into detail. *Couldn't.* He knew what he needed to know. Any more would simply be me sounding as though I were looking for sympathy, and nobody who hadn't slept rough *could* sympathise, not really.

Mac looked at me levelly. He was an outline of shaggy hair, incipient beard and careful solicitude. 'Then you should sleep now,' he said quietly. 'You're safe.'

I pulled my sleeping bag up to my ears and lay down again. He was right. I was safe. And there was a measure of security in knowing that someone was there who wasn't going to go through my possessions as soon as I fell asleep, or try to force themselves into my sleeping bag. Noises outside and enough snow to cover the front of the tent were nothing, merely circumstantial stuff. I was warmish and with someone who knew my fears and was trying to avoid exacerbating them with an almost comic degree of care. For the first time in a time so long I really didn't want to think about it, I let myself fall into a deep sleep.

7

I woke to the sounds of shovelling from outside. Mac was still asleep, curled up away from me with one arm thrown out above his head. Random bits of hair were all I could really see of him – that, and a hand in a mitten that curled upwards slightly. I hoped he was still alive in there.

'Are you two all right?' It was Sebastian's voice calling in through the flap. 'Your tent is practically buried!'

'Tracks,' I said blearily.

The sound of shovelling stopped. 'I'm sorry?'

'We heard noises. In the night. You might want to check for tracks around the camp.' I sat up and rubbed my face to the sound of a whispered conversation outside. It sounded as though Sebastian and Junior were at the sharp end of the shovels, with Ruth and Kanga hovering around on the periphery, waiting to hear whether we'd survived the night, like a kind of mining disaster only with more tea.

'It's all been pretty windswept.' Sebastian came back to the flap. 'Junior's going to go and look, but it snowed all night and the wind will have...' He stopped and there was more whispered conversation. 'Junior says the wind will have made tracks difficult to read. Oh, and the motion-sensitive camera has stopped working too, he says. Rain got into it, or something.'

I could feel my face puckering into a 'well, isn't *that* convenient?' expression, which was wasted on the still-sleeping Mac. So, if any of our party *had* been out there planting fake evidence, then their tracks would also have been obliterated, while making everything obscure enough to look real.

'We're digging you out now,' Sebastian carried on. 'Your tent got the worst of it. Kanga and Ruth are going to make breakfast,' he added hopefully. 'There's bacon.'

Mac stirred at the mention of food. 'Great,' he grunted sleepily. 'Fry up'll do.'

'Oh, you *are* still alive.' I felt odd towards him today. Last night's confessions had been an aberration in the dark. A baring of a soul that today felt raw and defenceless. I fell into sarcastic attack in an attempt to make him forget those moments of intimacy; at least if he was inwardly calling me a cow, he'd not be dwelling on what I'd told him. 'I thought rigor mortis had set in over there.'

'Nope, no, I'm fine.' Mac sat up and rubbed at his chin. 'God, I need a shave. And a shower. *Bits* are beginning to come loose, and I daren't go and look in case they are things that are supposed to be attached.'

His levity was both unsettling and reassuring. It had a slight overtone of 'I am not going to mention what we talked about' beneath 'until the time is ready for me to do so'. I really hoped he wasn't going to start trying to bring it up every time we were alone. My sharing had been done in a moment of weakness and was not for discussion.

'We're not supposed to use the water for washing.' I parroted what Dax had told us when we'd first arrived at the camp. 'So we don't run out of treated drinking water. I think we're supposed to strip off and sluice ourselves in the river, or something.'

'And now all the loose bits have retracted into my body cavities at the thought.' Mac gave a dramatic shiver. 'Right. Where's this bacon?'

'On it now!' came Ruth's distant call, filtered through presumably quite a lot of snow, from the amount of shovelling noises, and eventually daylight burst in through the tent flap, accompanied by Sebastian.

'Glad you're both still alive,' he said cheerily. 'Was worried you might have suffocated. But the back of the tent is clear – if it hadn't been for the rock face, we'd have tried to dig you out that way.'

I crawled out, to be met by what looked like an overexposed photograph. There was sun, but the way it reflected off the snow took any detail from the surroundings, and the valley was a white dip amid white folds and creases, like the memory foam mattress of a very heavy person. 'Ow,' I said. The light was so bright that it hurt.

'It's like an illustration of a hangover, isn't it?' Sebastian asked, still way too cheerfully.

'And the smell of bacon frying adds to the verisimilitude.' Mac crouched his way out of the tent beside me. 'It's beautiful, though.' He looked at me. 'Don't you think?'

He sounded as though he really cared about my opinion, so I tried to form one as best I could. Now my eyes had adjusted, I could see the faint peppering of the snow's surface where the tips of heather and whin had scraped their way clear from beneath, and the humps and bumps that yesterday had been landmarks were now ironed smooth under the weight of the snow. Rocky outcrops were either wind blasted to a stark black clarity against the whiteness or capped with rakishly angled bonnets of snow. Features that had become familiar had vanished and new landmarks had been wind-carved over the top of them, so that the whole moorland now looked as though Barbara Hepworth had had a hand in its construction.

It was beautiful. Mac was right. Stark, glaring and freezing, but beautiful.

I was about to tell him this, but when I looked in his direction, he was looking down at me with an expression that stopped the words in my throat. He looked – it was so incongruous that I could barely consider it – hopeful. I nodded and wondered if I'd been mistaken. After all, most of us barely had enough face visible for any kind of expression to be readable; the men were bearded and the women had their coats pulled up past their chins to achieve the same warming facial effect. We all wore hats nearly all the time, tugged over ears and hair so low that we were all basically down to emoting purely with our noses.

'It's lovely,' I said. 'But bloody freezing.'

'Well, this camping experience hasn't exactly been noteworthy for its clement weather so far, has it?' Sebastian shouldered his shovel. He was up to his thighs in snow, but had cleared a path to the cook site, where Ruth was setting up pans and a kettle. Kanga was lurking on the periphery, stacking and restacking the food boxes. She didn't look as though she was being much use, more trying to look busy. She looked a bit fed up too, not like someone who has spent a night being sexually satiated. Junior was bent double, crouching his way through the snow and zig-zagging his way down towards the track, presumably looking for prints. The other tents were mostly clear of snow, ours had obviously been where the wind had dumped the majority of the storm. But none of us were hypothermic, we'd all survived the night, which was a bonus.

And there was bacon. The smell of it frying perfumed the air and I was grateful that all the food was kept in containers, with any medication and, now, the gun. I'd watched that locked away and been part of a brief discussion where the rotation of 'The Keeping of the Key' had been timetabled in as serious a way as Frodo and Sam had talked about carrying The One Ring. I still felt a bit guilty about the way I'd raised the subject of Junior being armed and it made me want to be more friendly towards him, so I followed him down to where he was criss-crossing a section of snow between the camp and the river.

'Have you found anything?'

Junior straightened up. 'Wind's taken the detail,' he said, which didn't mean anything to me. 'Look.' He pointed at a blur in the snow. Something that *could* have been a pawprint or a depression caused by something beneath the snow, or even where an object had scuffed its way over the surface. 'Looks like it was headed over there.' He pointed down the valley. We both gazed in that direction, although with the sun bouncing off the snow, it was hard to look anywhere except at our feet without squinting. The light was almost blue and edged with the frosting of breath.

'What could it have been?'

Junior shrugged. 'Cat. Dog. Something big, anyways.'

I looked at him. He was wearing what looked like an army-issue parka coat with the hood up, very utilitarian and with enormous pockets. 'I'm sorry about the gun thing,' I said eventually. 'I never meant to imply that I didn't trust you with it.'

He gave me a big grin. 'Nah. You're right. I'd have done the same thing in your place. Don't trust anybody, y'know?'

I remembered Dax's long visit to Junior's tent. Was this Junior sending me a covert message? Was *he* not to be trusted? Junior would, after all, be ideally placed to fabricate evidence.

'How does this compare with tracking Bigfoot?' I asked. I had a vague idea that I could catch him out in his answer, but then realised that I knew as much about Bigfoot as I did about big cats, and this approach would never work.

Junior grinned again and threw his arms out to indicate the scoured white landscape. 'No trees,' he said. 'You got distance sightlines.' Then he went quiet, eyes still fixed on the horizon. 'You can see the future from right here.'

I wished I could. Even a glimpse at the next five minutes would be something. 'I hope it's a bright one,' I said quietly.

Equally quietly, he replied, 'I sure as hell hope so.' Then he looked down and caught my eye. Junior was usually as impassive as a rockface, so I was surprised to see a look that was almost a rueful sadness on his features. 'I sure as hell hope so,' he repeated.

'You and Kanga seem to have, um, hit it off.' I wondered if he was contemplating a future that had coupledom in it, and wasn't sure if I'd wish Kanga on anyone not armour-plated.

'Kanga.' He sounded almost surprised by the observation. 'Yeah. She's – yeah, she's one hell of a woman.'

I wasn't going to deny that. And I certainly wasn't going to mention all the other things that she was, not to a six foot ten bloke with muscles like airships, who'd spent much of the last two nights with her and just might be thinking of a relationship.

Junior gave me a slow nod, as though we'd shared a secret, then he slapped my shoulder and moved off down the hill, still winding along an unseen path, leaving me wondering about our conversation. Had his words about trusting no one meant that he knew this track had been faked? But if he thought that, he was putting an awful lot of effort into following it, wading through the deep drifts where the snow had piled into the side of the valley and blown to fill unseen pits and holes. It dampened sound too, so I hadn't heard the others calling my name until I turned back towards camp.

'Izzy! Food's ready.' Ruth, wearing an apron quite frankly ridiculously over about fourteen layers of clothing, brandished a plate at me. 'Eat before it gets... well, it's probably already cold, given the temperature. Eat it before it sets.'

Bacon sandwiches had never tasted so good. Kanga flourished a pot of tea and I stood beside my tent eating and drinking. The cup would have been too hot to hold on a normal day, but insulated by my mittens, the warmth seeped through to thaw my fingers. The cold was metallic and hard around the edges, but the sun gave the illusion that we were all basking in warmth, only the sheer amount of clothing gave us away as frozen.

I put my cup down and wandered over towards the Portaloo, slapping off my camera as I went. Everyone else was eating and drinking, so I might as well take advantage, while it wasn't occupied. But as I was about to go in, I spotted something in the snow. Half buried, surrounded by scratch marks, at first I thought it was a stick, but then I saw it was something else. Maybe human. I looked suspiciously behind me at my fellow campers. Surely not. The Portaloo was *right there*! None of them had mentioned any kind of digestive issues that meant having emergency access to the toilet, and this – I glanced down at the object – didn't look like a hurried situation. But someone had tried to bury it, wind had stripped the snow covering away and left it... well.

I raked in my pocket, found a plastic bag, and carefully picked up the lump of poo. Dog? From the dog that had almost certainly roamed around the tents last night? Whilst the paw prints could still be planted evidence, surely nobody would think to plant a lump of poo?

Another look behind. No. *Surely not.* Gingerly, I placed the plastic-wrapped lump into my pocket. DNA was in poo. So if someone *had* planted this, Dax ought to be able to establish who it was, which would pinpoint our faker. Or prove the dog theory. Prints weren't evidence. *This*, I determinedly kept my hand out of my pocket, might be. I found my face falling into lines of pure disgust at the thought of one of our number purposefully pooing in the snow to provide pretend evidence, although I did have to admit to a certain admiration for their dedication.

And there would still be the pay for being here. There would still be the £3,000, my safety money. That was enough.

I availed myself of the facilities, which were slightly less smelly than usual thanks to the cold, and then rejoined the rest of the crew at the camp.

'We're going to check the whole valley for tracks,' Mac said. 'Junior says the animal seems to have come up that side of the valley and then back down this side, so we're going to split up and try to find the point of origin.'

'But you can't tell what made the tracks.' Kanga looked accusingly at Junior, and I wondered how long their relationship would last. 'She's one hell of a woman,' Junior had said to me. Maybe the emphasis was mostly on the 'hell'. 'So why should we follow them?'

'It's something big,' Junior said, pulling his parka hood down to reveal that he was growing a decent crop of hair over his shaven head. 'It ain't rabbit or badger. Could be cat, but the track's too degraded to see claw marks. It's kinda spread, which is typical of cat, but could be a running dog. If we can track it, we've got some idea where it came from.'

'Do we *want* to know?' Kanga, hatless again, shook her hair out, then made a little face of disgust at the feel of it against her skin. 'God, I have *got* to get a decent wash.'

'Quarter of a mill says yeah.' Junior flashed her a smile, which seemed to hold – something. Not necessarily fondness, but a certain understanding. He hadn't been there for the discussion where none of us had wanted to shoot the animal, of course. He still thought we were here to win the big prize and I was very glad that Kanga hadn't pillow-talked him into the knowledge that we'd agreed not to try for that one.

We paired up for the tracking. To my slight disappointment, Sebastian decided to pair me with Kanga, sweeping the lower valley for any trace of anything, whilst he and Mac went right out beyond the camp and Ruth and Junior tried to pick up anything on the ridge that lay behind the tents. Kanga seemed to feel the same way about the matching up, and so we stomped through snow that came up to our knees, down in the direction that Junior had taken earlier, towards the river, in a sullen silence.

By now, the sun was melting the edges of the snow into transparent crystal knife-blades, which crunched and cracked under our boots. We left a trail of dark footprints all the way behind us, and in front of us the reflections off the ice at the edge of the river were blinding. Amid its frozen extremities, the river still ran, thick and black, carving a channel between the ice cavities at either side, like a huge punctuation mark in the landscape. We marched downhill towards it, in a silence as chilly as the air, with me scanning the surface of the snow for marks, and Kanga half-heartedly gazing out at the high horizon. The far side of the valley was in shadow, and the contrast between its crepuscular shading and the blazing, overdone light our side meant that our eyes had trouble focusing on any kind of detail further away than the ends of our legs, so I didn't know why she was even bothering to pretend.

'I can't see anything, can you?' I finally had to break the silence. 'I think whatever made the tracks that Junior saw must have gone higher up.'

'Mmm.' Kanga continued tramping on down to the edge of the stream. The edges were frozen to sheet ice, but the trickling water had kept the middle from freezing. For a moment, I wondered if she was about to jump across, and went to put out a hand to stop her – the running water part was only about a metre wide, but the frozen edges added another couple of metres to the width.

'We can't see tracks on ice, Kanga.'

She whirled around, pulling off her hat. 'I'm not tracking. I want to wash my face in some clean water.'

I looked at the stream. 'Clean' was not the word that sprang to mind. It was dark with peat and run-off from who knew where. 'Why not grab a handful of snow and rub it on your face?'

'Because god only knows what has peed on it, or walked across it!' She gave me a look as though I were an utter simpleton. 'I want to wash the ends of my hair too, and Sebastian won't let us use the water up at camp.'

'Well, no, because that's been treated for us to drink,' I said reasonably.

Kanga took a couple of steps out onto the iced edging, hands held out sideways to keep her balance. It creaked.

'I don't think you should walk on that, it doesn't sound safe,' I carried on, even though my rationality didn't seem to be having any effect, other than to give me an 'I told you so' opportunity.

'It's fine. It will bear my weight, anyway. *You* might not want to come out on it.' She gradually slithered and inched her way closer to the running brook. 'And I won't be here for more than a minute, just to wash my face and dip my...'

She bent down, presumably to splash water onto her skin, and the ice beneath her gave way. She plunged face-first a surprisingly long way, the water was deeper than it looked, and the current inflated her clothes and carried her downstream.

'Kanga!' I have no idea why I shouted her name, she already knew what was happening. She gave a short, high scream and then went silent, stunned by the sheer cold of the water and the force of it, which was sweeping her relentlessly down into deeper water, through the narrow channel cut in the ice.

'Try to grab hold of something!' I shouted, pelting along the bank to keep pace with her, as she bobbed and flailed. Fortunately, about fifteen metres downstream, the river narrowed even further into not much more than a gulley, and Kanga fetched up against the iced-over rocks that formed its sides, grasping out to try to stop herself being carried further on. I reached her as she jammed in the gulley entrance and, by grabbing hold of a nearby gorse bush to anchor myself, managed to get a hold on her soaking coat sleeve to stop any further forward motion.

'Can you slide out?'

She'd gone very pale and quiet. Shock, and the temperature of the water, had rendered her mute. She shook her head.

I flicked a quick look up at the sides of the valley. There was nobody about. Everyone had gone in the other direction, and the sides of the gulley hid us from their view. I couldn't pull her out without getting in the water with her, and she seemed to have lost the ability to move herself.

'You need to move, Kanga. You can't stay in the water, you'll die.' I gave her sleeve another tug. 'And whilst your weight may only register in the grams, you're still too heavy for me to pull. Can you touch the bottom?'

Kanga shook her head, her wet hair flipping droplets that stung my skin with the cold. 'Too deep,' she said, through chattering teeth.

I yelled, 'Help!' a couple of times, without any real hope of anyone hearing me. The snow deadened the sound, funnelled my voice back down the slope to me so that my words landed flatly. Nobody could have heard unless they'd been standing close enough to already see what had happened.

I was too precariously balanced to do much more than hold her sleeve and try to stop the drag of the water pulling her further along. The gorse bush I had hold of was bending and flexing in a way that indicated it might snap and precipitate me on top of Kanga, and the rocks on the river's edge were slick with ice. I couldn't get enough grip with feet or hands, but she couldn't stay in the water.

'Come on, Kanga, try! If you can kick yourself up onto the side, I can pull you from there.'

Kanga was looking as though only the freezing temperature was stopping her from bursting into tears. 'I can't. I can't move my legs!'

So, this was it, this would be how it ended. With one of us dead, the rest of us carted off in disgrace. Dax had said that they could afford to lose our entire segment of the programme, so that would be the end of it. I hated to admit it, looking down on Kanga's slowly blueing skin and chattering teeth, but I was mainly thinking of the money again. *Still* not enough, not enough for a deposit, first month's rent up front. Condemning me back into sleeping in basements, on buses, the odd sofa and spare room here and there.

The thought gave me a burst of adrenaline which lent me fake strength. 'Come *on!*' I let go of the gorse bush, leaned forward across the ice and, with feet slipping across the shiny frictionless surface of the rocks, I got my hands on Kanga's shoulders and yanked. Once she was above the water level, she managed to get her arms under her, and with all the grace of someone landing an enormous fish when they'd only gone out for minnows, I managed to drag her clear of the stream.

Kanga lay on her stomach, inert. Unmoving.

'You're not dead, so don't even pretend,' I said snappily. 'But you will be if we can't get you back to camp and out of the wet clothes.'

'I can't move,' Kanga said to the snow. 'My legs are numb.'

I rolled her over, she was already starting to freeze to the ground. Her make-up was streaked down her face, mascara giving her eyes the appearance of a Halloween ghoul. Wet hair draggled and stuck to her head and she suddenly looked very small and rather frail. I took my outermost coat off and the wind hit me.

'Let's get some of this wet stuff off.'

Kanga began to cry. 'Am I going to die, Izzy?' Her voice had gone small too. 'I'm so cold...'

'Not if I've got anything to do with it.' I unzipped her soaked coat and peeled it off unresisting arms, like undressing a three-year-old. I absolutely was *not* going to admit that it was the fear of losing pay, not altruism, at work here. 'If you put a dry layer on over the top, it should get us up to the tents.'

I shoved her into my coat and did it up around her, then stuffed her into my thin inner jacket over the top, pulling her wet hair free from the collar. Adrenaline was beginning to leach out of me now, meaning I could feel the bone-cold of the wind bouncing off the snow, niggling its way through the rest of my clothing. I took off my fleecy trousers and worked her legs into these, fortunately big enough to go on over her boots. She flopped, unresisting, boneless with the cold. 'But you will need to walk.'

'I can't,' she said again, pathetically, through tears. 'I am going to die, aren't I? Oh, god, I'm going to freeze to death out here, with my make-up all runny.'

'You are with that attitude.' Now the wind had got through the thermal leggings I'd had on under my trousers. My knees ached with the cold. 'Come on.' I managed to haul her upright.

'I can't.' She sat back onto the snow. 'I really can't.'

'Look, Kanga—' I made my voice stern, although it wobbled a bit with the exertion of trying to get her back up.

'My name's not Kanga, really,' she said, still in that small voice.

'I don't care if your real name is Simon right now.' I jerked at her shoulders again. She had to get up, she *had* to. I was beginning to shudder with the shivers. 'But you are *not* going to die!' Her lack of effort irritated me almost as much as the fear of losing money did. 'It's not that far to camp, and once we're up on the ridge, I can yell to the others and get help. You need to *walk*.' I dragged at her, and managed to slither her body a few metres, carving a trail through the snow as we went. But uphill, with her a deadweight? I wasn't sure I was going to manage it before *both* of us died.

'It's really Kellise.'

'What is?' I was out of breath already.

'My name. Kellise. I didn't really grow up in a Kensington mansion and I don't really live in Notting Hill. I live with my mum and my brothers in a council flat in Wandsworth.' She looked at me with a childlike expression of mingled bravado and shame, as though she'd just done something praiseworthy yet secret.

'Oh, Kanga.' I tugged again at her sleeve. 'This isn't the place for—'

'Only, if I'm going to die out here, you have to tell them. So they can tell my mum.' She took a deep breath. 'Because Sol said that these shows like it if you've got "background", and he told me to make myself sound fancier, so I could get the "posh totty" slot, you see.' Then, with a flash of spirit, 'Sol's my agent.'

For someone who couldn't put any effort in to walk, she was managing to find enough impetus to talk. My back hurt already from trying to get her through the grabbing heather under the snow. 'Come *on*.' I tugged with as much strength as I had, and noted that it was a lot less strength than I'd had a minute or so ago, as though everything was leaching out of me as the cold came in.

'I want my mum.' Kanga's lip trembled again. 'I can't die. I want my mum.'

'Kanga, you are *not*...' I stopped. Actually, given how wet she was, that she couldn't move and that the camp was half a mile away, uphill, her death was starting to look not totally improbable now. Only the effort of trying to move her was keeping me warm enough not to start to lose feeling in my extremities. For a brief second, the thought that we might *both* die, huddled together here in the snow, crossed my mind. And then I wondered whether my mother would even miss me, whether she would bother to turn up for my funeral. Paul would.

He'd probably do the 'distraught and grieving step-father' across my coffin and insist on me being buried with my childhood toys and a photo. Of him. Urgh. The thought made me shiver more than the cold.

I put my arm around Kanga and sat back on the snow next to her to try to get my breath back. She had begun to cry, with a weak, fading sort of sound, as though she were giving up and I needed to keep her motivated. I needed to give her something else to think about other than our current situation. 'Look, you're not the only one telling porkies out here,' I said, uncertain of the wisdom of exchanging confidences with someone like Kanga, but needing to keep her engaged, to keep her focused. 'I'm homeless. Away from all this, I'm sleeping in empty kitchens and any spare room that will have me.'

It worked. She stopped crying. One runny-mascaraed eye fixed on me. 'Oh? I thought you were all educated and that.' Her accent wavered for a moment. 'Never had you pegged for a bag lady. Well, yeah, actually, you are a bit scruffy...'

'You can be educated and homeless, you know,' I said sharply and stood up again. 'It can happen to anyone.'

'Yeah, but...'

'Look, this isn't about our relative living conditions, or about how many lies we've told. It's about getting us out of here!' I grabbed another hold of her multiple coats and pulled. 'I only told you because – actually, I've got no idea why I told you, so let's just shut up and make some effort here, all right?'

I tugged a bit harder. Kanga's unresisting form slid a few metres then jammed against the friction of the undergrowth. My muscles were already protesting, and her hair was going stiff, beaded with snow and plaited with water, like the hairdo of a snow bride in a children's story. I yelled again a few more times, but my voice was beginning to sound weak too, so it came out as a feeble squawk, nothing that would reach up over the lip of the valley.

We'd stopped talking. I needed all my breath to drag her along and besides, the past felt unreal, maybe because a future was beginning to seem decidedly uncertain. I began to doubt the wisdom of showing Kanga who I really was. It was a stick that she could well use to bludgeon me with, should she choose to.

'They'll miss us in a minute,' I said between chattering teeth. 'Someone will notice that they can't see us, and they'll come to look.' This was pure hope, of course. Trying to encourage Kanga, to keep her spirits up. It wasn't cold enough for us to freeze to death here instantly, but it *was* cold enough to sap all our strength and mean that we'd probably become hypothermic long before we could crawl our way out of this scoop in the hills. *Would* anyone notice us missing before then?

'Please, try to walk.' I was practically begging Kanga now. The water was seeping through her clothes, even the dry jackets I'd put on top, and my leggings weren't keeping the wind off my bottom half quite as much as I'd like. My knees were numb. 'We have to get up the hill.'

'I really *can't*,' Kanga whined. She slumped, silent, on the snow for a moment, then brightened. 'But, if I die here, I'll be famous, won't I? I mean, it will be a tragedy, my picture will be in all the papers an' that.' Her accent, usually so carefully crafted with its round vowels and enunciated consonants, slid around the map from Berkshire to Estuary.

'Probably. But being famous for being dead isn't going to be half as good as being famous for surviving, is it?' I tugged at her again. 'You can sell your story, if you're alive.'

A look of greedy acquisition came into her eyes and displaced the hopeless self-pity. 'That's a good point.' She clutched at my ankle, the deathly cold of her fingers cutting right through the thermal factor.

I spared a quick thought for Dax, whose burgeoning career in film making would probably not be done much good by having someone die during a programme, and got my hand under her arm to lever her upwards. I didn't know how we were going to do it, because we'd barely made it ten metres and I'd already lost all my strength, but now Kanga was feeling more positive and actually helping, we might get—

'Izzy!' It was Mac. Mac galloping down towards us through the snow like a St Bernard approaching travellers lost in a storm, the tassels on his stupid hat swinging and his boots kicking a bow-wave of snow in front of him. Behind him, Sebastian was coming more slowly, in his tracks. They'd clearly run quite a distance, because Mac was flushed and there was a crust of sprayed snow frozen to the front of his coat; Sebastian was high-stepping like a show pony in his footsteps, both of them coming downhill at us from the opposite ridge. 'Are you all right?'

I slumped with relief and Kanga slid back down onto the snow again. 'Kanga fell in the water,' I said. 'We're wet.' I could barely get the words out around the chattering of my teeth.

'We know.' Sebastian rammed his hat over Kanga's head, whilst Mac wrapped me in his warm, warm coat. 'Let's get back to camp.'

'Kanga can't walk.' Tears of relief were pricking my eyes and all the strength had gone from my muscles, as though they'd been replaced by overstretched elastic bands. 'We were afraid that...' I tailed off. Didn't need to finish the sentence.

Sebastian and Mac exchanged a look. 'Yeah,' Mac said. 'Dax was afraid of that too. He saw you go into the river. Apparently it was a very "televisual" moment. But when he lost both of you, he buzzed me.'

'Kanga's camera went off when she fell in the water,' Sebastian put in helpfully, over Mac's shoulder.

'And yours is under another layer.' Mac flipped at my gilet, now on top of my jacket, on top of Kanga. 'But Dax got the film of you pulling Kanga out of the water.'

'Oh.' It was all I could say. I *wanted* to add, 'So, what took him so long to call for help?' but I didn't. I could imagine Dax, revolving with anxiety watching the film, gleeful about the potential of real threat on screen, and then realising that it wasn't just a threat, it was a promise of death. Weighing up the audience excitement, the Must Watch TV potential, seeing his programme grabbing headlines, raking in the publicity – and then setting it against people actually *dying*.

I didn't want to think that maybe it was the thought of us dying *off camera* that had really spurred him to call for Mac to help us.

'Let's get you back to camp and warm.' Mac put an arm around me, stopped, looked into my face. 'Are you all right if I help you like this?'

I almost laughed. He was being so careful. 'Yes, Mac, I'm fine,' I gibbered.

'Only I don't want to cross any boundaries...'

'Mac, we are freezing to death out here. I think my boundaries can flex a little bit so as not to die.' I gave him what I intended to be a smile, but my lips were numb, as was my chin, so I had no real control over the expression that resulted.

'Ah. Okay.'

With Sebastian half-carrying Kanga, and Mac bundling me along like a shoplifter under arrest, we staggered our way back up the slope to the track and the tents.

8

After we'd been fed hot tea, rubbed with towels warmed by the fire,
changed into dry clothes and generally thawed out, Kanga retired to her
tent. She wouldn't meet my eye now. I didn't know whether it was because
her vanity had nearly caused the pair of us to freeze to death, or whether
she felt horribly embarrassed now that I knew she wasn't who she said
she was. But then, she knew about me too. At least the cameras were
already either ruined or obscured by the time we'd confessed, so the
public would never know. Just Kanga and me. It was either going to result
in an uneasy truce or blackmail, and with Kanga, you could never be sure.

When Junior and Ruth returned from their unsuccessful mission to
track further along the ridge, he was sent to try to 'warm her up' by Sebastian, who was storming around looking upset about the disorganisation
involved. He'd done a lot of shouty directing of action once we'd got back
to the camp, and his sergeant major act had made me roll my eyes more
than once.

I stayed by the fire. My legs were tingling as the life gradually came
back into them, but at least they were still attached and not going black.
They could still take my weight, although relief and stress had made them
a bit trembly, which was why I stayed where I'd been put, wrapped in
several sleeping bags, within the heat range of the campfire. Under the

guise of starting to prepare a meal, Sebastian was keeping an eye on me, and occasionally stopping in front of me as though he wanted to say something, but always hesitating and then going off to find onions fascinating, or to poke around the storage boxes, muttering something about gravy.

Eventually he straightened his shoulders and came back again. 'Look,' he said, and he was trying to sound definite and firm. 'I think we should call this off, okay? Get Dax out to pick us all up and write it off.'

I sipped at my fourth mug of tea. My insides had lost that 'swallowed a cold rock' feeling now, but Sebastian's words made it refreeze a little. 'Why?' I asked, trying not to sound too pathetic.

He threw his hands up into the air, causing the fork he'd been holding to fly several metres and land with a plop in a snowdrift. 'Because it's a complete bastarding waste of time, that's why!'

It was strange, seeing the composed outdoorsy Sebastian losing control. He'd always seemed the most ploddingly unimaginative of all of us, bossing us about in a way that brooked no denial, which probably stood him in good stead as a farmer. Now he looked as though this abandonment of common sense was as odd to him as it was to me; as though he didn't know quite what to do with himself.

'You could both have died out there today.' He lowered his voice a touch. 'I mean, I think we've all been looking on this whole expedition as a bit of frivolous fun, haven't we? Pretending to track something, to be looking for a big beast that I'm pretty sure nobody believes in. Grubbing about in the mud and following paw prints that could be made by anything – and all for what?'

'Around three grand,' I said, simply. 'And that money might make quite a difference to some of us, Sebastian.'

He deflated. His shoulders came down and he stuck his hands, which had been expressing his dissatisfaction with our mission to the detriment of at least one fork, into his pockets. 'I *know*,' he said dejectedly. 'Honestly. It's a greater part of my winter feed bill. I need the money too, Izzy. But... *you could have died.*'

My heart was thumping and, had I had the energy and sufficiently obedient legs, I would have jumped up. Instead, I settled for trying to influence him with calm. 'But we didn't.' We'd agreed that if a majority decision decided to cancel, it was over. And I couldn't go back, not after all this. 'It will make brilliant television, a bit of drama and peril. And Kanga and I are fine.'

At least, I hoped Kanga was fine. She and Junior were very quiet in that tent.

Sebastian deflated another notch. 'I know. I feel...' He took a deep breath. 'I've become a kind of leader here, haven't I? You all seem to look to me to be the organiser and all that. So I'm supposed to – oh, I don't know. I'm supposed to make sure everyone is safe. And I didn't.'

'You've got children, haven't you, Sebastian?' I remembered him telling me about his wife, his family, keeping the farm going whilst he was out here.

He looked taken aback at my sudden derailing of his angst. 'Er, yes. Three. Two boys and a girl, why?'

I had the feeling that I was talking for my future. That if I let Sebastian follow his trail of parental guilt to its natural conclusion, he would persuade a majority to head back to civilisation and call this whole thing off. I *needed* to get him to see that we had to continue. My mouth went a bit dry with the urgency.

'Do you think you might be infantilising us, a bit?' I went on. 'We're not your kids. We don't need you to keep us safe, we can do that for ourselves. And if we cock up and, well, end up in a freezing river, that's on *us*.'

He frowned. 'Er.'

'After all, that's why we're out here, isn't it? We could have set up some remote, motion-activated cameras and be sitting somewhere in a hotel in Pickering, watching in rotation for a big cat to come past? This' – I waved a hand to take in the moorland, now becoming slightly blotchy as the snow melted off the bushes and rocks – 'is kind of the *point*?'

'Oh. Oh, yes, I see.' Sebastian took his hat off and scrubbed a hand through his hair. 'Is that what you think I'm doing? Treating you all like you're my children?'

'Little bit.' I smiled at him. 'We're all adults capable of making our own decisions about safety and stuff. You don't need to tell us to keep away from deep water. Well, except Kanga, of course, obviously, but then I think she's stuck somewhere around fifteen anyway. What?'

Sebastian was looking at me in a very peculiar way. It was almost as though my forehead had become glass and he was seeing through into the workings of my brain. He stared for a moment longer, and I realised that he wasn't actually seeing *me*, he was looking at his own thoughts. Eventually he said, 'Thank you, Izzy. No, really, thank you.'

I didn't know how to reply. There was something in his voice, something almost abject. Something humble. His expression was that of someone having an epiphany.

'What for? Telling you that you are treating us like juvenile incompetents?' I cupped my hands more forcefully around my tea mug, in case this was all about to go south very fast.

'My wife,' Sebastian began, then glanced around the camp to check to see if anyone was listening. I opened my mouth to remind him that we'd got our cameras on and that half the country would be listening soon, if Dax, the advertisers and the TV listings had anything to do with it, but then shut it again. 'Look.' Sebastian half turned away as though he were ashamed, and then whirled back and began talking quickly. 'My wife suggested that I tried for this show. It's not quite what I told you, I mean, *yes*, I do want to find evidence that what I saw on the Downs that day wasn't an aberration, but – look, well, we're having a kind of trial separation is what it is. Oh, not a real one, well, sort of a real one, but...' He tailed off, scratching at his blond beard, getting his thoughts in order.

'Sebastian?' I prompted, trying to make my voice gentle because the mixture of emotions that were crossing his face looked painful.

'She says I treat her like one of the kids,' Sebastian said, with the words rushing out as though they'd been dammed up behind hope, worry, fear and a little bit of cognitive dissonance. 'She says that she wants to be treated like a woman, like someone who's equal on the farm. I'm not including her in decisions and I'm expecting her to be there, working away like I do with the tractor or the harrow and when I talk to her it's a sort of "patronising chat", she calls it,' he finished sadly. 'And now you say I'm doing it here as well, so I think she might have a point.' He took a deep breath. 'I really, really love her, Izzy. I don't want to lose her.'

Now he was looking at me as though he thought I'd have answers. In fact, I had nothing but a mug of rapidly cooling tea.

'But I'm beginning to see.' He sounded a bit happier a bit more definite. 'It's become my default. I don't want to try to excuse myself or anything but – farming, when you've got children, is a complicated exercise in trying to stop accidents, make money and juggle an entire life. I didn't realise... but now I do.' He stared in a really concentrated way at my shoulder, and I wondered if I'd got something big, creepy and poisonous on it for a moment, until he spoke into my camera. 'I'm sorry, Caroline,' he said. 'I'm really, really sorry. I can do better. I *will* do better.'

Then he swept off towards his tent, still with that rather fixed expression.

I retrieved the fork from the snowbank, refilled my mug, and sat down again. 'Well, that was unexpected,' I said aloud.

'What was?' Mac had come up behind me.

'Oh, nothing. Watch the finished result, unless Dax edits all this out.'

'Dax is coming tomorrow again. To film so that you and Kanga can give the full, unexpurgated, "what it was like to nearly die" stuff to boost the ratings. And to bring a replacement for her camera.' Mac pulled up another chair and sat down, hands stretched out to the fire's warmth. 'I think he'll want you to lay it on thickly, so you may want to practise what I think is known as your "shocked Pikachu face". Oh, and cry a bit.'

I'd never really done the 'sarcastic silence' before, but now seemed the perfect time to practise, so I pulled a face and looked at the snow.

'He's got a helicopter. Apparently,' Mac went on. 'Quite frankly, I've got no idea how he's pulling any of this off. He works out of a studio that's held together with Blu Tac and sweat. Anyway. How are you doing? Any extremities fallen off yet?'

'Are you jealous?' I asked suddenly. Sebastian's self-realisation, combined with Kanga's confession as we froze on that riverbank, had given me a sudden insight and, combined with the near-near-death experience, I was riding high on a cloud of 'nobody is quite what they seem'. It wasn't just me doing it, we were *all* projecting an image.

Mac did what Sebastian had done earlier. He went very still. I didn't prompt him. I kept sipping at my tea. After a long pause, during which I could hear Ruth singing to herself somewhere on the other side of the camp, and some muffled noises which may have indicated that Kanga had now reached normal body temperature and was trying to redo her make-up, Mac shuffled his chair a bit closer to mine. He'd turned his camera off again.

'Please would you...?' He jerked his head towards my shoulder.

I obliged, but sighed. 'Honestly, it's like the bloody hokey-cokey with you and these cameras.'

'I don't like my life being documented on film, that's all.'

'That's a strange thing to say, for someone who films his life day by day in foreign places, *for a living.*'

'I do my own editing. I cut out anything that looks personal.'

'But isn't that what people really watch this sort of thing to *see*?' I had a sudden flash-back to being younger, being safe, sitting on the sofa with Mum watching a bunch of people performing tasks in front of a camera. I couldn't even remember which programme it had been. Mum, crying in sympathy with a girl revealing her tough home life, and saying, 'That poor girl,' over and over. Relishing, I now realised, *not* being 'that girl' and having her own cosy domestic existence.

I wondered if she ever thought of me now.

'Maybe. Probably. I don't care, they're not rummaging about in my private life.' Mac hunched himself forward. I wasn't sure if he was trying to get closer to the glowing warmth of the fire or protecting himself.

'So. You and Dax.' I watched Mac's good-looking face, with his hair squeezed to his eyebrows by his hat, and his dark beard coming up the other way, so that his ears were basically invisible under both directions of growth.

His eyes were downcast, watching the fire flame and spit. 'He's my brother,' Mac said at last. 'Two years older, that's all. But I *think*, and this is only a suspicion, that our parents hadn't planned on a follow-up. He was supposed to be the Son and Heir.' He pronounced the capital letters with a certain twist of bitterness.

Well, this was turning into quite a day. Kanga, Sebastian and now Mac, all choosing me to confess their secret other life to. What had I done to deserve this? Then I reminded myself that, in Mac's case, I had actually *asked,* so it was probably my own fault. And that Kanga had thought she was going to die, so she had an excuse, and Sebastian had had his great realisation – that was it, I was going to spend the rest of this month with my mouth firmly shut.

'So you're perpetually in his shadow?'

Or maybe I could go off and study psychology somewhere? Become a therapist, because at least then I'd get paid for what I was, currently, doing for free. I smiled inwardly at the thought. That would require money and a fixed address and time to study and read and write essays, all things that were at a premium when you worked on your feet twelve hours a day and then always volunteered to be the one to lock up at night and open in the morning so that nobody would suspect that you slept on the kitchen floor.

'Mum and Dad are both in the TV business. They got Dax his start, working with friends of theirs, getting experience. I had to get my break making YouTube shorts.' Mac sighed. 'But hey, it's all working out. I get to make programmes for people who like to watch other people go on adventures when they're never going to further than commuting from Giffnock into the city, and maybe a package to Portugal in the summer.'

'You said that you only came here because of family blackmail?'

'Mum. She told me it could ruin Dax's best opportunity of getting himself noticed. This whole thing' – Mac gestured at the fire pit and the food storage area, but I supposed he meant the programme – 'it's going to be Dax's calling card to go on to bigger things.'

'Dax's *Love Island*?' I asked, acerbically.

He didn't answer, just poked at the glowing red embers deep in the fire, with a stick. 'So, yeah. Family pressure. Mustn't ruin my brother's big chance, must I? Even if it means cancelling my own job.' His tone was mild, but I guessed only because he'd said those words to himself so often that the bitterness had been used up.

'So, do you want us to succeed, or not?' I drained the last of my tea and put the mug down in the little patch of thawed ground beside my chair. 'You seem pretty much anti the idea of there being a big cat out there for us to find.'

'I think the whole concept is flawed.' Mac stood up. 'I told Dax he'd be better off making a programme about punters learning to track ordinary animals, rather than this sensationalist crap of trying to find something that isn't there.' He jabbed once more, quite savagely, at the fire. 'We might as well be ghost hunting. At least we'd be indoors, in the warm.'

Then he stalked off, straight backed. I wondered if he felt embarrassed for having said so much, or whether the phone had been vibrating away in his pocket with Dax's eager injunctions to 'turn your fucking camera back on'.

9

The next day, as I spoke to Dax about our 'falling in the river' experience, I looked at him with different eyes. Now I knew, he obviously had all the hallmarks of the favoured child – a certain confidence in himself that Mac lacked. An air of security, almost as though he knew that, should this whole venture fail, there would be other opportunities. As though his path through life had been steam-rollered flat by the sheer force of protective parenting, and any failures would be swept away under the impetus of upward movement. Dax also had an easier way with people, I thought. Mac had been grumpy and awkward when I met him, hell, he was still pretty grumpy and awkward, and it was only the fact that I'd come to like him that meant I could overlook it now. Dax dealt with us smoothly, as though he'd been greased.

Before he helicoptered his way back out of our lives again, I caught him checking the food supplies. 'Er, Dax.'

He turned and I saw the dealing-with-difficult-people smile descend onto his face from his hairline where it had been lingering. 'Oh, hi, Izzy! Yeah, great insert there, you rescuing Kanga from the river, that's going to look fabulous when I've brushed it up a bit and cut it for the screen. Lots of peril, lovely!' He seemed to turn the memory over. 'Yes, lovely,' he reiterated in an emphatic tone. I hoped it wasn't a hint that he wanted more of the same, because there was absolutely *no way* that I was going to put myself in the path of anything more hazardous than a paper cut from now on.

'I wanted to give you this.' I handed him the little plastic bag of potential poo. It had somewhat suffered alongside Kanga, during our drag through the snow, and had been squashed into a small, flat disc.

Dax looked at it with suspicion. 'Yes, and?'

'I found it – er, out where we were tracking.' I didn't want to admit to finding it near the Portaloo. I could already imagine Dax's somewhat fastidious reaction to being told that. 'I thought it might be a sample of...' I groped for the word. 'Spoor,' I finished, dragging out my memory of Junior's tracking lectures.

Dax took it with his fingertips and held the bag by the corner furthest from the sample. 'Does it smell?' He looked at it as though he thought it was about to explode and cover him in excrement.

'No. I sealed it in the plastic as soon as I found it. I think it's fine. I thought, well, maybe it should be tested? It might be – proof?'

The only proof I thought it might really contain was of the fact that the camp was almost certainly being visited at night by the dog which barked so frantically on the farm further down the valley. That, or one of our number ought to see a doctor. But at least it showed I was taking this beast hunt seriously, and it might help to allay some of the rumours of big cats up on the moors.

'Right,' Dax said slowly and dubiously, still handling the plastic as though he feared he was already contaminated with most of the major forms of death through its protective layer. 'Well, I'll get it to the labs.'

'It might make a nice – insert,' I suggested and he brightened.

'Oh, yes. We can film its journey – we've not had much in the way of evidence from the other groups, except the Cannock Chase guys found some hair, but that turned out to be badger.'

It seemed that 'the Cannock Chase guys' were our main rivals in this. I had a brief, but amusing, fantasy about sabotaging their expedition, then realised that I had absolutely no idea how I would go about this, and suppressed it.

'Right. Off I pop. See you all again in a week or so.' Dax, still keeping the bag at a distance from his body, headed off towards the helicopter, which was beginning to whirl its rotors, sending surface snow flying and making the tents flap. 'Oh, and remember.' Dax lowered his voice in a confidential way. 'Drama. The more drama you have, the more chance you've all got of making yourselves a Name. Column inches, opening civic buildings, *Celebrity Countdown*, all that.' He gave me a bright smile and dashed off to climb up into the helicopter and flew off out of the camp with a sense of thankfulness that streamed off him.

On the other side of the camp, I could see Junior watching Dax's departure with his hands in his pockets and his shoulders hunched. I wondered why he was there. Had they been planning another meeting that I'd ruined by arriving with my little bag of poo? Had Junior been waiting for more instructions, more plans to plant evidence?

'He didn't bring any peanuts.' Mac emerged from the shelter of the rockface. 'He said he'd bring me some peanuts.'

'Maybe next food drop,' I said absently, thinking that all this suspicion was not doing me any good, and that I wasn't sure I ever wanted to achieve the dizzy heights of *Celebrity Countdown*.

'Bastard. I should have been in Croatia right now, and he couldn't even bring me a packet of peanuts.' Mac stood beside me and together we surveyed the scenery. The snow was thawing now, chunks of moorland appearing through the dwindling whiteness like a soggy magic trick and the crisp, ironed-fresh look had given way to a slumped patchiness. 'But this has its own charm.'

'Does it?' I watched a large lump of snow slide inelegantly from the rocky overhang above the tents to burst on the ground outside Kanga's accommodation.

'Yes.' Mac gave me a sideways glance. 'It does.'

Kanga erupted from her tent, ready to accuse someone of throwing things at her, I thought, only to catch the second lump of snow's descent on the top of the head and to disappear in a cascade of whiteness.

Mac and I stood and watched dispassionately.

Kanga shook herself free of the snowfall, glanced over to where we stood, seemed about to say something, didn't and retreated back inside her tent. 'She's improved since she fell in the river,' Mac observed. 'A few days ago, she'd have tried to turn that into a Great Moment in Television.'

I thought back to Kanga's trembling fear of dying on that riverbank. 'I think she's had enough Great Moments,' I said. 'Maybe nearly being a tragic heroine has convinced her that she's done enough to be famous.'

'Plus I think Dax came with an offer for a photoshoot for her.' Mac had turned back to the hillside. 'Some camping equipment place wants her to be their Face.'

'Hang on, people are actually *watching* this?' I looked around me at the piebald mud of our surroundings.

'Advertisers watch the rushes. They want to make sure they're getting their money's worth out of us. After all, they want to be ahead of the game when this gets transmitted – no point in being a "celebrity" from a programme that's over and done with.' Mac grinned at me. 'We're only valuable as it's screening, once it's over, we're has-beens. But they can build our profiles before the show goes out.'

So, that was it for Kanga. Objective achieved. All right, it might not be modelling for whatever fashion line she favoured, but it would be a decent earner. Might even get her a stint on *Countryfile*, or *Springwatch* if she played her cards right. Fame and fortune, sort of.

'Good for her,' I said, and surprised myself by meaning it. My feelings towards Kanga had softened since I'd found out that she was playing a part as much as I was. Then I spoiled my magnanimity with, 'She could be the new Tenty McTentface.'

'When this is over' – Mac was keeping his eyes on the far horizon and ignoring my prejudicial utterings – 'would you like to go to dinner, sometime?'

Startled, I tried to look at him, but he was rotating away from me, so all I could really see was flicking ends of hair and a lot of bobble hat. 'Dinner?'

'Mmmmm,' he said to the general direction of York. 'You know. Out for a meal?'

'Mac, I'm a waitress, I'm perfectly well aware of what dinner is,' I said and then regretted my tone. 'Why?'

His anorak shrugged. 'You're nice. You've got no ties, you're free to go where you want without anyone missing you.'

'Oh, and that didn't sound creepy at *all*.'

Now he turned around properly to face me. 'I want to ask you to come with me.'

'Mac, you are really not making a lot of sense here. Is it the lack of peanuts?'

Now he laughed. It was the first time I'd heard grumpy Mac laugh, and it gave his face an animation that made him look like a real person rather than a set of features under a big hat and above a huge coat. 'Look, I really like you. We get on well, you're not precious about where you sleep or what you eat; you're practical and down to earth and I think you and I could make a good team. I'm pretty much running out of places I can go solo and make interesting – how about we branch out and start showing places people can go as a couple?'

My stomach bubbled. At first it was hunger, but then I realised that it was something else. I wasn't entirely sure *what*, and it could yet turn out to be last night's Three Bean Stew, but there was a fizz about it that had all the hallmarks of potential. 'But we aren't a couple,' was all I could say.

'Neither are most TV couples,' he said. 'We wouldn't actually have to *be* a couple to film as one, you know. *Doctor Who* isn't real either.' He gave me a grin. 'Sorry.'

'I...' I said, but could come up with no more words and stared at him.

'I have a reasonable audience, fair bit of advertising revenue, some of the kit is sponsored. I can't exactly offer you much in the way of money, but it's a way to see the world, fully paid for and, you know, maybe have a good time.' He looked at me dubiously, as though my lack of effervescent delight puzzled him. 'Er. You *did* say you wanted to see the world?' he finished, on a note of such doubt that it made me smile.

'Well, yes, I did. And I do. But I don't really know you, Mac. I can't run off to some warm, sunny place to live in a tent with a man I don't know.'

'But you *do* know me.'

'Not well enough for that. I mean, thank you for the suggestion and all that, but be real. I think this forced proximity thing is getting to all of us a bit.'

'Oh.' He looked downcast and bedraggled. 'I just thought... it seemed like a good idea. It's work, you know, proper work. Not all lying on beaches or eating in fancy restaurants.' He frowned for a moment. 'Actually, there's a fair bit of lying on beaches and eating, now I come to think of it. I'm not offering you this because I feel sorry for you or anything. I'd really like to, well, see you. After all this is over.'

I looked at the brown eyes, slightly puckered by a worried frown. 'I think I'd like that too, Mac,' I said. 'But shall we start with dinner, and work up to the running off across the world with a tent? In fact, let's start with getting off this moor without being eaten or savaged.'

'Kanga's not *that* bad,' he said, and grinned, and at that point, I knew it was all right, he hadn't taken offence at being turned down. While it was tempting – yes, *very* tempting – to think of running off with Mac, I *didn't* know him.

My inner voice whispered *yet*, which made me smile.

I looked over at the saggy nylon of my tent, still half-covered in rapidly melting snow. Although it was a depressing sight, somehow the knowledge that there was a future out there for me, that I *could* make a go of life, made the yellow fabric gleam a little brighter, and the sullen sky that was allowing glimmers of sun to poke reluctant holes in the sky a little less forbidding.

Mac liked me enough to see potential in me. *Someone* believed in me. The fact that this was a strange sensation showed me how much my mother's rejection of me had reduced my own opinion of myself. Not that my opinion had been exactly stratospheric to start with; the ending of my relationship, which had begun in High Romance and Grand Gestures and sunken into arguments about putting away laundry and stacking the dishwasher, had reduced it quite a long way already. The plans we'd made had fallen further and further down the ladder of lifetime achievements. We'd started out planning backpacking trips around Australia and, by the end, been unable to organise a weekend in Rhyl without arguing. The quotidian had eroded away a love of adventure and driven me back to my mother's spare room, to craft bookcase ornaments and earn barely a living wage. And then I'd been driven from there to a life of sleeping in unoccupied buildings and asking if people would like some sauces and did they need fresh cutlery?

But there were other lives. My relationship might have failed, and my mother and I were now estranged, but I was still here. Still existing. I'd been down, but there was an 'up' beckoning. All I needed was that down payment for a flat, and I could make myself a new life. And a rather gorgeous, although grubby, man liked me enough to want to have dinner with me. I could see a dim outline of a faint future again, and it made me want to dance my way through the snow.

'We're on cooking duty.' Ruth had come up behind my chair. 'If you're feeling up to it. I can get Mac to take your turn if you're still recovering.'

'It happened yesterday,' I said, still scanning the faint blue line of horizon as though I were waiting to see the topsail of a schooner bearing my mariner husband and enough of a whale to keep us in blubber for six months.

'Kanga says she's not going to be able to do any tasks for at least a week.' There was no judgement in Ruth's voice, which was admirable. 'She's got to get over the shock, so she's staying in her tent.'

I briefly wondered if Kanga was really staying in her tent so she didn't have to talk to me. Whether seeing me made her embarrassed that she'd confessed her real self. And then I remembered it was Kanga, and she'd probably had embarrassment removed with all her body hair and replaced with cool when they did her eyebrows. Plus, if she stayed in her tent, there was less chance of her blurting out *my* story to anyone. I'd worked out what I'd say if she did – some convoluted tale involving partial truths and the probability of Kanga mishearing me – but it was still a possibility that was making me glad that she wasn't around.

'No, I'm fine.' I stood up. Ruth was looking at me with her hands on her hips and her jacket unzipped to reveal a startling red sweater underneath. 'What?'

Ruth tilted her head. 'You seem very – chipper.'

'Chipper?'

'Yes. You look lighter, somehow.'

Gosh, she was perceptive. Or maybe Mac's offer of a job, accommodation, the possibility of a life that didn't consist of putting on an apron or learning to deal with leery remarks really had taken some of the strain out of my face. I wouldn't be surprised. Homelessness and living on a pittance had certainly given me lines that I wasn't sure I was ready for yet.

'Mac's offered me a job after all this is over. Filming. Travelling.'

'And will you take it?' She tilted her head the other way and her pony-tail flopped over her shoulder.

'No. But it's made me realise...' I trailed off. I didn't need to involve Ruth in the grimness that was my life. 'It cheered me up.'

Ruth nodded. 'God had a plan for you when you came here,' she said sagely. 'That's why He didn't let you die in that river.'

'To be fair,' I said carefully, 'that *was* mostly down to Dax seeing what happened and calling Mac to help us. I'm not sure God is all that hot on phone calls.'

Ruth gave the soft smile of one who is so used to having her beliefs challenged that it barely even registers as an offence any more. 'Maybe God told Dax to watch over you,' she said pertly.

Preferring not to think of Dax, with his strange hairstyle and offhand manner towards peanuts, as any kind of guardian angel, I followed her to the food locker and started pulling out supplies to cook for our collective dinner.

10

It thawed all night. Water dripped and plopped and trickled and I woke in the early hours to find my sleeping mat surrounded by rivulets of meltwater, turning me into a huge sleeping island in a sea of soggy groundsheet.

I climbed out of my sleeping bag, pulled on boots and went out of the tent. A full moon gleamed off the remaining patches of snow on the high points of moor around us, but the valley below was stygian in contrast. I could see the occasional glitter of water, bouncing starlight around as it cascaded, swollen with melting snow from further up on the moors. There was a distinct gurgle and swoosh coming from it now, and it carried enough force to sweep along the odd branch, visible only as a ghastly outline coming in and out of vision, like a subtle horror film.

Something moved. Just in the corner of my vision, near the top of the valley on the other side. A shape, a shadow in the dark, a reflection off something that had come around the top of the moor and was descending towards the river. I squinted. The moonlight was too intermittent for me to properly see anything other than a quick angle that *might* be a limb, or a movement that *could* be a tail. All I could really tell was that it was something sizeable and mobile. It could even have been a sheep, isolated from the rest of the flock, making its way towards the farm, picking its way through the fingers of undergrowth.

I kept watching, more to give my eyes something to look at than out of any desire to distinguish what was out there. Trails of water were slithering down the hill like the tracks of really enormous snails, bubbling into cataracts over rocky descents as the snow capping the high moor melted. The shape was making its way delicately around these proto-streams, I could see it emerge into moonlight and then vanish as the moon was subsumed by a block of cloud. Just a shape. Probably that dog from the farm that crept about at night and visited our camp. That dog that left tracks in the mud, blurry enough for Junior to be unable to definitely diagnose it as a bullmastiff or some kind of collie cross. The dog that was the entire reason we were able to string this whole thing out for a month and earn enough money to be able to envisage a life.

I whistled. Through my teeth, like I'd seen the shepherds do when Mum and I had had a brief holiday to the Lakes when I was ten. In sheep-herding language, I'd probably told the dog to do something physically impossible involving pitchforks, but it got the attention of the animal moving across the valley. I saw a movement as a head came up, and then a brief shine as eyes caught the moonlight, then it was gone. Sunk into shadow, it vanished, running back towards the head of the dale and quickly invisible as the moon vanished behind another cauliflower of cloud.

Dog. Yes. Obviously, it had to be a dog. The dog that barked so frantically, unseen, on the farm. *The dog that was barking right now, far away, on that farm down the valley.*

Okay. So, not *that* dog. But another dog. There must be other farms, other houses up here, where the dogs roamed loose at night.

But. Just for that one second, when the animal had raised its head and looked at me, for that brief, tiny moment, it had looked as though it had a round head with a short muzzle. A cat's face. Small ears, eyes huge in the dark.

There were dogs with round heads and short muzzles, weren't there? Big dogs. I'd had a friend, back in the days when we'd socialised as couples, who'd had a Dogue de Bordeaux. It could have been something like that. Only black.

Who, in their right mind, would let a big dog out at night to prowl around the valleys like that? No wonder sheep got killed and stories of pumas and panthers spread around, when appalling, irresponsible dog owners like that existed. It was only surprising that people weren't being attacked; that ramblers weren't reporting the Hound of the Baskervilles roaming the moors, I thought, heading back into my tent to find that the water had formed an attractive feature right through the middle and I had to drag my sleeping mat into a corner to stay dry.

In the morning, I agonised over whether to tell Junior what I'd seen. On the one hand, he'd get a day's tracking out of it and we might even find out where the dog was coming from. On the other, wouldn't the proof of dog short-circuit our entire venture, have us called off and, therefore, deprive me of the rest of that three grand? We'd been out here for a fortnight. Would £1,500 be enough to make the deposit and rent on a little flat somewhere? No, I needed choice, to give me security.

I decided not to say anything. After all, the beast had been a long way off, I couldn't accurately tell Junior where to start looking for tracks. And there might not even *be* any tracks, it was mostly heather and bracken over there, especially now the snow had gone. Yes. Saying nothing would be best.

So, as instructed by Dax, via Mac, we scanned our usual sites for tracks, looked around for 'other evidence' – Dax hadn't mentioned my little bag of poo to anyone else, so he'd delicately phrased our search as being for 'traces' – and argued lightly, itched, rinsed our faces in meltwater, cooked and adjusted the tents, which were all beginning to lean slightly. I stuck with Ruth, because she didn't seem to feel the need to confess an entire traumatic back story to me and her tendency to defer to me, and then to God, was refreshing.

Kanga stayed in her tent. Presumably, the prospect of modelling camping wear was enough to prevent her from wanting to be the centre of filming attention for a while, and maybe she genuinely was shaking off a nasty case of shock. I was a little surprised that Junior carried out his usual ranging about, scanning the ground, tasks rather than stay with her and build on their putative relationship. But then, any hint that there was anything between them other than the tent sharing and Kanga's presumably physical persuasion to get him to relinquish the tranquiliser gun mostly came from Kanga herself. Junior was neither confirming nor denying anything, and, in fact, seemed actively to avoid her most of the time.

But then, so was I. Every time I saw Kanga, I felt another hot backwash of shame. Every meal she deigned to join us for meant that our eyes would meet and our glances would slide off into a morass of embarrassment and discomfort. We knew about each other. That knowledge kept us safe from one another – I didn't think Kanga would tell my secrets as long as I was keeping hers – but the fact that she knew made me itchy and hot inside my jacket. None of the others seemed to notice our awkwardness around each other. If they did, they probably put it down to Kanga not liking the fact that I'd saved her life. But I knew she knew. And while her secret was nothing more than acting a part, mine was... mine was something that would make the others think of me differently. I'd seen the look on Mac's face when I'd confessed to him, the 'but only losers end up homeless' look. Even though he hadn't said it, probably had only thought it for one brief moment, the look had been there. And I didn't want Sebastian, Ruth or Junior to wear that look either.

It was probably a permanent fixture on Kanga's face, along with the tattooed eyebrows and the lip fillers. So, all in all, I was very glad she chose to stay away.

Sebastian had come over very domestic, taking on the cooking and camp-tidying tasks. He stopped trying to marshal us into a team and lost the paternal attitude. He was doing his best, I guessed, to show his wife that he could change. It was rather sweet, although he did forget at times and bark orders like a frustrated scout master, but at least now he apologised afterwards

Mac was – about. He was collecting firewood, tending to the fire, checking food stocks, being busy. We didn't find the opportunity to talk properly again for a few days. It was surprising how fast the hours went by now, almost as though we'd forgotten any other life existed out beyond this scruffy little campsite in the middle of nowhere. But then, as we rose with the daylight and went to bed not long after dark, the actual hours were quite short.

I was draping my sleeping bag out to air over the roof of my tent, wrestling it inside out and pulling out the liner, which came accompanied by a worrying puff of dust which I feared might be my actual skin. It had been so long since I'd had a proper wash of any parts of me that didn't see daylight that I was beginning to think I might be eroding. If I got fully undressed, I might discover that I was nothing more than a flaky shadow and a strange smell.

'Hey.' Mac came up from around the rocky backdrop that sheltered the tents from the worst of the building wind. 'How are you?'

'Pretty much the same as I was at breakfast. Is Dax going to bring any more bacon? We're scarily low and I fear there may be rebellion if we run out.'

'Haven't heard from him.' Mac slipped a hand into a pocket. I presumed he was touching the phone, to reassure himself that it was still there and the silence from Dax wasn't because the phone was under four feet of undergrowth. 'Which is slightly concerning.' He leaned against a boulder.

'Are *you* all right?' I asked, lowering my voice slightly in case I was about to be privy to another family revelation. I'd only just got over being the repository of everyone's secrets and I didn't think I could stand another outburst. Mac was looking a bit awkward, as though he didn't know what to do with his body.

'Yeah. No, I'm fine. Fine,' he repeated. It didn't look true.

I raised my eyebrows.

'Well, no. I'm thinking. About what I said the other day, about you and me – about going filming.'

'It's fine. Don't worry.'

Mac pushed away from the rock and came over. 'I phrased it all wrong. I made it sound – I've gone over and over it in my head and I should have said it differently. I didn't mean it to sound like a pity offer. I don't feel sorry for you.'

The words came in an odd mixture of staccato and rush, as though he were an old-style record, sticking and then jumping. Mum loved vinyl. We'd played her old collection of punk rock records until they wore out, dancing round the living room, in the old days. Before Paul.

'Why the hell would you feel sorry for me?' I finished draping the sleeping bag. It now looked as though my tent was wearing a particularly unflattering hat, but then, we all were.

'Look.' Mac put his hand on my arm. The wind blew the bits of his hair that protruded from the beanie hat, as though it too wanted to touch me. 'It was a genuine job offer. I think I made it sound like I was wanting to rescue you from... from...' He looked over his shoulder in an almost comic way, but there was nobody about to hear our conversation. 'From *being homeless*,' he whispered. 'I didn't mean it to, honestly. I don't have some kind of saviour complex – I really, genuinely like you and I think we could make a good work team. And all that stuff I said about you not having ties – I could kick myself.'

'Don't worry, I'll do it for you. Easier for me to reach.' The leaden heaviness of lost potential was evaporating the more he spoke, and being replaced by the buoyancy that I'd been riding on since he mentioned the job offer. It made me more effusive than I might otherwise have been. 'To be honest, Mac, I'm not all that worried about your motives.'

He stared at me. 'That's, er, that's very... actually, it's probably not good.'

'Only if your motives are to kill me, or chain me up and keep me as a sex slave,' I said friskily. 'Believe me, anything else will be an improvement on serving pasta to overweight middle managers and their girl-friends and then sleeping between the fridges.'

'I wanted to tell you, that's all.' Mac's eyes were intense. 'I didn't want you to think that I'd offered you a pity posting. I really do think we could work well together. But no sex slavery, promise.'

I had a sudden image of what Mac would look like, stripped of the multi-layered look we all wore. I remembered the first day we'd all met, when we'd been given our kit and told to put it on in the minibus on our way to the moor. He'd been wearing slim-cut black jeans and a jumper that made him look slender and active. To be fair, he'd probably still got them on underneath, but it would be a task akin to a geological expedi-tion to find them under all those coats.

I wondered how he remembered me.

'Well, not slavery, anyway,' I said, feeling myself heating up inside my clothes. It wasn't an unpleasant feeling.

He caught my meaning and gave me a grin that contained promise and mischief and a certain degree of smoulder. '*Definitely* no chains.'

'Spoilsport,' I grinned back. The heat was coming up the back of my neck in little puffs when I moved.

'Oh, we would have made such a great team.' Mac raised one eyebrow. His grin was now broad enough to crease his cheeks and give him very appealing dimples.

'Look, I've said I'll have dinner with you, isn't that enough? As long as we can eat somewhere warm.' I flapped a soggy-coated sleeve and gloved hand to indicate the damp moorland. 'Or at least, above zero?'

'How do the islands of Croatia grab you?'

There was still mischief in his eyes and his face was very close. I really hoped that we weren't going to try to kiss. I didn't want his first experience of a decent snog with me to be complicated by escaping layers of skin, although I was beginning to realise how very desperately I *would* like to kiss him, and also that the feelings of guilty inadequacy that usually twinged in the back of my head whenever my lack of a permanent address was raised didn't bother me when Mac mentioned it.

'As long as they are above the water table, they would be an improvement on this place.' I heard a noise and looked up. 'Oh, hi, Kanga.'

Kanga had slithered from her tent and was turning her face up to the watery sun. She looked in our direction and then stomped off, shrugging her shoulders in a way that conveyed annoyance even through layers of cagoule.

'She looks a bit miffed,' Mac observed, watching her march off to the side of the camp. 'Maybe you could talk to her?'

'Must I?'

'It'll look good. For the cameras. You two bonding after your near-death experience.' Mac grinned at me sideways. 'Besides, you're the only one she doesn't sneer at. Well, not as much, anyway.'

I wouldn't say that, I thought. But he was right, I couldn't ignore Kanga for the whole of the rest of our time out here just because she made me feel awkward and pathetic. 'I'll have a word with her,' I said, starting to move away and realising that I was moving reluctantly, not wanting to relinquish this cosy almost-closeness.

Mac grinned and pulled his hat more firmly over his ears. 'I'm on "looking for tracks" duty anyway,' he said. 'Apparently. This is going to be the most boring viewing since I made an entire segment of video about a fishing trip to Devon.'

I opened my mouth, about to tell him about the creature that I'd thought I saw across the other side of the little valley. But that had been a few days ago and I could have been mistaken, so I didn't.

'I'll catch you later.' He patted my arm and, with another hat-pull, moved away off over the heather. I paced after Kanga, who had placed herself, staring wistfully into the distance, off to one side of the camp. I wondered if she was practising to be the Face of Tents. I didn't want to tell her that, from the direction I was approaching, her backdrop was the Portaloo.

'How are you?' I tried a tone of mixed jollity and tactful gentleness.

'I'm...' She pulled her hat off and let the wind stream through her hair. It was less of a stream and more of a flop because of the general level of damp and unwashedness, but it showed willing. 'I'm recovering. Slowly.'

'Hmm.' It was all I could say. She was recovering so slowly that she seemed to have become exempt from all chores around camp.

'You and Mac seem... very close.' She was still staring at the slope of hill opposite, looking winsome.

'We're... friends. Yes. Friends.' It gave me a nice warm feeling to say that. Friends. With a tiny little side order of *potentially more*.

She rounded on me now. 'But *I* was supposed to be the one who found a love interest!' There was an edge of tears in her voice. 'I was going to go to the magazines, and everything!'

'Well, you and Junior...' I began cautiously.

'He's *gay!*' she snapped. 'And he's not even American, he's from Barnsley!'

The words dropped into a silence that I could feel the edges of. It lasted for a few seconds before I got my mouth and brain lined up. 'He's very convincing,' was all I could say.

'Yeah, well, he's lived over there since he was eight, when his parents emigrated. But he's not at all what I thought, and it's *rubbish* because I wanted a photoshoot and everything!' Her eyes were bright with the tears of having her expectations dashed.

'But you've got the whole camping thing, haven't you? Modelling for them? It's better than...' I stopped suddenly. I had been going to say that it was better than a council estate in Wandsworth, but that would make her think about my situation again and that conversation had been private. Not to be raised ever again. 'Better than nothing,' I finished.

Kanga looked at me now. I saw her understanding of what I'd been about to say, what I'd *actually* said, and how everything was balanced on the keeping of confidences. The realisation of the power we had over one another hovered darkly deep in her eyes. 'Oh, I will make it amazing,' she said.

'And it's probably a stepping-stone to other things,' I added.

'Undoubtedly.'

'So you really don't *need* the whole coupling up, selling your story, *Hello* magazine photoshoot, do you? You can do this on your own.'

Kanga smiled and tossed her hair again. Some of it clonked. 'Of course I can,' she said, as though the matter had never been in any doubt, which I thought was a bit rich, but didn't draw attention to. 'I'm going to have a Future.'

The subtext of 'which you won't have because you live on the streets' ran beneath her words like double underlining but, again, the balance of power between us prevented it from breaking through. It didn't need to anyway, the look on her face was worth an entire dismissive paragraph. Then she stalked off, presumably in search of someone else to annoy, but she looked more relaxed and her stride was designed to be photogenic as she marched through the heather. She'd been worried, I guessed, that I might blow her cover story and ruin the illusion of her being Posh Totty, but she'd kept my secret. I owed her my silence too. At least, for now.

Plus, Sebastian wasn't exactly spreading his story about his worries for his marriage about, Mac hadn't come clean to everyone about his sibling rivalry and Junior *definitely* hadn't let anyone, apart from Kanga, in on his background. He was still out there in his vest, playing 'American Celebrity Big Foot Finder' to the hilt. At this rate, Ruth was going to turn out to be a devil-worshipping polyamorist. I turned around to see her blamelessly tidying up the cooking area in a way as unlike a satanic orgy-fan as possible and shook my head. Ruth, despite my early impressions of her, was the most normal of all of us.

Suddenly Kanga, who had clambered up onto the rocks above the campsite to gaze picturesquely into the middle distance, presumably in case any of us were filming her, gave a shout.

'There's something out there!' She pointed, although the distance was such that her finger encompassed several hundred acres. 'Over there!'

I swivelled in the direction she was indicating. Saw Ruth turn too, and Mac, who'd got as far as the track, stopped and looked out over the valley.

Sebastian bounded from wherever he'd been and looked up at Kanga on her perch. 'What is it?'

'Something big. I saw it move, over *there!*' Another outflung arm taking in most of Yorkshire.

I couldn't see anything. From their various expressions, neither could anyone else.

'It *was* there. It *was!*' Kanga sounded almost tearful in her urgency. 'It ran across that gap out there!' Still unspecific, her arm at least indicated a general direction.

'What did it look like?' Mac bounded up the hill to the top of the rock next to her. 'Big cat?'

'I don't *know.*' Kanga burst into tears, flinging herself into Mac's arms with a fervour that nearly sent the pair of them tumbling down onto the tents. Mac looked down at me over Kanga's heaving shoulder, and widened his eyes.

I smiled.

'Do you think she saw something?' Ruth whispered to Sebastian and me. 'Only she may still be in a state of shock from the river.'

'Or outright lying to get some attention,' Sebastian said acerbically. He clearly hadn't quite forgiven Kanga for trying to seduce him, on camera.

So, did I do the decent thing and make myself look like someone who was trying to keep secrets from the team? Or did I go along with the definite fact that Kanga was a fame-seeking, media-hungry girl?

'She may have seen something. I saw a dark shape moving across there the other night,' I said and kept my eyes on the ground as I felt everyone shuffle round to face me.

'Izzy?' Sebastian was right beside me. 'You saw something?'

'And you didn't say anything to anyone?' That was Ruth, reproachful. 'We could have taken photographs!'

'It was dark,' I muttered. 'Middle of the night, you were all asleep. By the time anyone got out here with a camera, whatever it was would be gone. And anyway,' I looked up now and I could feel the heat in my cheeks rising to burn behind my eyes, 'it's a *dog*! We all know there's no big cat out there prowling around. Don't we?' I appealed to Sebastian. 'We're all hanging on out here because Mac doesn't want to let his family down, Ruth wants the money for her church's Good Works, Kanga wants the fame and publicity, Sebastian wants to show his wife that he can be an equal partner and I...' I took the vehemence down a notch. 'I want as much money as I can get,' I said quietly. 'None of us really believes that we're going to catch ourselves a puma, not really. Well, maybe except for Sebastian.'

There was silence. It was broken occasionally by Kanga hiccupping theatrically, and the susurration of wind through bracken, but nobody moved. Nobody spoke.

'Do you think this is all pointless, then?' Ruth eventually said. Her voice had its usual gentle tone, but she looked rather sad. 'That we're waiting it out to collect the money for being part of the show, and that's it?'

I shrugged. It was *exactly* what I thought and, in fact, what I'd said. But reiteration seemed too cruel.

'Okay, group vote.' Sebastian straightened his back, then seemed to realise that he'd sounded dictatorial. 'I mean, if everyone wants to, that is.'

Everyone else looked thoughtful, as though they were all weighing up the potential for getting off this moor and into some clean dry clothes. I felt guilty as hell. I hadn't meant this to happen. I'd thought I was being the voice of rationality, of reason.

'There could be something out there, though,' I said, hurriedly 'There's all these stories, after all, and Kanga and I have seen—'

'We should still vote on staying.' Sebastian frowned at me. 'We can't have dissention, it could be dangerous.'

'How?'

'You could go mad and run away from camp because you've decided it's all a waste of time,' Kanga said, sounding slightly hopeful. 'Or something bad could happen.'

'Teamwork,' Sebastian said firmly. 'We have to be thinking and working as a team.'

Mac led Kanga, who was still clinging to him in a way that made me slightly uncomfortable, down to the tight group that had formed by the fire. I was on the outskirts, almost as though they were making a deliberate decision to exclude me, and I felt my eyes bulge with tears. I wouldn't cry, though, not in front of everyone like this, not with Kanga showing how it should be done, prettily and emotionally and with not a trace of snot.

'Is it really necessary?' Mac disentangled Kanga from his coat. 'Izzy's entitled to her opinion, isn't she?'

I wanted to hug him. Damn it, I was so grateful to have someone on my side that I practically demanded to be allowed to conceive his children right here.

'*Everyone* is entitled to their opinion,' Sebastian said. 'Hence the vote. If Izzy is so unhappy with everything, maybe others are too.' He looked around the group. Everyone else looked at the ferny floor. 'So. Does everyone think we are wasting our time?'

More silence, while the wind whistled across our ears and tugged at our clothing like a hyperactive toddler.

'I think,' Ruth finally broke the still air, her voice small, 'that I'd really like a shower. But God put us here for a reason, so I want to stay. But I really *do* want a shower,' she added, with a slight tone of defiance.

'And I have to stay.' Mac came closer to me, until his multi-coated bulk nudged against my shoulder. 'Family unity and all that. Dax would never forgive me if I was part of a walk-out, although Dax never speaking to me again would have its advantages.' He flicked me a quick look. 'I think I've gained a lot already from being here.'

'And I never said I wanted to call this all off!' Mac's proximity gave me a bit of courage. 'Just that I don't believe there's a big cat out there for us to find.'

'Kanga?'

At Sebastian's voice, Kanga raised her head. Diamond-tears sparkled along her enhanced lashes and highlighted her cheekbones. 'I saw *something*,' she said. 'I know I did.'

'That's not really the question, Kanga.' Sebastian sounded a bit tired. 'Do you think we should call this off?'

She tipped her chin further towards the clouds. On cue, a shaft of sunlight broke through and haloed us all in its watery gleam, making Kanga's tears shine like cosmetic glitter. 'No,' she said, injecting a tone of brave defiance into her voice. 'I want to stay.' Then, less dramatically and more prosaically, 'I might get a presenting deal out of this yet.' She tossed her hair. 'Channel Five are recruiting.' And then, slightly more quietly, but with a fierce undertone, 'I saw *something*.'

'Dog,' said Mac and I, in unison.

Sebastian looked around the group. The weight of being our leader seemed to be heavy on his shoulders now, or maybe it was the fact that he was trying to balance leadership with not telling us what to do, to honour his on-camera promise to his wife. But how can you lead without taking control of a situation? I felt a pang of sympathy.

'Maybe,' I said slowly, and watched Sebastian's eyes swivel toward me now, 'maybe we should concentrate on proving that it *is* a dog?'

Mac gave me another encouraging shoulder-bump. 'Keep on tracking, you mean?'

'Well, yes. We're here to prove the existence *or otherwise* of big cats in the British countryside, aren't we? If we can prove that this particular example isn't one, then at least it's a result of sorts for Dax. We'll get the three grand for being out here for a month, Kanga gets her modelling contract, Sebastian learns to deal with conflict without being bossy and Junior gets to demonstrate his skills. We're all winners, maybe not of £50,000, but how many of us really thought we were going to find proof of a puma?' I looked around the group. 'Let's do what we can to prove that there *is* something out there, and what it is.'

The dog down the valley began its hysterical barking into the silence.

'Right. That's sorted, thank you, Izzy.' Sebastian did a dramatic mime of dusting his hands. 'It may well not be a large cat, but let's aim to prove that. As Izzy says, we're all gaining from this experience, one way and another.'

'And there's definitely *something* out there,' I added, helpfully. 'You never know, there may be a reward, if it's a lost dog, and if it is then it ought to be got off the moor before it starts worrying sheep.'

A loud bass roar made us all turn round. Junior was advancing up the slope of the hill, his vest shining under the sun's rays, like the approach of a cleaner Bruce Willis. Because of the deep undergrowth, he was even moving in slow motion, as though he were wading through surf. 'There's more tracks!' he rumbled. 'Down over there!' He pointed, and it looked as though he were indicating the general direction in which both Kanga and I had seen our 'something'.

'We ought to let Junior know what we've decided,' I said.

'He still thinks we ought to capture it.' Kanga tucked her hands into her pockets. 'Who's got the gun key today?'

'Me.' Ruth unzipped a layer to show the key to the locked food box around her neck on a piece of string.

'I'll tell him.' Sebastian squared his shoulders. 'We're still needing him to track, though, right? I really don't want Junior angry at me when he's got those boots on.'

'I'm going to put a big pan of water on to heat.' Ruth put an arm around Kanga. 'There's plenty of drinking water left, let's say "blow it!" and at least wash our hair, shall we? It will make us feel much better.'

'And a shave.' Mac tugged at his chin. 'God knows I need rid of all this beard.'

'Amen,' Ruth replied, robustly.

'Let's have a party,' I suddenly said. 'A rummage through the food boxes, build up the fire, let's all get changed and washed and pretend that we're here having a good time.'

Mac put a hand in his pocket.

'We could put some music on,' Kanga said hopefully. 'And dance.'

'And toast marshmallows – if there are any in the food box – and drink and relax a bit.' I was pleased with my idea. 'I know there's no alcohol...'

Sebastian, looking slightly ashamed, cleared his throat. 'Er. I *did* smuggle a few beers in my rucksack.'

'And I've got three bottles of Prosecco in mine.' Kanga looked matter of fact, as though it would be taken for granted that she wouldn't travel without sparkling wine.

'I think I may have a half bottle of vodka somewhere about my person,' Mac put in.

I looked at them. 'You *all* broke the rules?'

There was a sort of combined mutter and I wished I'd thought to pinch a couple of bottles of cheap white wine from the last restaurant I'd worked in. But 'No Alcohol' had been at the top of the list of instructions that Dax had given us.

Mac had pulled the phone out and was staring at the screen. 'Dax says that a party sounds like great television, but can we keep the drinking to a minimum, or at least, off camera.'

Junior had reached us now, wading to the shore of camp with his newly grown hair fluttering in the wind. Even *he* wasn't what he seemed to be, although there was no trace of Barnsley in his deep American intonation and his bulging musculature. I looked at him, and wondered. Did he really know that we were tracking a big dog? Was he keeping anything else from us, apart from his background and his sexuality? 'Are we going to investigate, or what?' he boomed.

'Ah. There's been a wee change of focus.' Sebastian led him away, presumably to explain about us dog-detecting and, hopefully, about the party too. I wouldn't have liked to spring anything unexpected on Junior.

11

And so it came to pass, as Ruth might have said, that we partied. It wasn't exactly a nightclub, and the booze didn't exactly flow like water, but, for a bunch of people isolated on the moors without any dry clothing, we did our best.

Mac channelled his Spotify playlist through the phone, and then blasted music into the night. We built up the fire with a kind of 'it's all going to hell anyway' insouciance with the firewood, and Ruth made some food that we could eat with our hands while we danced.

It must all have looked a bit pagan from a distance. Mac, Kanga, Junior and I danced wildly around the fire, fuelled largely by a mixture of alcohol that any of us would have turned our noses up at, had things been normal. We became ethereal, flickering things, half-seen as we twisted in and out of the light, laughing. Even Junior let some of his hair down, dropped a lot of the gruff persona and entered into the spirit of things, with moves that told of an awful lot of time spent on a dancefloor, supple hips and waving arms. He danced with Kanga, mostly. I guess because her knowing about his sexuality made him feel more secure with her, but as it suited the narrative that had been built around the two of them sharing a tent, Dax would be happy. He would probably edit out Kanga's blurted admissions anyway.

Mac and I danced on the periphery. Uneven ground and unexpected alcohol making me fall over meant a lot of time spent with him catching me and setting up upright again and I had to admit that *some* of my stumbles were more for the pleasant feel of his arms pulling me in against him. I hadn't realised how much I missed that. Pure physical contact from another person hadn't been a thing for a long time in my deceased relationship and since my mum had stopped hugging me. Since she'd started to look at me sideways whenever I'd been alone with Paul.

Had she *really* thought I'd been seducing him? Or was she so entrenched in Paul being her last chance at a relationship that she'd wanted *not* to see what was going on? Either way, she'd stopped snuggling up with me on the sofa even when he was out. Stopped hugging me before she went on one of her weekends away. And I was beginning to realise how much I'd missed that closeness, that warmth.

Now, here was Mac. Treating physical contact as though it were the most natural thing in the world; laughing as he lifted me up from yet another ankle-snagged tumble amid the heather and bracken that we'd danced out into. Now we were on the edge of the firelight, seeing one another in cut-up flickers and long shadows that added an extra frisson to the hand-clasps and half-embraces.

Over nearer to the fire, Ruth was in charge of the music now, staring down at the phone screen. Kanga was doing what I always thought of as 'club dancing', with lots of eye-catching arm movements and enough hip-wiggling to cause apoplexy in our target viewing audience, while Junior matched her wiggle for wiggle. They seemed to have come to something of an understanding, or were using one another to boost their televisual presence, because they were grinning at each other and occasionally bumping hips. Sebastian was in charge of the booze and we'd decided to keep him as much 'off camera' as possible, in case Dax came charging in, in his hired helicopter like a literal *deus ex machina* to stop our fun. Which meant we tried not to point ourselves at him, and he was mostly sticking to the darker corners of the camp, where he was pouring vodka into beer and shoving enamel mugs of drink into the hand of anyone who came past.

I stopped to draw breath between songs and looked at the campsite as

I blew heavily, hands on knees and my head forward. The semi-circle of tents abutting the outcrop of rock felt like home now. The firelight was throwing all kinds of atavistic shadows over us, and making the tents look as though they were moving, dipping under invisible weights and billowing in unfelt breezes. It looked at once both cosy and alien.

'You all right?' Mac bent beside me. Since we'd all had a decent wash and sacrificed enough water for the men to shave and everyone to wash their hair, his face looked different. Shorn of its increasing mat of beard, he looked more open. More approachable. *Sexier.* The new cleanliness made his eyes look bigger than ever, and the curve of his smile was now properly visible, rather than subsumed into face covering.

'I'm all right.' I straightened up. 'How about you?'

'Me? Och, I'm good. I'm always good. Why wouldn't I be?'

'Because we've downgraded ourselves to basically hunting down a stray dog, and you and I drove the downgrade? I'm not sure the others have forgiven us yet.'

He turned away to look over at where 'the others' were partying. Kanga was holding her hands above her head and twirling slowly, whilst Junior put his arms up in imitation and copied her rotation. They looked like a pair of figures on a fifteenth-century clock, about to strike the hours. Ruth was consulting Sebastian about the music, heads bent together over the tiny glowing screen.

'How are you charging the phone?' I asked absently, taking a swig out of the plastic cup of Prosecco in my hand.

'Dax gave me a battery pack,' Mac said, absently, as though he were thinking of something else, staring off into the darkness over my shoulder. 'Same as we're using for the cameras. Izzy...'

'I was wondering, that's all.'

'Yes, I can understand that. Izzy...' He still sounded vague, as though he really wasn't listening to what he was saying.

'I think I really like you, Mac. I'm looking forward to that dinner, when we get out of here.'

His attention snapped back to me. 'Oh. Oh, that's great. That's... really great.'

I moved in a bit closer. Felt the warmth from his skin where he'd been dancing. 'You don't sound so sure now,' I said. 'Is it still on?'

His eyes had gone off into the dark again. 'What?' He drew his focus back to my face. 'Yes! Yes, of course.'

His eyes were huge. They moved as though he were taking in every feature on my face with a kind of calliper-measuring precision. As though it was about to become very important that he knew the *precise* width of my lips and the colour of my eyes down to the merest fleck.

We'd been drinking and dancing and the somewhat enforced intimacy of the camp and spending practically every waking moment in one another's company compounded things, and I found that I was reaching my arms up to put behind his neck and he was leaning in, and there was a heat and a scent that I'd thought I'd forgotten rushing through my mind.

Our lips had barely touched when Mac gave me a sudden shove that sent me down to the lumpy ground with more force than any of my half-drunken stumbles. I landed on my back with the wind knocked out of me by a branch that jutted somewhere round my midriff. I gasped, and flailed for a moment, not sure whether I was more hurt by the impact or by his physical rejection of me, then realised that Mac was down here beside me, there was shouting and the music had stopped.

'What the hell!' That was Sebastian. Ruth was screaming.

I heard Junior say, 'Gimme the key, Ruth,' and then sounds of scrabbling.

'Stay down,' Mac hissed into my ear among the confusion and I felt his arm come across me, pinning me to the undergrowth, from where dampness was sponging down my dancing warmth like a cold shower.

Flashes of light. Someone had taken a piece of flaming wood from the fire and was whirling it about, trying to illuminate the scene, running from side to side of the camp. I assumed it was Sebastian, I could still hear Ruth screaming and Kanga was sobbing, a panicky, deep kind of sob, nothing like the cosmetic crying she'd done earlier.

'It's gone.' Sebastian. Lowering the branch so that the light died back to join with the flickers from the fire.

'I'm going out anyway.' Junior, swinging a coat over his shoulders. 'Everyone, stay close to the fire. Don't move.'

Gradually Mac released the pressure over my chest and gave me a little push to sit up. He rolled himself upright alongside me.

'What happened?' I began to pick itchy bits of plant out of my clothes.

'I saw...' Mac began, then rubbed both hands over his face. 'Just a shadow. Something dark, moving, behind you. Then you... well, you distracted my attention. I thought it was only the wind, making the plants move about and the firelight making it all look as though it was running, and then something huge and black came out over on the edge of the camp. Ran across in front of Ruth and Sebastian and then away.'

I sat silently for a moment. My heart was thumping sickeningly and the recent winding didn't help the awful feeling that we'd all had a near miss.

'Sorry I pushed you,' Mac went on. 'But I didn't know which way it was coming and I didn't want you to get bitten.'

'Gallant of you,' I said, somewhat breathless.

Sebastian was comforting Ruth, I could hear his 'ssshhhing', and thought that a paternal figure wasn't always a bad thing at times like this. Hopefully it had all been caught on camera, and Sebastian's wife would realise that his taking charge could be a good thing sometimes.

'What *was* it?' Kanga, seeming to need the reassurance of others, came over. 'I couldn't see. The fire is too bright.'

'Dunno.' Mac gave her a brief pat on the shoulder. 'I couldn't see, either. Just a shape and movement. But it was big.'

I seemed to be the least shocked of the party, but then I'd not seen anything. I'd had my back, apparently, to whatever it was, whilst I'd been talking to Mac, and he'd pushed me down before I caught a glimpse of anything coming into the camp. Indignation, and being winded, had meant I'd not even looked up.

'Dog?' I asked.

Mac shrugged. 'It was a reflection of light on some kind of fur and then I panicked. It must have been.' He reached out a hand and pulled me upright. 'I need to talk to Dax. He can look at the film, we all had our cameras on, right?'

Kanga nodded. Sebastian looked up from patting Ruth. 'We did. But

I'm not sure we'll have caught anything, like Kanga said, the light of the fire meant it was nothing more than a moving shape.'

I made a noise born of frustration and a little bit of discomfort, I was definitely bruised somewhere around the midsection. 'Oh, that's typical! Big beast, we've all got cameras, we could have *proved* something, one way or another!'

And, whispered my tiny inner voice, if it was a cat, you could have got yourselves £50,000 if only your cameras had been facing the right way and the light had been right.

'But it's like what I saw before, up on the Downs,' Sebastian said, his voice steady and reasonable. 'Just a glimpse, much too fleeting and fast to ever get a picture. And so there's no real proof. As yet,' he added. 'Which is why we're here.'

There was a moment's silence. 'Are we really bad at what we do or something?' Kanga asked hesitantly. 'The *whole point* of us being here is to get evidence. And we're totally shit at it. Why didn't you think to set a trap?'

Her voice trembled on the edge of tears again, as she rounded on Sebastian. I thought back to her confession. Council flat, mum and brothers. Modelling camping gear would be all very well, but it wouldn't make her fortune, whereas £50,000 would be enough to set her up. Kanga and I were here for the same reason. I just hoped she wasn't going to choose now to blurt out her real background, because that would leave me without cover.

I tried to catch her eye and send her mental 'calm down' messages, but she'd got Sebastian in her sights and wasn't looking at me.

'We didn't know it would come into camp.' Ruth, equally wobbly, but with a sort of defiance. 'You can't blame anyone.'

'I *told* you I saw something! Earlier today, I said I saw a shape! Why does nobody listen to anything I say? We could have been attacked and eaten!'

We all jumped as the sound of a shot pierced the valley, a sudden noise of destruction and anger into our slightly tetchy enclave. Ruth started praying, quietly.

'*Why* aren't we doing this properly?' Kanga's voice was rising to a semi-hysterical wail. 'We're bumbling about looking for tracks and stuff but we're not setting traps or keeping watch or *doing anything*! It's like we're all treating this as a really shit holiday and playing at trying to find this creature. Now we know there's really something out there...' She stopped.

'You think we've been playing?' Mac came in close now. We'd all shuffled closer to the fire, as though the dying warmth and light would protect us from all the beasties of the night.

'Well! None of us really care if we find this thing or not, do we?' Kanga looked around at the group. 'We're only here for the money. We don't want to know what it is, or why it's here or anything like that. We're not *investigating.*'

Inside my chest, my heart did a weird double-beat, *Not now, Kanga, please, not now.* Under my jacket, I broke out in a sweat. *Why* had I told her? Why hadn't I kept my mouth shut? This was Kanga, who had all the altruism of the average camel, and I'd given her access to a secret that would make everyone look at me differently. As though I were an object of pity. Or scorn.

'Look...' I began, trying to mitigate any damage before it started, feeling that awful tightening of my skin that came with the shame. 'We...'

But she ignored me and put her hands on her hips. 'Junior told me that half the tracks he's found have been badger anyway,' she finished defiantly. 'He's only pointing them out to string this along. And because I asked him to make it exciting, so we get viewing time.' Her voice was a bit sulky now, but I admired her honesty. At least, I admired it when it didn't involve her spreading my life out for examination.

'Kanga...' Sebastian moved forward as though to reassure her, but she shook her head, newly washed blonde hair streaking the night in the firelight.

'I'm going to my tent,' she said, with dignity. 'But *I* think we should set up a watch rota. I don't want to get eaten in my sleep.' She whisked off, ducking under her tent flap, and I saw the flashlight go on inside, making her tent shine like a beacon for any quadruped with ill intent.

The remaining four of us stood in silence. Then Ruth said, 'She's got a point, you know.'

'She's actually got several.' Sebastian sighed. 'If this thing, whatever it is, *is* going to be dangerous, then we should set up a watch. We *have* been going about this rather half-cocked, haven't we?'

'Our methods have somewhat lacked scientific rigour,' Mac agreed.

'But we said we didn't want to shoot it.' Ruth sounded a bit breathless now. 'We agreed we wouldn't let it be put in a zoo. Not even for money.'

'But if it tries to kill us?' I asked. 'Surely we defend ourselves.' I was surfing on the backwash of relief from Kanga not having trotted my past out for consumption, so I may have sounded a little more stridently anti-creature than I would have otherwise done.

Ruth's face took on a 'set' look. 'But it didn't. It came right into the camp and nobody was hurt.'

I rubbed my sore back ruefully, but had to agree.

'It *didn't* attack. It could have, we were absolutely unprepared, but it didn't. It ran through and on into the night, and it was so fast that we couldn't even tell what it was!' Ruth took a deep breath. 'I don't want any part of hurting it. I couldn't see an animal that was born wild put in a cage. Especially not an animal that isn't harming anyone. God said, "Thou shalt not kill," and taking something off these moors and keeping it in a zoo would be the same thing as killing it.'

With those biblical words dropping into the cold dark like stones into a deep lake, she turned on her heel and walked a few paces away, clearly distancing herself from our raging bloodlust.

'Ah,' Sebastian said, somewhat inadequately.

'Maybe it's all academic?' I pointed out down the valley. 'Maybe Junior shot it just now and he's dragging the sleeping body back here at this moment?'

I could almost feel the cash-registers in our heads start to click as we all mentally spent £250,000, and then reality asserted itself once more. 'Whilst I don't doubt that Junior is terrific at what he does, I'm not sure that shooting a moving animal in the dark is going to take one shot,' Sebastian said cautiously, with one eye on Ruth. 'This isn't the Wild West.'

'It's not Barnsley either,' I observed, and my tone was a little more waspish than I would have liked. I'd been *enjoying* myself, dancing with Mac in the firelight, nearly kissing him. I'd been having *fun* without worrying about where I was going to sleep or how safe I was, for the first time in ages, and that had all been ruined by that running dark-furred shape. 'Maybe he killed it. After all, does anyone know what dose those darts carry? Is it the same for a big cat as for a wild dog?'

Nobody asked why I'd brought blameless Barnsley into the conversation. Presumably they all thought I was just overwrought. Ruth made a small, strangled noise. 'Oh, no! That poor damaged creature!'

'That poor damaged creature that tried to come into our camp,' Mac said, dryly. 'Kanga was right. Anything could have happened, and we're a long way from help, even if Dax was watching the live feed and sent someone straight out. You can bleed to death in minutes, Ruth.'

This mad escapade had stopped being enjoyable. That was what I was finding so difficult to process. For all the cold ground and the damp tents and Kanga falling in the river and nearly freezing, we'd been going about camping and tracking as though all we wanted was the money for being here, anything else was a bonus and hopefully wouldn't come at the expense of attacks and blood and someone carted off to hospital. Suddenly, the potential for severe injury and killing an animal, accidentally or otherwise, was front and centre.

'I'm going to draw up a watch rota,' Sebastian said, sounding slightly shaken. Perhaps he'd had the same realisation that I'd had. 'And I *think*, maybe, whoever is on watch ought to have the gun?'

Ruth made another little noise.

'If it comes down to one of us being attacked or potentially killing whatever this thing is, I'd rather we all made it out alive.' Sebastian sounded more resolute now.

'Plus, we could always fire into the air. Scare it off,' added Mac.

'And I don't think any of us are exactly skilled marksmen. Women. Markspeople. Persons,' I added, trying to be as accurate as possible within gender lines. 'The chances are that nobody is going to shoot the creature. As long as we don't shoot each other, we'll be ahead of the game.'

Ruth looked slightly pacified. She tugged at the end of one of her bunches and frowned. 'I don't want anyone to die,' she said. 'But then I don't want *anything* to die. But if we shoot it and tranquilise it, what do we do? Leave it to come round with a headache and attack us all? Oh, I don't know.'

'If it's a big cat, then presumably the dose of tranquiliser will knock it out. We could take pictures of ourselves with it, then get Dax to come and get us but only after the cat has come round and we've let it wander off, while we hide?' I suggested. 'And we can say, "Whoops, sorry, we must have mistimed things; oh, look, here are some wonderful photographs of us with the unconscious cat as proof."'

Ruth gazed at me, her eyes big and round. 'But it's not a cat, is it? You said so. And if it's a dog, then the tranquiliser dose might kill it! Or not be enough to knock it out and then it's just us and a very cross and absolutely enormous dog.'

Junior arrived back then, storming through the heather behind us and scrambling, unnecessarily, over the rockface down to where we were huddled. He was without any sign of having been savagely attacked and he didn't have anything strapped to his back either.

'We heard a shot.' Sebastian sounded rather interrogative, and seemed to realise it, because he cleared his throat and softened his tone. 'Are you all right?'

Junior looked uncharacteristically sheepish for a moment 'Yeah.' He hunched his shoulders and rubbed a hand over the top of his newly shaved head. 'Got a bit trigger-happy down there. Thought I saw something move. Yeah.'

'And?'

'Er. I shot a tree.'

The release of the tension that we'd all been holding brought on a fit of laughter. First Sebastian, letting out a big shout of a laugh, then Ruth and I began giggling. Even Mac relaxed enough to grin.

Junior looked annoyed for a moment, and then joined in. 'It's okay. I hit it quick and clean. It's going to have a headache, that's all.'

The realisation that Junior could have a sense of humour made my giggles intensify. I'd been thinking of him as little more than a walking hunk up until now; an emotionless slab of a man whose reasons for being here, apart from avoiding Bigfoot, were sketchy. But now I was learning so much more about him, it was as though he were coming gradually into focus. From being an outline of a human to a fully drawn character. I wondered how a gay guy from Barnsley had made it in the Sasquatch world.

And, again, just *why* he was here.

Real life, I reflected, as we all went to our tents, leaving the fire banked up and burning and Junior and Sebastian on watch, was beginning to hit us all. The whole 'kill or be killed' was how our ancestors must have lived; there probably wasn't a Palaeolithic hunter out there who'd hesitated over the ethics of killing in the face of a charging mammoth. Now, when life revolved for most around doing the laundry, going to work, making sure you were eating the right things and exercising enough...

I lifted the tent flap and sniffed the air. Bruised shrubbery wafted in, from where we'd danced on the grass and heather. The smell of water, brassy and green, from the river. The comforting smell of the fire and the peat that ran down the sides of the valley. The smells hadn't changed over the millennia. Those hunters would have smelled these things too.

I let the flap drop. Not having a home, not having somewhere I could close a door and call a space mine, had obviously got to me. I was beginning to identify with people who hunted with spears and lived in fear of bronchitis, rather than those who cooked elaborate meals and phoned in sick with a hangover.

Maybe because my present life was closer to that of the early occupants of Britain? Was that it? Maybe I'd got a feel for what it was like to have a precarious existence because I didn't have a 'safe place', and I was over-identifying with the early hunter-gatherers, because, whilst serving overpriced white wine to trendy accountants wasn't exactly stalking deer, trying to find somewhere to sleep afterwards where I wouldn't be mauled or robbed was certainly closer to living in a skin tent among ravaging beasts. I looked around at the resolutely nylon walls of my current tent, had a brief imagining of a ravaging beast scything its way through them in order to get to tender, tasty me, and pulled my sleeping bag tightly up around my neck.

Those early hunters, those without a place to call home, wouldn't have had this feeling of humiliation, would they? The feeling that everyone else had somewhere to live, leaving only those of us who had failed catastrophically at life to dot the streets and people the unattended build-ings. It made me realise even more forcefully that was all I wanted now. A door to close behind me and a piece of floor that nobody else was going to walk over.

And the fact I hadn't got one was all my own fault. If I'd stood up to Paul right at the beginning, rather than trying to be 'nice' for Mum's sake... maybe he wouldn't have got the idea that he could put his greasy hands on me at every opportunity. If I'd shut him down when he whis-pered those things to me, if I'd insisted on going with Mum on her week-ends away, perhaps she wouldn't have been so ready to believe that I'd *wanted* to be alone with him.

And I'd still have my room. My things. My job, and my mother.

I'd agreed that Mac and I would take the late-night watch. Mac woke me by poking the side of the tent with a stick.

'Hey,' he hissed from somewhere outside. 'Are you up? It's our shift.'

'Ow. Yes, I'm up. What?' I was still half asleep. It was dark and cold, that metallic kind of feel that you really only get at about two in the morning, when the night is well established and there's no kind of day on the horizon.

'I'll make some tea. But it's pretty chilly out here, so I'd hurry if I were you.' Then he stopped the poking, and the shadow that he'd thrown across the fabric moved off. There were distant noises of fire building, and I sighed and climbed out to go and join him.

The rest of the camp was utterly silent. Even Junior and Sebastian, who must have only recently come off their watch, had vanished into dark and quiet. The only light came from the sullen red smoulder of the logs that Mac was teasing back into life, and the small bright eyes of our cameras, which didn't illuminate anything, just a laser pinpoint on our shoulders.

'You okay?' Mac poured tea into a couple of tin mugs.

'You're very perky,' I said, sitting somewhat sulkily on one of the camping chairs and cupping my numb fingers around the mug.

'I'm used to being up and about at night. Makes for better filming, you don't get loads of wannabe TikTok stars trying to crash through your set-up.' He put another couple of dry branches on the fire and flames began to twist through the dark. 'But I don't usually have company.'

'No hordes of women wanting to accompany you on all-expenses-paid trips to obscure places?' I tried to make it sound light and jokey, but I'd been wondering about this. About how someone who seemed likeable and attractive managed to stay solo, or whether he'd really been running a harem of women, travelling for a season and then discarding them. Not that it was any of my business, really, after all, I'd only agreed to go to dinner with him. I looked sideways at Mac's profile as his eyes reflected the red glow of the fire and wondered if I'd been mad to turn down his offer to travel with him. He'd said we could travel as friends, as work-mates, it didn't have to be a 'thing' between us. Pretend couples worked out all the time in the media, after all. But maybe I'd read one too many 'fake relationship' books to believe that it could end with a merry hand-shake and cards exchanged at Christmas. Perhaps I didn't want a 'fake relationship'. I wasn't quite sure what I *did* want.

Then I stopped myself, as I'd got going with a runaway fantasy of living on some tropical beach with this man; the two of us, a tent, all the coconuts we could eat and no other people intruding. No. The runaway fantasy was just that. Running away. I didn't need that. I needed a life, a real, proper life, with somewhere to live and a job. I *could* run, of course I could, like I'd run here to this damp camp site, but I couldn't *keep* doing it. One day, I'd need to turn around and face what was following me.

'Oh, they're keen enough to come,' Mac replied, with his tone as light as mine, but there was a heaviness underneath, a kind of dip to his head as he sat beside me. Something that told me there were a lot more sentences waiting to be said on this subject, but that he needed to form them inside his head before he put them out into the world. They were sitting like an incomplete craft project somewhere in his mind, and he knew that finishing them off and putting them out there was going to take effort and time. So I didn't push the subject.

'Have you got the gun?' I sipped at my tea. It was bitter and stewed, but hot enough for me not to care.

'I didn't bother with it. Junior offered it to me, but I've locked it away again. I have absolutely no confidence in my ability not to shoot you, set fire to the tents and possibly cause a minor earthquake, should I try to fire it.'

He seemed grateful that I wasn't going to make him talk about women, and if talk about shooting was lighter for him than talking about women, then I had the feeling that he might be in for a long and painful process to get around to them.

We sat in silence for a while. The night sat around us. There was the occasional lone baa from an isolated sheep, and the whisper of the wind as it tiptoed through the gorse bushes behind us, but no other sound. The crackle of wood twisting in the fire made me jump.

'Well, this is nice,' I said eventually, because all this quiet was getting to me.

In a move that was so quick and seamless that he had to have been planning it, Mac slapped off his camera, then leaned across and turned mine off too. 'How did you come to be homeless?' His change of subject was so abrupt that at first I thought I'd misheard him, and my brain strained to make sense of the words.

'You know how,' I said eventually. 'My mum threw me out of the house because of Paul.'

'But didn't you have friends you could move in with? Nobody who wanted to go in on a flat share or anything?' He looked at me, brown eyes flaring along with the dry twigs in the firelight, above his mug. 'Most people – I mean, not that I've known many, but there have been a few, whose relationships have ended, they've had places to go. There always seems to be someone wanting an extra person to take the spare room or whatever. You didn't have that?'

I let my mug drop onto my knees. The enamel was scalding against my fingers, contrasting with the chill of the night. 'All my friends were... they're all in couples. *I* was in a couple. We had couple friends. Nobody else had broken up and they were happy to have me on the sofa for a while, but they didn't have spare rooms to offer me. Any spare rooms were offices or nurseries, and I didn't have the deposit to move into a flat share.' I tried to judge his expression, but it was hard with the darkness and a big white mug taking up most of his face.

'Plus, I think my mum may have talked about me seducing her partner, and mud like that sticks. Suddenly, nobody in a relationship is keen to have a single woman with a reputation for breaking couples up sleeping on their futon. You know what it's like.' I didn't go into the shame and humiliation that resulted from everyone believing that my mother was right and that I was the kind of woman who would behave that way. It had come a little too quickly from many people that I'd thought were good friends.

The camping chair swayed as he stood up. 'Not really. I don't have friends like that.'

'What the hell kind of friends *do* you have, then? Basement-dwelling perpetual bachelors who never go out in daylight?'

'Not friends whose relationships I know anything about. I travel. I make programmes about travelling. It means never being in one place for long enough for anyone to rely on my friendship.' There was a loneliness to his tone, as he spoke to the night. As though he'd learned to be self-contained and not need that friendship, but that he desperately wanted it. And I thought, *yes, you're running too.*

'Why?' I stood up as well. I couldn't have this conversation to the back of an anorak and the bobble of a hat. I needed to see his face. 'Why did you take up the travelling lifestyle? You could have stayed in Glasgow and made, oh, I don't know, wildlife films or something?'

There was a long silence. Even the sheep had stopped baaing, although that dog, wherever it was further down the valley, had begun to bark, short staccato barks, as though trying to draw someone's attention to something.

At last Mac turned around. His newly shaven cheeks were sucked in as though he were chewing the inside of his mouth, biting down on words that were trying to come out. 'Do you remember,' he said slowly, 'when I said I'd had a... friend, who was raped?'

'Yes.' I made my voice gentle. There was genuine anguish on his face.

'It was my girlfriend. Callie. We were at university together, very much a couple. I loved her, she loved me, we were great.' He took a deep breath. 'She was raped, one night, walking home from a late class, and I was an absolute *shit* about it.'

Again, that silence. The wind hissed its disapproval and the fire spat. Mac's breathing was loud now, as though he were panting.

'I couldn't get my head round what it meant for her. I thought it was, oh, I don't know. Like getting punched outside a pub, or something. A thing. A thing that happened. And I couldn't see how much it was going to affect her life, and who she trusted and how she lived. I mean, obviously I didn't think she should shrug it off and pretend it never happened. I went with her to the police station and all that, I tried to support her, but...' A deep sigh. 'I kind of *blamed* her, if you see what I mean. If she hadn't been walking home, if she'd called me to meet her, if, if, if...'

Now he bent slightly, so that he could see my face, his eyes looked into mine with an intensity that almost hurt. 'I was useless. I couldn't help her. She was feeling things that I couldn't relate to, and that I couldn't deal with. And we split up.'

Part of me wanted to berate him but he'd clearly spent years beating himself up, any chastising I did would be superfluous and cruel.

'So, what happened then?' I touched his shoulder. 'Mac?'

'I finished uni and started travelling. My family were all in TV production, so it was all I knew how to do; they weren't a lot of help and I figured I was better off alone, so I started making the YouTube films, got myself a sponsorship deal, and here I am. I made myself learn more about what Callie had gone through, I talked to people, I got educated. I never wanted to feel that lost, not knowing what to say, what to do, again. But what happened kind of hindered my relationships a bit. Made me wary, let me know that I can't always keep someone safe and that I can be an utter plonker when things get beyond me.'

'You are not telling me that you've not had a relationship since. I will not believe that,' I said sternly, because I feared he was going to fall into a black hole of self-pity and recrimination.

Mac grinned, which stopped the look of drawn-in unhappiness and self-reproach, and made his eyes spark a little. 'Thanks for the vote of confidence there.' The grin broadened until his teeth also gleamed in the firelight. 'I was beginning to wonder what you thought of me.'

'I think you *were* an idiot. But you were very young, it must have been hard for you to know what to say. And you've worked on it.'

'I never wanted to feel helpless again. Not like that.' He raised a hand, as though to run it through his hair, encountered the woolly hat, and lowered it. 'There have been women. Here and there. But I'm not in one place long enough to really build anything long-lasting. Relationships, friendships, any of that. I've kept moving.'

'So that you could never be *expected* to build anything?' I asked.

He shrugged. 'When you find yourself behaving in ways that you don't like in your formative years, it kind of makes you wonder. If anyone could ever put up with you.'

'But you asked me to travel with you.' What he'd asked, the importance of it to him, was dawning on me.

'Yes.'

I raised my eyebrows at him. 'You had better not have thought that I was such a pushover or so desperate that I would put up with anything.' I tried to make my tone light, to make it obvious that it wasn't what I thought at all. That what I *really* thought lay underneath the words. I was beginning to realise how much I liked Mac, with his honesty and his beanie hat.

'Quite the opposite. You're together, you know what you want. You didn't *have* to come on this expedition. I'm sure there are easier ways of making some money for a deposit on a room rather than camping in the wilds of Yorkshire with an assorted bunch of weirdos. But you came. You're here. And you are, quite often, the only one of us talking sense about this whole fiasco.'

We stood, side by side, my hand still on his arm, looking out into the darkness.

'There aren't that many ways of making three grand, you know,' I said at last. 'Not legally, anyway, and I absolutely was *not* going to take to Only-Fans. It was taking me forever to save money, even eating leftovers and sleeping on floors. Plus, I never want to see chips again, ever.'

Mac bumped his shoulder against me. 'We make a good team,' he said quietly. 'I don't really like chips much, either.'

We both sat down again. There was a new kind of tension between us now, not the tension born of unspoken things, but one that came on the edge of something that might be a future. That almost sexual frisson lasted right up until Mac shifted, and the nylon of his chair gave way along the back and he wobbled, then pitched over backwards into the heather, all insulated arms and legs waving like a gigantic marshmallow falling off a toasting stick.

Both of us started laughing. Just like earlier, when we'd laughed with Junior, I hadn't realised that I'd held so much tension, until it started to come out, and now I was laughing so much that I was breathless and had to grab at my knees to steady myself. The ridiculousness of everything, from what we were doing out here to the fact that I couldn't bend over because I'd got so many clothes on; that we were trying to last out the month for an amount of money that most people would have put on a credit card, that it was dark and cold and here we were sitting around waiting for an imaginary animal – well. It was funny. Probably only in that minute, and only between Mac and me, but it made us laugh.

I hadn't laughed like this for a while. I had to rack my brain to remember when I'd last really had the chance. I'd smiled at a few customers occasionally, maybe the odd giggle to try to get them to tip me more, but – laugh? No. You had to feel safe to laugh. Suddenly it dawned on me that, precarious though our situation was out here on the edge of tho moon, in the middle of the night and with a potentially dangerous creature stalking around out there in the dark, I felt safe with Mac.

Eventually we stopped. Mac hauled himself up out of the damp undergrowth and perched on what was left of his chair, now converted into a stool, and we sat together, looking out into the dark. 'Are you ever going to speak to your mum again?' Mac asked, in such a complete non-sequitur that I was sure my eyes bulged.

'Sorry?'

'To tell her she was wrong? For the sake of closure?'

I stayed silent. The laughter that had held us together in that bubble of broken tension had gone. It had evaporated into the night, leaving a cold, bitter residue, not unlike what was left of my tea. All I could see was my mother's face, twisted and dry as the stems of the heather that were reaching their jagged way to the sky.

'No.'

'Why not?'

All trace of humour was gone now. The man who sat next to me didn't feel like Mac any more, with his big brown eyes, ridiculous hat and corkscrew hair poking from underneath its ribbing. This man was challenging me. Asking me to do something that I'd sworn to myself I would never do – after all, why should I? She'd taken the word of a man she had known for a matter of months over her own daughter. She'd swallowed his lies because she'd wanted to, and kicked me out of my security, without the means to earn a living, because she'd needed to believe him over me. I didn't want any further part in that.

'Because I don't want to.' I said it as lightly as I could manage, but there was a gruff depth to my voice that gave away some of the emotion that I was packaging down as tightly as I could.

'Don't you want to get it out in the open? Show that Paul up for what he really is?' Mac's voice was gentle, although the words were addressed to the velvet sleeve of night that contained us rather than to me. He was looking out over the little river valley as though he were focusing on something moving over there, for which I was glad. If he'd tried to meet my eye, to see what I *really* thought, I would have had to get up and walk away, and it was surprisingly comfortable in this camping chair with the cold mug between my fingers.

'How can you tell me to do something like that, when you won't even talk to your own brother honestly?' I surprised myself with the words. It was as though I wanted to make Mac feel the way I did, and I'd hunted around for something that made him vulnerable, although I hadn't even been aware of the thought processes. 'All that resentment you're carrying around, you should at least tell him that you know he's the favoured child and all that.'

Mac wriggled on the stool. One leg sank into the grassy surface as he moved, pitching him forwards now. 'This bloody thing has got it in for me,' he said.

'All camping furniture has an inbuilt desire to kill us and run free.' Clearly neither of us were very good at actually talking about what really ran beneath our reasons for being here, but I felt I'd done far more in the confessions stakes than he had. It gave me an unfamiliar feeling of pride. I'd not talked to anyone about what had happened at home, in that moment when Mum had been screaming, accusing, not listening, with Paul standing in the kitchen doorway, watching it all with that smile on his face that told me he'd not got quite what he wanted, but this was a good second best. The way I'd not even bothered to try to argue with her, past my initial contradiction of his statement. What I'd said to Mac had been the nearest I'd ever been to coming to terms with it.

Although I hadn't, had I? If I'd come to terms with it, I wouldn't get such a kick in the stomach whenever I thought of it, or feel the hot tight pull around my neck of that stranglehold of guilt.

More silence. The fire was dying now, not even crackling, only a sullen kind of hiss came from it now and again. The wind had vanished too, the air had taken the sort of stillness that comes before dawn gets going and the day decides what sort of weather it's going to adopt. Even the dog on the farm down the valley was quiet. There was the odd static-laden shuffle as someone behind us moved in one of the tents, the almost musical plonk and gurgle of the full river at the bottom of the gulley as it ran its silken way over submerged rocks, but nothing loud. Nothing intrusive. As though even nature and our surroundings were waiting for the next move.

It never came. By silent agreement, we turned our cameras on again and stayed there, sitting without speaking, until dawn underlined the clouds on the horizon, when we could leave our posts and head to sleep. From my side, there didn't seem to be anything to say. Mac didn't know, how *could* he know, that when I'd walked away from my mother, I'd promised to myself that I would never have any more to do with her. He didn't seem any keener to explore his relationship with Dax than I did to go back, so I reckoned we were even.

And maybe it was that sense of shame that gave us that unsaid sympathy for one another. He was clearly ashamed of the way he'd behaved towards his girlfriend and I – well. I'd only just started to unpack that emotion that kept me from confessing the reason I was homeless. I usually skirted over it. Pretended I was just between places. Looking at options. Wanting to remain mobile and free.

But really what I was was ashamed, of my mother, and of myself. How did a nicely brought up, and, although Kanga had practically weaponised the word it still applied, *educated* girl end up sofa-surfing?

As I lay down in my sleeping bag, listening to the sounds of the day dawning outside my tent, I wondered for the first time. How had my mum managed to fall so completely under Paul's influence that she'd believe him over her own daughter? She'd known me for all twenty-nine years of my life, whereas he'd only been with her for six months; how had all our family history come to be so swept away by the word of a man?

The heat of sheer indignity flooded through me. I'd been thrown out on the streets for the sake of a man. If I'd only done something earlier – said something, kicked Paul in his no doubt inadequate groin, screamed when he tried the handle to my room for the third time in a night and the chair under the handle had scuffed back a few centimetres on the worn carpet – if I had *done something*, could it have been prevented?

That shame weighed me down. The feeling that, somehow, it was my fault that I'd ended up like this stopped me from confessing. The sense that I should have had savings, should have had somewhere else to go, and that I'd screwed up my life because I hadn't had the foresight to predict that this could have happened, kept me quiet.

I fell asleep with the familiar beat of the words 'it's all your fault' drumming through my brain like the world's most persistent earworm.

12

I slept into the day, but woke up when Junior and Mac started cooking lunch. A wonderful aroma seeped under my groundsheet and I sat up like a corpse reanimated by the prayers of the faithful, pulled on my hat, and slipped through the flap to find out what was smelling so good out there.

Mac was stirring a pot on the fire, while Junior chopped things up and flung them in. They were both chatting about previous outdoor experiences, like a pair of fur trappers at the ends of the earth, rather than over-privileged campers who were brought regular fresh supplies. We'd got *basil*, for goodness' sake.

'And, once, in this here camp, we'd heard sounds of Bigfoot in the night, and when we came out, we realised that all our fresh meat was gone!' Junior said as he added onion to the pot. 'Had to live on beans and scallions until the trip was over.'

'I stayed in a bivvy up a Tyrolean mountain for a few days in a snow-storm,' countered Mac. 'Couldn't get out and had to eat dehydrated rations dry out of the packet.'

'Uh huh.' Junior stirred the pot. 'Hard times, eh?'

Mac nodded and I had to suppress a smile as they competitively tried to outdo one another with tales of deprivation. I could have joined in, told them about the days with no food, between jobs, then sneaky eating of people's leftovers on my way between the kitchen and the food bins. Times when you had no idea what it was that you were eating, when it was cold and congealed on the plate, but it was food and you didn't care. But I didn't. That was then, in the past. Despite my thoughts about my mother last night, I'd decided to cast off the past, hadn't I? This damp campsite and composite mud was my new start, stretching out in front of me like these moors, almost glittering under the sharp sunlight.

'Ah, Izzy, come and stir this, will you?' Mac stood up and handed me an outsize spoon. 'Ruth and Sebastian have gone down the valley to look for any evidence and I promised I'd bang a plate when the food was done.' He gave me a smile which held no sign of our minor disagreement last night. 'Like getting the cat in.'

I took the spoon. 'No sign of anything moving last night, then?'

'Nope. We're on first watch tonight, so we can catch up on our sleep. Dax is coming over to record us talking about the creature that came into camp. And bringing peanuts if he knows what's good for him.' Mac began heading off through the heather, climbing up around the back of the tents to the high point on top of the rocks. I watched him go. There was a lithe suppleness to the way he moved, as though he were used to vertical slopes over crags, and I thought he was heading up there to avoid me mentioning his brother. He was clearly no keener to talk to Dax about their relationship than I was to face my mother.

I watched him clamber to the top of the outcrop, armed with a tin plate and a teaspoon, which he brought together with a distinct amount of drama, like a very cheap remake of the Rank gong striking. I wondered if he was doing it because he knew I was watching, which gave me a little warm glow. It had been a long time since a man had cared whether I was looking at him or not, and Mac was – well, he was *Mac*. Confrontation avoidant he might be, but people in glass houses and all that, and hadn't it been conflict avoidance that had got me where I was?

'What on earth is that all about?' Kanga had appeared at my elbow. Her hair was loose again, cleaner and blonder since we'd had the chance for a proper wash, and she was obviously taking advantage by letting the wind ruffle through it.

'Mac's calling Ruth and Sebastian in for lunch.'

'Oh.' Kanga moved away, heading towards the camp stools and the cauldron of bubbling goodness over the fire, then seemed to think again, and came back. 'Izzy,' she said, with an odd tone in her voice. 'What I said, the other day. About my background.'

She wasn't looking at me, she'd got her eyes firmly on the toes of her boots. The wind cobwebbed her hair and she looked young and rather fragile suddenly.

'I haven't said anything, and I won't,' I assured her. I still had half an eye on Mac, who was now slithering down the bank from the promontory, with a lot less grace than he'd gone up. 'It's your business, not mine. And you've been keeping quiet about what I said about being homeless, so I'm not likely to, either.'

Kanga raised her head. Her eyes were very, very blue, I noticed. 'Oh. Right. Only, I just wanted to say that I lied. I'm not from Wandsworth at all, I only said that to... to make myself sound more relatable, do you see? If anything had happened – I mean, obviously we were safe enough and nothing *too* dreadful could ever happen really – but in case, I thought I'd make myself more of an everyman. Not everyone can muster up sympathy for someone who grew up with my advantages. But obviously I won't say anything about your... situation. Because I'm sympathetic to the fact that not everyone can have my support network.'

I wondered if the blue of her eyes was tinted contact lenses and suppressed the desire to poke her in one.

'Whatever,' I said, tiredly. I'd been feeling more warmly towards Kanga since our mutual confessions, but her retraction – lie though it obviously was – sucked all that warmth back and made me want to put slugs in her sleeping bag. 'There's nothing to be ashamed of in having no money, you know.'

But wasn't I ashamed of that very thing? Hadn't I agonised last night over 'might have beens' and 'should have dones'? I regretted ever having confessed anything to Kanga in the first place, and wondered about the new uncertainty. Was she building up to throwing my life to the wolves? Or did she think doing that might take the attention away from her?

'Well, yes, you *would* know.' Kanga pulled a scarf more tightly around her neck, giving me dark thoughts about wanting to help her with it.

'Obviously.' She looked me up and down briefly and then headed off towards the food again.

Ruth and Sebastian were coming back into camp from opposite directions down the valley. Ruth had been on the track, now not sandy but more gritty mud, whilst Sebastian was picking his way carefully from the boulder-strewn dale head. They both looked as though they'd been doing this for years now and I wondered if we all looked like that – acclimatised to wearing seven layers of clothing and walking as though every footstep might land us in a bog or a snare of undergrowth.

'Find anything?' Junior's voice seemed to have gone down the register even further. 'I should be out there, y'know. I'm a hunter, I'm not down for cooking detail.'

'We all have to take turns,' Ruth said, reasonably. 'And I couldn't really see anything much.'

'I did.' Sebastian panted into camp. 'Well, I think I did. I'm not completely sure, of course, it could be wishful thinking, but I'm *almost* certain that I saw marks along by the river.' He pointed. 'Where the ice has gone, it's left mud and there's marks down there. Junior, I'll show you after we've eaten. I tried to film them, but all you can see is splodges in brown, I can see why they'd want more definite evidence before we win any money.'

A silence resulted, as we all inwardly processed once more the fact that the bar to us actually winning any money was so ridiculously high that it could have a jaguar weighing it down and we still wouldn't be able to reach it.

'Okay, then.' Mac picked up the pile of plates and began handing them out. 'Food.'

We sat, or squatted in Junior's case, to eat and I thought again of how quickly we'd adapted to this lifestyle. None of us wondered about what was happening in the world outside, we all carried on as though our little enclave was all that was left of humanity. I looked around at the motley crew and wondered if civilisation would survive if it was down to us.

'So, you gonna show me these tracks, right?' Junior finished first, flung his plate and spoon into the soapy water bowl and stood up. 'Before they wash away?'

'Mmmm.' Sebastian scooped down the last of his stew and the three men headed off out of the camp to view whatever Sebastian had seen. Kanga, predictably enough, went to perform her yoga to help her digestion, leaving Ruth and me with the dishes.

'Well, that's one way of avoiding the washing up,' Ruth said, rather tersely for her.

'It is what we're here for,' I reminded her gently. 'We won't win any cash for having the cleanest plates.'

She sighed. 'I know. I'm being – well, it doesn't explain Kanga, does it?'

'Kanga is...' I tailed off. I really didn't want to try to explain Kanga, and even summoning all the religious education I could remember from school, I could not come up with a biblical parallel for her. 'Sometimes we have to learn to live with people who are...' Nope. I still had nothing.

Ruth didn't seem to be listening. Her head kept coming up as though she was scenting the air funnelling down the gulley towards us, and she was evidently watching the men picking their cautious way through the scratchy heather growth. 'I mean, I've prayed for guidance and patience and all that but...' she went on. The downcast look wasn't like Ruth at all.

'Is this all getting to you a bit?' I asked gently, as we started to scrape and wash the plates.

'A little. Perhaps.' Ruth looked up and out over the valley again to where Junior and Sebastian were crouched at the edge of the river. Mac was standing, pointing at something. 'And...' She stopped again. Her face had gone a little bit pink. 'I shouldn't say anything. It's wrong, I know it is. But I can't help... And then I wonder why God would let me have such thoughts.'

'Ruth?' I touched her shoulder and, to my horror, she burst into tears. She'd always seemed composed, the most 'together' of all of us; content with herself and her god. Her tears made me realise that she was struggling as much as any of us with the miles of isolation and fruitless searching for whatever was out there. 'Ruth?'

'It's stupid and wrong and I know I shouldn't!' She sobbed and flung herself into my arms, crying wetly against my neck and scattering eco-friendly bubbles all down my legs. 'But I think God is tempting me because I drank alcohol! I've always tried to be a good Christian and live by His teachings, so why...?' She broke off again and all I could do was pat her back and try not to say anything that was going to sound stupid. But I genuinely had no idea what she was on about.

'Why don't you sit down here and tell me about it?' I half pushed her into one of the camp chairs. 'I'll make some tea while the water's hot.' Surreptitiously I turned her camera off as I eased her into the chair, and, not knowing what might come next, I turned my own off too. Ruth's confessions might be innocent but I felt I owed her her privacy. The thought of whatever indiscretion she considered worthy of this many tears being put out in public, where anyone from her church might see it, made me cringe. Dax would probably be livid, but was hopefully on his way here, so he wouldn't find out our cameras were off until it was too late.

Ruth hiccupped and bent forward over her knees. 'I shouldn't say anything. It's my own private pain,' she whispered, which made me roll my eyes and brought another realisation of how young she really was. Even being a good Christian girl was evidently no protection against talking like Taylor Swift lyrics.

'But I might be able to help.' I pushed a mug of tea at her.

'There's nothing anyone can do,' Ruth continued to channel every emo ever. She kept looking up and out over the untidy twiggy growth that waved in the wind, towards the group of men now trudging downstream, following the little river, and I had a sudden realisation.

'Ruth, have you got a crush on Sebastian? Or Junior?' I didn't mention the possibility of her having a crush on Mac, not because it wasn't possible, but more because I didn't want to have to wrestle her to the mud.

A sad little nod over the mug.

'Junior's... err... unavailable,' I said, swallowing down the word 'gay' as hard as I could.

'It's not Junior.' Her voice was tiny, but unconcerned.

'And Sebastian's married.'

Another pathetic nod. 'That is one of the reasons it's so wrong. I mean, I *shouldn't* have feelings for him, I know that.' A pair of tragic eyes met mine. 'And I would never, *never* tell him and you mustn't either, Izzy.'

'Of course I won't.' I'll just add it to my list of things people have told me that I'm not allowed to tell anyone else and hope that the list doesn't overbalance and send me into insane ramblings, I thought, and then felt bad. This was clearly Ruth's first exposure to a full-blown crush, and the fact that most of us had passed through this stage at about twelve, over some spotty idiot in the year above, didn't help her. 'As long as you absolutely promise that you're not going to act on it.'

To my surprise, Ruth gave a tear-salted laugh. 'Izzy, I think I am the *last* person who would ever admit something like this. I don't know if I would even tell my vicar.'

'But you told me.'

'Yes.' Ruth's eyes met mine. 'But you are different. You're the one of us who usually talks sense, aren't you?' She sniffed and stared out across the acres of wilderness again. 'You remind me of my house mother when I was at school.'

Oh, great. I'd gone from being the cheerleader of the group to the one the audience loves to hate, and now I was hanging somewhere around middle age, wearing a cardigan with hankies up the sleeves and dispensing Werther's Originals. 'You'll get used to having a crush.' I tried to sound cheerful and upbeat and not one step away from orthopaedic shoes. 'Honestly. We've all been there, and it dies away eventually.'

'But how?' Ruth hunched over her tea and I could almost feel the drag as she pulled her eyes back from watching Sebastian.

'Oh, I don't know. One day you look at them and think, "What the hell – I mean, what on earth was I thinking?" If you're very unlucky, you find out that he wears his underpants for a week without changing them, or something else that puts you off. Otherwise, it sort of wears away.'

'But you don't understand. I've never felt like this about anyone before.' Ruth looked so abject that I almost wanted to laugh, but I didn't. For her, this was serious stuff. 'I think it might be God punishing me. When we had that party – I tried some of the beer that Sebastian had in those bottles. I *knew* it was wrong, but I did it anyway, and what if this is God's way of showing me how my life could be if I stray from the path? I've been brought up so much within the church. My parents, my school – this is my chance to grow up.' She sniffed dismally. 'I didn't know growing up could be so painful.'

I wanted to agree, but equally I didn't want her to feel that adult life was a world of suffering, just because mine was. 'This bit is. But it does get better. And I very much doubt that God would want to punish you for a mouthful of alcohol. You will fall in love, properly, with someone more... accessible,' I said delicately. 'Maybe this is God's way of showing you what you're capable of feeling.' I was quite proud of myself for this bit. It managed to make her feelings sound temporary without dismissing them, and I made a note to remember what I'd said, then realised that I would probably never need to say it again. 'Just try to stay away from Sebastian, if you can.'

'Do you think he's noticed?'

I watched the three men, tightly grouped, walking along the edge of the river. They were far enough away that they weren't distinct and we couldn't hear their voices, but we could see their shapes. Sebastian, slightly stocky, talking earnestly. Junior, huge and bulky in his jacket, newly shorn head bare to the sky, and Mac.

'I think we're all so caught up in trying to find out what's making these prints that it would be surprising if he had.' I was trying to be tactful. Mac had noticed things about me, after all. Sebastian was older, he'd likely been the subject of youthful affections before, but I trusted him, and his love for his wife, not to act on this particular one and take advantage of Ruth.

I got up and began washing the dishes, slapping my camera back on now the worst was over, and letting Ruth sit and finish her tea.

'Thank you for talking to me,' Ruth said from behind me as I clattered the melamine out of the bowl. 'I know the others think I'm young and silly, but you always treat me as an equal.'

Privately I thought she was rather young and silly too, but was glad that these feelings hadn't leached out into our conversations. 'Maybe we're not all used to dealing with someone who has a faith.' I stacked the plates. 'And you are much younger than the rest of us. Maybe we've forgotten what that's like.'

She sighed. 'I know. And that's one of the reasons I want us to win the money. I want us to get *something*, some kind of evidence here, if only to prove that having religious beliefs isn't a barrier to doing things like this.'

'Getting wet and cold and failing to find anything?' I dried my hands.

'But if we *do* find anything, it's like – well, confirmation, you know? I mean, I don't really know where the church stands on big cats roaming where they shouldn't be, whether it's against nature or whether it actually *is* nature, if you see what I mean. But my being here, being on television, talking about my beliefs and still hunting for this animal – it makes religion seem less...' She tailed off.

'Less compartmentalised? More a part of life?' I hazarded. Crushes, yes, I'd been there and felt confident in giving advice, but making religion seem accessible by tracking a probably non-existent creature across moorland – nope.

'Well, whatever. I feel as though I'm doing the right thing by my church.' Ruth nodded a very definite nod, and I was so grateful that the conversation had swung away from Sebastian that I ran with it.

'And you'd really give them all the money? If we won?'

'Oh, yes. Well, most of it.' She gave me a little tear-stained and somewhat sheepish grin. 'I mean, I'd like to go on holiday or something first. But yes,' she added quickly. 'Most of it to the church. We do a lot of outreach work, you see, and it would be so wonderful to be able to hand over a meaningful amount of money that could really make a difference.'

'What sort of outreach work do you do?' I finished stacking the plates and got rid of the washing up water. I wanted to keep her away from the subject of Sebastian and how wonderful she thought him because my camera was back on, but mostly for my own sanity.

'We work with the homeless,' Ruth said innocently, and I almost swallowed my tongue.

'Gosh,' I said weakly. 'That's interesting.'

'Yes, I was talking to Sebastian about it, when we all had to share tents the other night. He said...' and Ruth launched into a long and involved description of Sebastian's view of homelessness, as seen through Ruth's rather partisan filter, complete with descriptions of how he'd looked when he said it. The crush seemed well established but at least she knew it was wrong, and hopefully now, how to handle it.

I let her words wash over me. She seemed to have a slightly skewed idea of homelessness, dealing as her church did with those who were living on the streets due to addiction problems or the failure of the mental health system. But then, hadn't *I* also thought of the homeless as grubby men with no teeth, or women with straggled hair and a bottle in their hand, begging on street corners wrapped in old sleeping bags?

Now I knew better. Knew how easy it was to find yourself out there, paying for hotel rooms for occasional nights to have a safe bed and a shower. Sleeping with one eye open on floors in workplaces, knowing you had to be up and packed away before everyone arrived in the morning. Having to go to a friend's to pick up any post, because you didn't have an address to send it to and were using theirs. Never admitting to the failure that had brought you here, whether that failure was relationship or financial or having worn out the hospitality of everyone close.

'...and it would be lovely to be able to make a real difference,' Ruth finished, and I dragged my mind back from its dwelling on the cold, lonely, unsafe nights and the relief of morning.

'I think it would be a really good use of any money we may win,' I said, trying to keep her focused on anything that wasn't Sebastian. 'Of course, we have to win it first.'

'It's not looking very likely, is it?' Ruth's eyes swivelled back over the valley. 'All we've got is tracks and Dax keeps telling us they're not good enough. But there's the pay for being here, and that's enough for me to make a donation. After all, £3,000 could make quite a difference to some people living on the streets.'

It certainly could, I thought, pouring her another cup of tea while she sat in her Sebastian-related state of guilt and twisted pleasure. Down near the river, I could see Mac talking and pointing back down around the valley towards where the dog barked so furiously every night. Junior was standing, shading his eyes against the low slant of the sun, looking as impressively solid as the few scattered boulders that littered the moorland. Sebastian was still crouched, head down.

'Oh. That must be Dax.' Ruth stood up, as the sound of a noisy engine crept in underneath the constant boom of the wind in our ears.

It was a mark of how desperate we felt for contact from the outside world that Kanga had come out of her tent, and we three stood grouped to welcome Dax's arrival long before the Jeep even came into sight, jouncing over the low horizon with the usual team on board. They all looked a little jaded. Even Dax had lost his 'smuggler's coat' in favour of something that looked suspiciously like an army surplus parka.

'Where is everyone?' were his first words, as he jumped out of the Jeep, coat buffeted by the wind until he looked as though there were several ferrets in there with him. Camera-Callum and Sound-Steve climbed out wearily.

'Well, we're here,' I said, slightly smarting at the implication that the men were 'everyone'. 'The others are tracking. You all look fed up.'

'We lost Bodmin,' Callum said, avoiding Dax's thrown glance of vituperation by fiddling with his equipment. 'There was a fist fight, blood, everything. Had to pull them in.'

'Yes, well.' Dax gave himself a shake and the parka wobbled. 'We're over that now, aren't we?'

The looks that Callum and Steve gave him indicated that they, very clearly, were not over it, and might be suffering a degree of post-traumatic stress. 'We only asked them if they missed beer,' Steve said. 'And then it all turned ugly.'

'They were like animals,' Callum agreed. 'Raided the Land Rover, went through all our gear. They stole Steve's emergency whisky, didn't they?'

'And my crisps. I was looking forward to those crisps,' Steve agreed, mournfully.

'We've decided to keep their contribution in the final show.' Dax pushed his hands into his pockets. 'They were doing so *well!* I really thought they might be onto something with that creature they saw.'

'It was a dog, Dax,' Callum said, even more wearily. 'Even they said it was a dog.'

'Yes. Well. You go and set up. We'll chat to whoever's here first while we wait for the others to get back.' Dax spoke briskly, as though trying to distract from the awfulness.

'Did you bring peanuts?' I asked. 'Because I think Mac might come running if you rustle the packet.'

Dax ignored me, and went off to help set up the equipment in the shelter of the rocky outcrop. Maybe he feared a repeat of the Bodmin Incident if he brought out treats like peanuts. I could only imagine the state of deprivation that the Cornish team must have been in to have staged a mass attack on the camera crew. Then I remembered our party, with the smuggled beer, Prosecco and half bottle of vodka, and felt a bit guilty – maybe *we* would also have stormed this visit from civilisation had we been that desperate.

And bugger them for having a dog as prime suspect. That meant that I daren't even raise the fact that we thought our interloper might also be a dog, because Dax, in his current state of disillusionment, might call the whole thing off

'I'll talk to them first.' Kanga had retrieved a hairbrush from her tent and was busy sweeping her locks out over her shoulders. She'd done something to her face too, she looked dewy-eyed and fresh. Ruth always looked fresh; even with the recent traces of her tears over Sebastian drying on her cheeks, she was rosy and clear-skinned. I felt like a crone in comparison.

'Just...' I wanted to warn her but didn't know what to say. *Don't mention the dog? Don't say anything about my reasons for being here?* But then I reminded myself this was Kanga and she was more likely to talk about herself than lose the viewer's attention by mentioning someone else. 'They look a bit shell-shocked,' I finished.

Kanga gave me a shrewd look. 'We all need a month, I get it,' she said. 'I want the exposure.' Then she swept off to flirt with Callum and flaunt her hair at Dax, and I breathed a small sigh of relief. She knew. Kanga might seem to have all the emotional depth of – I looked around me for a suitable simile, but everything I could see was deep; heather, mud, puddles – of the average game show contestant, but she understood our need to run this right to the end. This was her way of getting out of a council flat in Wandsworth. Yes, she understood.

Ruth sidled up to me. 'If they stop the programme,' she said, 'if they decide to cancel all this... I'll never see Sebastian again, will I?' She was twisting the sleeves of her cardigan into little screws of knitwear. 'I mean, I know that's going to happen eventually anyway, but at least if we keep going...' She trailed off again. 'I know it's all in my imagination,' she said in a voice so tiny that the wind almost obliterated it. 'But at least I've got that.'

'There will be other boys... men,' I corrected myself. 'Honestly. It's not like we all only get one go.'

'The boys I know all seem so *churchy*,' she whispered. 'They're all sons of people my parents have known for years, or people I've known through youth club forever. None of them make me feel like Sebastian does.'

Here we go again, I thought, and had a moment of sympathy with Dax's present weariness. I really hoped this wasn't going to be the theme of the whole of the rest of our time in camp. 'They will grow up, though. They'll become men. And you'll meet others, really, Ruth, you shouldn't base your entire expectation of life on what you've seen so far.'

Her gaze had gone out again, trailing across the heather in search of Sebastian. The men had obviously seen the Jeep arrive and were heading back towards camp, Junior in the lead with his boots stomping down a trail and his gigantic muscles flexing sufficiently to cast the other two men into shadow. Sun streaked down across the scenery, and the undergrowth meant that they had to walk in slow motion up the hill towards us, lending a certain filmic quality to their approach, like weary soldiers toiling back to camp after a particularly ferocious battle.

I really hoped Dax was getting all this.

'I'm not saying that it's wrong to have a crush,' I whispered urgently to Ruth, wanting to get the words into her head before the men got too close. 'Of course it's not, it's natural. It only becomes wrong when you act on it. Keep your dignity, Ruth.'

Ruth gave a rueful little smile. 'Of course I will. I don't want to make myself look stupid, Izzy. Sebastian talks all the time about his wife and his children and the farm – he really and truly loves them and I'm not going to do anything to spoil that. Besides, I wouldn't know *what* to do, I'm not exactly experienced in the ways of love and all that. It's...' she drooped again, '...really hard loving what you know you can't have.'

Ah, we were back with the emo lyrics again, were we? Well, they were easier to manage than tears. 'You'll live.'

Ruth nodded, eyes still downcast. 'I think I may have to go and pray for guidance,' she said in a tiny voice. 'Will you talk to Dax next? When

Kanga comes back, I mean.' Then she headed off towards her tent, presumably to let God hear an Adele-worthy compilation of sadness.

I sighed. But at least she was actively trying to avoid Sebastian, who was plodding the last few metres behind Junior, which was hopeful.

'Did...' Mac was puffing a bit as the three of them arrived at the camp, '...did he bring the peanuts?'

'He didn't say. They're all a bit depressed.' I explained about the Bodmin fiasco.

Junior rumbled something. Whilst I'd got better at picking words out of the general background resonation, sometimes his *sotto voce* pronouncements were too far below my range of hearing and I usually waited to see what the reaction of others was before I answered. But this time they were all looking at me.

'Oh?' I hoped that would cover it, but clearly not.

'Junior's got a point.' Mac came to my rescue. 'If they're leaving in the Bodmin bit, that means that Dax told a bit of a fib when he said that he'd need to pull our entire section if he took us off the moor. Which means we sat it out in that snowstorm for nothing.'

'But if we'd packed it in then, we'd be home by now.' I almost stuttered over the word. Home. For me, for the last couple of weeks, that had been a small bistro in a backstreet in York, interspersed with nights in a tiny B&B that I couldn't really afford, when I was supposed to be on 'days off'; it was hardly a home.

I saw Mac give me a quick glance.

'I mean,' I carried on, hoping that nobody else had noticed the slip, 'we wouldn't be earning the extra money that we're getting for carrying on.'

Junior nodded thoughtfully.

'And I wouldn't be getting the chance to show Caroline that I'm trying not to be so bossy and patronising,' Sebastian said with a commendable lack of embarrassment. 'So it isn't just for the money really, is it?'

Mac was still looking at me. He'd got splashes of mud on his face like freckles over his bare, unweathered cheeks, and his hair was curling out from under his hat again. I felt my heart double-beat an acknowledgement as our eyes locked, and had a moment of fellow-feeling for Ruth.

Sebastian and Junior moved off, talking now about tracks and directions and whether we could set a feasible trap when we had nothing sturdier than a couple of food containers and a Portaloo with which to possibly contain a beast. Mac kept looking at me.

'What?' I said, eventually.

'You don't have a home.'

'Yes, I know. I told you that.' For some reason, the intensity of his stare was becoming disconcerting. 'It's kind of what "homeless" means. Home. Less. Go and look it up if you're still floundering.'

Mac took his hat off and the wind instantly swept his hair up above his head so that it looked as though he was about to be drawn up to the sky. 'I know. It's really only just dawned on me. Weird. You're not what I expect when I think of the word.'

'Don't be bloody daft.' I had to turn away. I couldn't keep looking at him because his expression had become dark and intense, the trace of the Scots accent very noticeable. It was horrifyingly attractive. 'Homeless people don't all have three noses or glow in the dark or something. Might be useful if we did, actually, people wouldn't have any excuse for tripping over us.'

Mac took a step forward and closed the muddy, heather-strewn gap between us. 'I'm really beginning to understand,' he said. 'Of *course* you want the money.'

'Again, not news to me.'

Mac cupped his hands over his face and blew out a breath. 'Okay,' he said, muffled through his fingers. 'And you absolutely *swear* that this isn't a set-up?'

I stared at him. I wasn't quite sure what to think, but there was a bubble of anger rising in my chest, so I went with that. 'You think...' the words came out more quietly than I'd intended, 'you *seriously* think that? *Now*? After everything that's happened?'

'I dunno.' He dropped his hands away from his face and put them on my shoulders. '*Something* is going on out here. Someone is behind it, they have to be.'

'And you think that's me? What about that dog that came into camp the other night? Do you think I could have set *that* up? How? Using the vast number of Bonios I've obviously hidden in my luggage?'

'No.' He was looking into my face properly now. Eyes moving, searching. For what? Truth? 'No. I'm just realising that, of all of us, you would have the most to lose if we don't find any evidence.'

I took a step back and his hands fell. 'I am,' I said, with dignity, 'more than a little insulted, Mac. I've assured you already that I am not Dax's stooge here, and I am not planting evidence for reasons of my own. I thought...' My voice broke but I carried on, despite the fact that emotion was pressing behind my eyes and in the back of my throat, 'I thought you understood that. I thought we...' That was it. I couldn't carry on.

With my words to Ruth about 'keeping your dignity' ringing in my ears, I turned and marched away, leaving Mac standing in the heather with his hair still tumbling around his face and his arms hanging by his sides.

How dare he? I wanted to flounce off into my tent, but Kanga caught me on her way back from filming her piece to the cameras.

'Dax is waiting,' she said, flipping her hair again. I wondered why Mac's hair was performing circus acts while hers was lying smoothly against her shoulders, and then reasoned that she'd probably got a lifetime's worth of hairspray stashed in her tent. 'You'd better go next. I think Ruth is...' She nodded towards Ruth's tent, where Ruth's muttering was audible. 'Well. She's doing something religious,' Kanga went on, pronouncing 'religious' as though it was some kind of perversion.

I set my jaw until my teeth ground together. How *dare* Mac even *think* that I was behind all the tracks we were finding? How *could* he even reason that I'd had anything to do with the creature that had crashed through our camp while we partied? Unless he assumed that Dax and I had set up the stunt between us, somehow? If he thought that, did he also think that anything we might be starting between us, any hint of attraction, was *also* a set-up and that I was only reciprocating his attention because I was being paid to do it?

The edge of bitterness swept me on, up towards the sheltered spot between the rocks where Dax, Callum and Steve had set up their filming station. By the time I got there, the anger that had set in at Mac's almost-accusation had risen to levels that that Ruth would have recognised from the Old Testament. I was only one step away from a flaming sword.

'Right.' I marched up to Dax, who was holding out a microphone for me to clip to my jacket. 'You need to talk to him.'

'Er.' Dax took a step back. The other two men instantly turned on their equipment. 'What? Who?'

'Your brother.' I advanced on Dax. 'He's got a huge chip on his shoulder about you, and now he thinks that you and I have set this all up between us.'

Dax was now backed right up against a big rock. His parka undulated. 'I have no idea what you're talking about.' He held the microphone up as though to ward me off.

'You getting all the family preferential treatment! You being the Golden Son! Him having to make his own way while you get a leg up! And now, you and me laying false tracks and somehow persuading some big dog to come leaping through our campsite!'

It had been me who had suggested the party, hadn't it? Maybe Mac thought I'd done it on purpose, set us all up to be a bit too tipsy and giggly to have the presence of mind to film the animal? Maybe he figured I'd used the party as a distraction to give Dax a chance to creep up and release something on us? The realisation intensified the anger.

'So you need to talk to him,' I continued. I may have poked Dax in the shoulder, I certainly had a forefinger raised in a menacing way. 'You need to *tell* him. A – that you and I aren't in league in setting this up and B...' I punctuated my alphabet with little finger-jabs. 'That you aren't using your advantage with your parents at his expense.'

'But they don't favour me.' Dax sounded as though I'd lost him somewhere halfway through Point A.

'Oh, really? So you've got your own production company, advertisers willing to put up the money for this show, all that, off your own efforts, at the age of – however old you are?' There was a feeling inside me, as though my core were on fire. As though my whole digestive system was filling up with acid. Partly at the injustice of how Mac was treated compared to Dax, but also fuelled a little by wanting to pour some of the anger that Mac had engendered in me over his brother.

'Um,' said Dax. 'Well, I may have had some advice from Dad...'

'So you're here, about to put your name to an entire series on main-stream TV, while Mac scrabbles about camping in Croatia and filming himself, for a YouTube programme? And you think that's *fair*?'

Dax was practically smeared across the rocks now, in his attempt to get away from me and my scary pointy finger. 'Well, no, but look, we've *both* got the money from our grandparents, and...'

'And you're taking advantage of being the favourite child to advance your career!'

I had to step back now or run the risk of actually lying on top of Dax, who was looking utterly horrified, with his arms held out in front of him and his back pressed against the rocks. 'I... I...' he stammered.

'*Talk* to him,' I snapped, whirled around and, catching sight of Steve and Callum exchanging a conspiratorial grin, added, 'and I don't think you two are blameless, either!' Then, with my back so straight that you could have ruled lines with me, I marched away from the filming site and down to my tent, where I would have slammed the flap shut had the technology been available.

13

I must have fallen asleep, because I was aware of sounds on the wind that entered my dream and became memories. My mother, red-faced, hands on hips, standing in the doorway, screaming, 'Why would he lie?' Me, hurtling up the stairs to my room and scooping things up off the floor, looking at all my tiny wood cutters and files and knowing I had to leave them, stuffing random clothes into a shiny plastic bag. Tears and pain and rejection all churning away inside me as I left my equipment because the cutting tool I really needed was too big, too firmly attached to a table, to take and knowing that my future was being rewritten in uncertainty by my leaving. Hating myself because I knew that if I'd been less of a 'good girl', if I'd made a fuss the first time Paul tried it on with me, that this might not have happened. Not this way, anyhow.

The shouting. The shouting.

Then the cough which woke me. 'Um, Izzy? Um, I wonder if you could come out here for a minute, please?' It was Sebastian. When I shuffled my way out of the tent, he was standing there with Ruth at his shoulder and in my half-dazed sleep state, I wondered for a second whether she'd confessed her crush and I was now going to have to stop the pair of them eloping.

'What?'

But I could hear the shouting for real now. Raised voices which came and went as the gusts of wind swept them along the valley.

'It's Dax and Mac,' Ruth said quickly. Maybe she'd seen the look in my eye. 'They're arguing.'

'Yes? And?'

'Well, we don't want Dax to shut the whole thing down, do we? I mean, if he decides he doesn't want anything to do with Mac?' Sebastian scratched at his chin. 'And you seem to get on so well with Mac, we thought you might be able to talk to them.'

'Make them stop fighting,' Ruth put in. 'You're so good at talking to people,' she added.

The shouts were escalating now and I felt a momentary guilt clutch at my heart. I'd told Dax to have it out with his brother. I'd told Mac he needed to tell Dax how he felt. What if they'd both chosen now to bring all their family resentments to the fore – out here on a November hillside? And then I remembered that Mac had accused me of faking stuff, and the guilt went away.

'Why don't we leave them to sort it out?' I suggested. 'They've got years of sibling rivalry to get over.'

A particularly high-pitched yell of 'It was *my birthday!*' washed over us and we all glanced towards the sound. It was followed by the kind of silence that is usually caused by two people getting physical.

'Oh, all right,' I said grudgingly. 'I'll see what I can do. Although, if I end up battering both of them to death with a packet of peanuts, you only have yourselves to blame.'

Ruth and Sebastian exchanged a look.

'And I hope the gun is locked away safely,' I said ominously, as I clambered out of the tent and headed towards the grunting, breathless, gasping noises.

Callum was filming with a kind of urgent happiness, whilst Steve ran about with a sound boom, trying to capture any moments of lucid conversation. Mac and Dax were down on the ground and trying to fight, but the sheer amount of clothing they both wore meant it was like watching two people in sumo suits attempting wrestling manoeuvres.

I watched, dispassionately, for a moment. Mac had Dax by a toggle and was holding him down, but Dax had pulled Mac's beanie hat over his face, so Mac couldn't see to land the punches he was vaguely swinging at the hood of Dax's parka. Their overpadded top halves rolled around one another like Weebles, whilst their trousered legs looked puny and feeble in comparison, trying to get sufficient grip in the heather to gain an advantage.

When I'd watched their rather pathetic attempts for a few moments, I finally gave in. Wading in between their struggling bodies, I knocked them apart with my boots. 'That's *enough*,' I said, injecting enough 'waitress stopping toddlers from running around my restaurant' into my tone to sound quite fierce. 'What the hell are you doing?'

The two men lay prone for a few seconds, getting their breath back. Finally, Mac rolled over, adjusted his hat, and looked up at me. 'He's jealous of me,' he said.

'No, I'm not! You're jealous of *me!*' Dax snapped, somewhat muffled by still being face down in the undergrowth.

'And fighting is stopping you being jealous – how?' I bent down, took Mac's hand and pulled him upright, then levered Dax into a sitting position.

There was a slightly embarrassed silence, broken only by the faint whine of Callum's camera. Steve had raised the sound boom on its stick and was sitting on a boulder, watching.

'You said we needed to talk,' Dax muttered eventually.

'Talk, not pull one another's heads off.'

They both shuffled about like schoolboys told off for stealing sweets from the tuck shop, and murmured something into the collars of their coats.

'Right. Come on. Down into camp and we'll sort this out within reach of a cup of tea and somewhere proper to sit.' I was still angry and it gave me the bossiness that Sebastian had lost. 'Callum, turn that camera *off*.'

Callum looked at me with huge disappointment all over his face, until I pointed at my own camera, light on, winking away, whereupon he gave me a thumbs-up and a nod and he and Steve sloped off back towards the Jeep, no doubt to eat any peanuts that might be going, and bitch about their boss. Then I led Dax and Mac, who walked with their heads down, still like scolded schoolboys, back to camp, which was conspicuously empty. I suspected that Kanga, Junior, Ruth and Sebastian were hiding out in one tent, listening intently, but for now I was happy at their absence.

'Right. Why are you fighting?' I sat them both on camp chairs and put the kettle over the fire, which was flaring and flaming as gusts of wind caught it, and reflecting pretty much how I felt right now.

Mac raised his head and looked me in the eye. 'I'm sorry,' he said. 'I'm sorry I ever thought you and he were working together. You're far too nice to ever agree to work with a fuckwit like my brother.'

'A little biased, but thank you. I'm not sure I've forgiven you, but the sentiment was welcome. Dax?'

''S your fault,' Dax muttered. 'You said I should talk to him, so I did. And then he punched me.'

'In the arm!' Mac retorted. 'You've got so many clothes on that you can't have felt it!'

I sighed. I *had* hoped that they would have raised their grievances with one another, talked them over and ended on a mutual handshake and a new fraternal relationship. Instead, I appeared to have a pair of five-year-olds on my hands, sulking for Britain and each regarding the other as the Golden Child of the family.

'He gets to do what he wants!' Dax suddenly broke out. 'He's jetting off all over the world filming and stuff and I'm stuck here with a struggling company, Callum and Steve and trying to make a film of people getting covered in mud and finding nothing!'

'You get all the family backing; buying your equipment, talking their friends into getting you resources and then strong-arming advertisers into bankrolling your stupid idea!' Mac retorted, then met my eye again and subsided somewhat. 'It *is* a stupid idea, though,' he muttered.

'So, *you* think Dax is using family connections to further his career without having to work for it, and *you*—' I rounded on Dax, who ducked, 'think that Mac has the freedom to do what he wants and make whatever programme he wants, whilst you are tied down by family expectations?'

Neither of them replied. They both seemed to have decided that their boots were objects of utter fascination and were studying them in close detail. Eventually Mac looked up. I raised my eyebrows at him.

'I didn't know, Dax,' he said in, I was pleased to note, a tone of contrition. 'I thought you'd got it all and they were leaving me to sink or swim.'

Dax, in a very un-Dax-like move, rubbed his nose on his sleeve. 'I wish they would let *me* sink or swim,' he said, dejectedly. 'It's all, "Oh, we'll introduce you to Lawrence and he can get you these contacts and I'm sure they'll sponsor an idea if it involves – oh, I dunno, some stupid bloody idea about filming people looking for wildlife that doesn't exist!"'

'I want to give up running around the world.' Mac looked at me again. 'I want to be able to stay in one place now. Have a proper home, make a proper relationship. Not be spending nine months of the year in a tent trying to remember which country I'm in.'

'And I want to be able to make the films *I* want to make, programmes that *help* people, not try to establish a name for myself as king of reality TV.' Dax was still talking to his shoes.

Mac stood up and held out a hand to his brother. 'Family, eh?' he said. 'Maybe we need to present a united front, rather than letting the folks decide what we do with our lives?'

Slowly enough for me still not to be certain that it wasn't going to involve punching, Dax stood up too. The brothers shook hands and then entered into a hug, with a degree of back patting that probably went unfelt in all the clothing.

'We should tell the parents what they can do with their offers of help. Tell them how we feel,' Mac went on. 'They can't *force* us to carry on doing what we're doing, can they?'

'There's always the guilt.'

'Oh, yeah. And Mum will cry. But if we face it together – I reckon we can talk our way out of it. We should at least try.' Mac stood away from Dax, still holding him by the shoulders, but looking into his face. 'Now we both know what we *really* want. You know, stand up for each other instead of letting them divide and conquer.'

Dax scuffed his sleeve over his face. His smooth cheeks and perky hairstyle now topped a wobbly lip. 'Can we?' he almost whispered.

'Aye. Reckon.' Mac's accent was suddenly broad, as though he'd reclaimed his childhood. 'We're no' wee wains any more, ken?'

'Oh, stop it,' Dax half-laughed. 'You didn't get that expensive education to have you talking like something from the Gorbals.'

'And you,' Mac dropped the Rab C. Nesbitt impersonation, 'are going to have to learn to stop talking like Mum. Yes, we had a decent education. But the parents paid for that of their own free will, they can't hold it over us to make us do what they expect of us for the rest of our lives.' Then he lowered his voice a little and looked straight into Dax's face. 'We have to be who we are, Dax,' he said, quiet and intense. 'Our *real* selves, and never mind what they think of us.'

It sounded like a part of a different conversation, one they'd had years ago. Dax returned Mac's direct look, held it for a moment, and then nodded.

I took a deep breath. It seemed to come from somewhere other than my lungs, as though it carried my own parental expectations out with it. 'Right,' I said. 'Right. That's all good.'

'I really, honestly, am deeply sorry about what I said.' Mac let go of Dax and came over to me. 'I'm just confused about what's really going on here.'

'Nothing,' Dax put in. 'There's nothing *to* find out here. I thought it would make good television, tell a bunch of people that they're going to track big cats, take them away from civilisation and see what happens.'

I gave him a stern look.

'Well, there *might* be cats out here,' he said, his tone full of self-justification. 'I mean, you can't prove that there *aren't*. And people have seen things.'

Junior was suddenly next to us. I must have been right about the others listening in from inside a tent, because he appeared, muscling his way out through Sebastian's tent flap like the Incredible Hulk bursting through a wall. 'You mean I'm wasting my time?' he demanded. 'What about the *tracks*, man?'

Dax took several steps back which, I noticed, put him behind me. 'I didn't mean that there wasn't *anything* out here,' he stammered. 'You're finding tracks, that's good. That's great!' he added, with a touch of the old Dax.

'I quit filming my series to fly over here to find big cats for you,' Junior rumbled on, threatening as an approaching avalanche. 'You said UK exposure would be good for my profile, and now I find that I'm here, what? To make up the numbers? Or do you try this crap on all your boyfriends?'

There was a silence that even the sound of the distant dog barking seemed to bounce off. 'Oh, shit,' Junior said, turned on his heel and did the 'bursting out of the tent' thing in reverse. This time he went into his own tent and zipped the flap behind him.

'Ah,' said Dax. 'Um. I think I may need to have a quiet word.' He followed Junior to the tent, unzipped the flap cautiously and crawled inside.

Suddenly a lot of things made sense. Junior and Dax's quiet moments of chat together hadn't been planning the planting of evidence. Junior hadn't been dragged away from Bigfoot TV, he'd come, presumably willingly, for his partner. They weren't in league, they were in love.

Mac and I, left alone in the middle of the blasted heath, looked at one another. 'Did you know?' I asked eventually.

'I'm not even sure what that question relates to,' Mac said. 'That Dax is gay? Well, yes, he's not exactly Out, but he's not exactly hiding at the back of the closet either. That Junior was his partner? No, absolutely not, but I did wonder where the hell he came in, apparently the other teams all got British guides.'

'Who got Bear Grylls?' I asked. 'I think Kanga might want to put in for a transfer.'

'But you were right.' Mac, quite properly, ignored me. 'We did need to have that conversation, Dax and I. We've both been so entrenched in our beliefs about one another that we never really thought to talk about the fact that it was our parents who were behind it all.'

'I'm sure they thought they were doing the right thing,' I said.

'Do you think your mother was "doing the right thing" by throwing you out?' The question was gentle, so I didn't take immediate offence.

'No. I think she should have talked to me.'

'And that's exactly what I think our parents should have done. Not assumed that Dax wanted to dash straight up to Head of Production, while I floated around the world making affordable holidays look enticing.'

We stood for a bit, looking across the camp. Knowing now that even *Dax* wasn't behind the planting of evidence and seemed to be playing the whole thing by ear as much as we were gave the whole place a new, slightly tawdry, air. Damp nylon, drooping because we hadn't tightened our guy ropes lately, trodden-down pathways leading from the Portaloo to the tents and across to the firepit, mud trails and dropped wood and general detritus gave it something of the look of decorations a few days after Christmas. Past its best.

'We can't call it a day, because we won't get paid.' Mac gave a sigh. 'And there's nothing to find, except shadows and a dog. Where do we go from here?'

'I suppose we sit it out.' I turned around to look at the moorland stretching its bleak way towards us. 'It's only, what, another ten days or so, then we can decently pack up and head... back.' I had been going to say 'home', but again, that word tripped me.

'Where will you go?' Mac wasn't looking at me. He'd pushed his hands into the pockets of his coat, elbows jutting at 'teapot' angles, and was scrutinising the dale down by the river. 'If you don't mind me asking.'

I shrugged. 'Christmas season is underway. There'll be plenty of impromptu shifts to pick up, and I'll get double time if I work Christmas Day. A couple who own a little restaurant down Walmgate are really kind to me and they let me doss in the office at the back and use the shower there, I'll be fine.'

It sounded pathetic. I realised immediately as I said it. I'd been thinking of it with plenty of positive spin – free Christmas lunch before evening opening, possibly a glass of wine and then somewhere safe to sleep. But it suddenly seemed rather pathetic.

'Look.' Mac sounded as though he was making up his mind on the fly. 'Why don't you come up to Glasgow with me? You shouldn't have to work Christmas Day. I'm having a bit of a rethink about my life and where to go from here, maybe you could come over, we could have Christmas lunch and you could give me some advice.'

'Plenty of people work Christmas Day,' I said. It wasn't an answer and I knew it. Over at camp, Kanga had squeezed out of Sebastian's tent and was looking around for the film crew, who I could see up on the hill, sharing a can of probably illicit lager. That left Ruth with Sebastian and I hoped she wasn't torturing herself too badly.

'But not if they don't have to.' Mac came closer. 'And you'll have the money from this.' He threw out his arms, almost tearing off his pockets. 'So, maybe, you know, you might consider, well. I've got a couple of spare rooms, very nice flat, just off the Byres Road. Only temporary, until you find yourself somewhere, there's a lot of flat shares going up there. Nothing keeping you in Yorkshire, is there?' He was looking out over the moor again. 'Apart from masochism.'

I felt a weird swooping sensation at the top of my stomach. It felt almost as though my life had been flatlining in the last few months, but had suddenly shown signs of waking up again.

'I know you said you didn't want to travel with me,' Mac went on, almost as though he was afraid to stop talking in case it gave me chance to break in with a refusal. 'And, yes, I get that now, it was a stupid suggestion. After all, if even I don't want to carry on trudging around the world with a tent, why should I expect anyone else to? But I need – I want to regroup. Think about my options from here on. I thought, well, you seem to need to do that too and maybe we could help each other? No ulterior motives, I promise. The flat is – hate to say it because it shows how much privilege I've got, but it's big enough for two people to rattle round in. Nice area, no drunks in the close, well, not many. Just think about it, eh?'

Then he walked off, leaving me feeling a weird combination of bubbling potential and an almost unbearable sense of hopefulness.

Callum beckoned to me across the camp. 'D'you think we can film you?' he asked. 'Only we're sitting here freezing our gulags off, there's no sign of the boss and this is costing about a thousand quid a minute.'

So I went and did my talking head to camera. I've no idea what I talked about, but I opened my mouth and disconnected words came out, covering the general unlikelihood of us ever finding anything bigger than a stoat out on these moors. I didn't care any more that Cannock Chase were ahead of us. I didn't care whether the Scottish contingent up in the Highlands might have personally wrestled a leopard to the ground, right now. I'd got Dax and Mac to talk out their differences, and the offer of a place to stay when this was over.

I was, I considered, well ahead of the game.

14

Early the next morning, I emerged from my tent to find Junior sitting forlornly over near the fire. He clearly had forgotten all his British training, because he hadn't even attempted to make tea. He was crouched on one of the stools, camouflage jacket draped over his shoulders and his head in his hands.

'Are you all right?' I filled the kettle and sat next to him.

He shrugged. It was a movement that lasted some time. 'I guess everyone knows now,' he said. 'That's the end of my career.'

'What, because you're gay? Don't you think you may be catastrophising a bit?'

He threw me a weird, hunted look. 'It was bad enough being black and tracking Sasquatch in the southern States, you wanna try adding gay to the mix?'

'Oh. I see.' The kettle began to whistle. 'So how did Dax get you on board? Er, how did he get you over? I mean,' I corrected myself, suddenly aware that I had begun to talk like a Carry On film, 'how did you come to be here with us?'

Another, gigantic, shrug. 'Love, I guess.'

Oh, no. I'd had quite enough of the 'tortured soul' lyrics from Ruth. I really didn't want to get into it all again with Junior, even if he did have a somewhat more worldly-wise approach. 'So, what's your new game plan? If you can't go back and hunt Bigfoot?'

'Try and make a living over here.' Junior rubbed his hands over his head, where stubble was beginning to appear over the shiny baldness again. 'But you don't have a lot of Bigfoot. Or anything else.'

I looked at his big, thoughtful face. 'I'm sure Dax will find a role for you. He was talking about making programmes to help people, maybe you could persuade him to make a film about rehabilitating gay black Sasquatch hunters?'

Junior gave me a grin. It held a twinkle of mischief, and I realised that there was a whole other person inside what we'd been seeing as the granite-hewn, single-minded tracker. 'I dunno,' he said. 'Maybe. As long as we can pretend I'm not from Barnsley.'

I grinned back and dared to give him a reassuring pat on his well-muscled arm. 'You will be fine,' I said. 'Dax brought you all the way over here, he must care a lot about you.'

Another grin accompanied a slap on the back that nearly catapulted me across the valley. 'He brought me here to this.' Junior indicated the damp little dale in front of us, grey with its carpet of old heather stems and wizened trees. Bleak patches of mud reflected the sky, like holes in the moorland. 'So, yeah.' Then he laughed. 'But I love him, so I guess I'm stuck with England now, hey?'

I made us both tea and we sat quietly together, watching the sun quiver its way up into the sky over the far horizon, melting away the overnight frost but leaving it in patches where the shadows of rocks and hillsides blocked the warmth. It made the whole moor look like a monochrome patchwork.

Suddenly, a movement caught my eye. Not enough to focus on, a flicker and twitch of the dead reeds in a patch of the river where the water hung still for long enough to swirl into eddies rather than run, up near the head of the dale.

'What's that?' I stood up to get a better look.

Junior stood alongside me, monolithic, between me and the sun. 'Something moving. Something big.' He was already shouldering his way into his jacket and putting down his cup. 'I'm gonna take a look.' He slapped at his camera, the little light winked on, and he was gone, surprisingly silently for such a big man, moving off obliquely through the thigh-high bushes.

'Where's Junior going?' Kanga, dressed and in full make-up as usual, was refilling the kettle.

'There's something moving down there. He's gone to investigate.'

'Oh. I expect it's that dog again.' Unimpressed, she brought out one of her herbal tea bags and poured on water that could only have been tepid at best. I shuddered. 'Honestly, after the way Dax left yesterday in such a hurry, I think they're going to call all this off. It's pathetic.'

'Do you think so?' My tea was cooling but I didn't want to top it up until the kettle reboiled.

'Well, we've got what we want out of it, haven't we? I've got a modelling contract – it may be camping materials now, but it's a stepping-stone to bigger things, and Dax told me – in strictest confidence, of course – that there have been approaches made to have me presenting a segment on *Springwatch*.'

She sipped at her tea, which was giving off a greenish steam that made me half expect her nose to melt off.

'Mac and Dax have made up and Sebastian has shown that he can dial down the sergeant major side of his nature. You wanted the cash, didn't you? Well, we've made a couple of grand, that should be enough, and Ruth's donating hers to her church.'

I wasn't completely sure that a 'couple of grand' would be enough. Glasgow, even if I could use Mac's place as a place to stay until I got somewhere of my own, would be expensive. And I couldn't afford to rebuild my book room kit yet, either.

'So I'm going to put it to everyone that we stop now.' Kanga made a face at her mug and put it down.

Not enough. But I could stay with Mac, pick up some work over Christmas in Glasgow to save for the equipment I needed... ten more days. Another thousand, and I'd have enough to pay my way.

'But there *is* something out there. We agreed we'd find out what it is.' I spoke quickly, aware that I was talking to save myself.

'Oh, yeah. But, you know, this whole thing has been a fiasco, is it even going to sell?' Kanga turned to head back towards her tent. 'Is anyone going to want to watch us wandering around this god-forsaken place in the rain, looking for things we don't find, to prove that there's nothing here?'

Sebastian was emerging, slowly, from his tent now. Stretching in the weak sunlight and dragging his sleeping bag out to air over the top of the tent. 'Are you talking about going home?' he asked.

'This is so done, admit it.' Kanga walked off and began trying to look as though she were tidying up, moving plastic plates about and restacking the food boxes which had been perfectly well stacked before.

'She's right.' Sebastian came over and shook the kettle. 'Even Dax has lost heart. Nobody is finding anything in any of the teams, the whole thing seems to be a glorious waste of time.'

'No worse than any other reality show, then,' I said gamely.

Sebastian pulled a face and poured the warm water from the kettle into a mug. 'I have to say, though,' he lowered his voice, 'that I won't be sorry now to get back. I've got new insights, mostly thanks to you,' he gave me a smile, 'and I'm looking forward to sitting down with Caroline and coming up with a game plan for our marriage.' A nod towards my camera. 'I really think we can do it now. This whole experience has made me stronger, made me realise that I can trust other people and I don't have to direct them every step of the way. Although,' and he lowered his voice, 'I'm afraid Ruth may have got a teeny tiny bit of a crush on me, which is proving a bit baffling. I don't want to upset her, she's a lovely girl, but...' he trailed off, shaking his head.

'*Has* she?' I asked brightly, not wanting to give Ruth away. 'I've not noticed anything.'

'Yes, well. She's started following me about. I practically had to beat her away from the Portaloo door the other day, and I've started only going when I know she's in her tent, asleep.' He picked up his mug of tea. 'It's playing havoc with my bowels.'

If this carried on, I thought, as I mooched off to the edge of camp to see where Junior had gone, I was going to have to draw up a flow chart to work out who knew what about whom. And there I'd be, sitting in the middle, knowing all these things about all these people, half of whom didn't even know it about themselves. It was tiring. To say nothing of confusing. But we *had* to stick it out for these last few days, the money would make all the difference, even if I was the only person it would make a difference *to*.

Junior was stomping back now, boots crushing the grey grasses and splashing, uncaring, through the little patches of bog.

'Anything there?' I asked.

'Nah. By the time I got there, whatever it was we saw was clean gone.' Junior looked rather pathetically at me. 'Whatever it is, it knows the moor. Knows how to stay under cover and move about.'

'No traces of anything?'

He shook his head, where the covering of stubble mitigated the shine. 'Nope. It's a fool's errand, Izzy. I told Dax. Whatever we're tracking, whatever is making those marks, we're not gonna find it. And it might not even be the same thing as came into camp that night. If there *is* anything out here, we're not getting any closer.'

He walked on past me up into camp and began an earnest conversation with Sebastian. Kanga was getting into her 'stretching' routine, although even that was half-hearted and didn't seem to involve nearly as much gyrating as it had before she'd been talked about in connection with *Springwatch*.

Kanga, Sebastian, even *Junior*, all seemed to want to go home. And to be fair, if I'd had a home to go to, I would probably have been with them. Junior was right, even if there was something here, we weren't the people to find it.

I took a deep breath. The air was warming a little, with the edge of the sun on it, but it still held the core of cold that the night had given it. Late November. Back in York, people would be Christmas shopping and having parties, all glammed up and sparkly. I remembered last Christmas, Mum and I had gone shopping together, having a giggly time fuelled by Irish Cream Hot Chocolate in the market, picking out little bits and pieces. She'd bought me a teeny jigsaw and varnish, essential equipment for the book rooms, because I'd broken my saw.

I found there were tears in my eyes. Last year, I'd been relatively secure. Paying my way, running my online shop, not making thousands but enough to help Mum with the bills and buy the odd treat and have a tiny bit of savings. She'd met Paul in February...

I sniffed hard. No point dwelling on it. No point. Plenty of people had it worse, I thought, and then remembered Mac calling me the 'cheerleader' of the group when we'd first met, because I'd learned not to look back. Face front, look forward. Only worry about things you can do something about.

Was that the right thing to do? If we all only dealt with 'things we could do something about', would Dax and Mac ever have cleared the air? Would Ruth have admitted her crush, would I know more about Kanga than I wanted to? Was it really better to sweep the bad stuff aside, trample over it in an attempt to reach freedom? Was *not* dealing with things sometimes worse than facing them head on?

'Mac...' I found him loitering on the outskirts of camp, sitting on a rock and swinging his feet. 'I want to borrow the phone.'

'Don't be daft.' He propped himself on his hands and leaned back to look at my face. 'If you get to borrow the phone, then everyone's going to want to. Next thing we know, we'll be up to our ears in paparazzi. Probably,' he added glumly, staring off across the dale. 'Although God only knows why they'd want to photograph us.'

'Nobody else would have to know,' I said, urgently.

Mac hopped down to land with a slightly muddy splash in front of me. 'This sounds a bit covert. What are you planning?'

'I need to talk to my mother.'

In the same instant, we both turned off our cameras. He was looking at me with a frown that creased his eyes. 'I thought you said you'd never talk to her again?'

'I've been thinking. If I want to move on, then I need to clear what's behind me. *You* said I needed to talk to her, anyway, remember? You can hardly act all surprised that I'm actually going to do it.'

'I bloody *can* act surprised. Nobody ever listens to anything I say.'

I had a sudden image of what it must have been like to have been the second, overlooked son, growing up. Disregarded and disenfranchised. It was a wonder that Mac had turned out as balanced as he was. Maybe travelling the world alone with nothing but a tent had given him insights into people he'd been denied before.

'Well, *I* listened. And you were absolutely right. Even if it's just to get my point across, I need to give her my side of the story before I can – well, move on with life.'

Silence. The kind of silence you only ever got on this piece of moorland, where the quiet only lay in the foreground. Behind us were birds twittering, distant voices of our fellow campers, the baa of a sheep in the valley and the almost constant far-off barking of the farm dog, in a multilayered soundscape.

'I shouldn't,' Mac said slowly. 'I mean, it's favouritism. I wouldn't let Kanga call out, when she asked.'

'Did she want to talk over a family fracture that left her homeless?' I asked, rather tersely, because I could guess the answer.

'No, she wanted to phone her agent. But even so.'

'I want to talk to my mother because I want to tell her how much of an utter dick Paul is, so that I can walk away with my head held high,' I said, in a rush. 'When she – when they threw me out, I didn't even *try* to defend myself. I packed and left, while he slithered about with a smirk on his face, because he *knew* that Mum would believe him over me. And now I'm starting to wonder if she took my leaving as guilt. The longer I go on, the more I think I want to shout in their faces that none of it was anything to do with me.'

Mac pulled a face. 'Before, you told me that it wouldn't do any good, that she'd take his side anyway.'

'Yes, but at least I'd have the peace of mind of knowing that I'd tried. If I really am never going to speak to her again...' My voice broke. All the memories of growing up, just me and Mum, came flooding in. All the times she'd sat with me when I was ill, talked me down over teenage rivalries, fed me cake and ice cream when I'd had my heart broken. Then she'd taken me back in after the breakdown of my relationship, fed me more ice cream, helped me set up my business in the back bedroom and taken an interest in the orders coming in. We had all that history. She was my *mother*. If I didn't try, if I never told her how much of a creepy pervert Paul was, hadn't he won? She might not listen, but I might plant a seed of doubt in her mind that would make her look at some of his behaviour differently.

'And if I want to spend Christmas in Glasgow, then I ought to make sure that she knows where I am,' I finished, rather feebly. 'I don't want to find that police are looking for me or something, and ruin Christmas Day by having the Scottish constabulary breaking down the front door as we finish boiling the sprouts.'

'You haven't cared about her knowing where you are thus far.' Mac sounded very sensible. I hoped he had taken in the fact that I'd accepted his invitation to spend Christmas at his place.

'I know. It's...' I tailed off again. It was different now. Now I'd met him. Now I had done this show, which, if we could last it out, would give me a new kind of future. Now I'd got a chance at something more, I wanted her to know. I wanted *Paul* to know he hadn't won. 'And Dax called you when Kanga fell in the river, to come and get us,' I said. 'So there's sort of a precedent.'

Mac bit his lip. He was obviously thinking hard, because he was now frowning so much that his hat had come down almost to eyebrow-level.

'If,' he began hesitantly, 'if I let you call, can we make it look like an accident?'

I stared at him. 'How? Do I fall on you and my hand flukishly manages to dial my mother's number as we land?'

He laughed. It made his hat retreat several centimetres, and allowed curls to replace the furrowed forehead. 'No, I mean, I could leave you alone, in my tent, and I could just *happen* to also leave the phone there, unattended, and you could see it and...'

'And you could pretend you knew nothing about it.'

He grinned and shrugged. 'I don't need the Wrath of Dax heaped on my head. We've started ironing out one set of problems and I'm not about to provoke another set. You could make your call in private, and nobody need ever know.'

'But what would I be doing in your tent for you to leave me alone with the phone?'

Mac gave me a look. It was very even and steady, but there was the hint of a dimple among the stubble, and a half-lift to his mouth that caused a rush of heat up my body. 'I can think of a couple of things,' he said.

I could feel my face getting red as the heat dashed through my layers of clothing in an attempt to reach cooler air.

'Although, of course, we don't actually have to *do* those things,' Mac went on, with his smile broadening. 'We only have to make the others think we are.'

There was something about the way he was standing, planted firmly in the hillside mud, with his hair escaping the confines of his hat to coil down over his cheeks, that made me suddenly very much want to do those things.

'I promise not to tell,' I half-whispered. 'Er. About the phone thing. Dax need never know.'

'When would you like to do it?' Mac paused, and then went pink. 'Use the phone, I mean. We could go now?'

'No point. Mum will be at work and she's not allowed her phone on the wards. Unless it's her day off, but then she might be out with Paul, and he often doesn't let her take her phone if they're out for the day. It "ruins the atmosphere" apparently.' I didn't even attempt to cover the bitterness in my tone. Paul had always taken *his* phone when they'd gone out. He couldn't ruin his own atmosphere, obviously, and never mind Mum. 'How about tonight?'

'That will probably be more plausible to the others too.' Mac took his beanie hat off, as though his head had got too hot. We both seemed to be overheating somewhat during this conversation.

'Right.' I unzipped my jacket a little, to let some cool air in.

'And maybe we should – well, pretend to be a bit, you know. Like, close? Today? So nobody questions what we might be up to?' Mac ran a hand around inside the collar of his coat. 'If it doesn't upset you. I'm not going to start groping you or anything, but maybe a bit of...' He waved his hands about.

'Okay.' I had to grin. His mind was obviously running along ahead of him and he was trying desperately to derail it. 'Within defined parameters.'

'Oh, yes, goes without saying. Yes. Parameters.' He blew out a long breath, which scribbled its way upwards in the cold air. 'Er. What are they, exactly?'

I took a small step closer to him. 'Well, we have to make it believable.'

He also moved a little closer. 'Believable. Yes.'

'So, touching is fine.' I put out a hand and laid it against the prickle of hair that ran from his chin to his cheekbone.

'More than fine.' His voice was a little hoarse.

'How do you feel about kissing?' I was looking into his eyes now. They were very deep brown, with straight brows and dark lashes. Attractive eyes. *Very* attractive eyes, in fact.

'I am right there with the kissing.' His eyes moved, from gazing into mine, to looking at my mouth. 'If I can practise beforehand.'

'Be my guest.'

And, as simply as that, we were kissing. The sounds of camp melted away into the overall buzzing in my ears that was my blood pounding its way through my veins as Mac's mouth met mine. His hand swept up to drag my hat from my head so he could push his hands through my hair and hold me steady. I didn't need my hat anyway. Or, from the heat of the kiss, the top three layers of my clothing. In fact, I probably could have stood here naked and let the east wind wrap itself around me and I would still have glowed.

The kiss had depth. It had *something*, something like passion but better. It wasn't the kind of kiss that is a precursor to tearing off your clothes, or the duty kisses I'd got used to at the end of my relationship. It was a kiss that said, 'This is just the beginning,' like the throat clearing before the soliloquy. I could have stayed in it all day.

We may well have stayed there all day, if it hadn't been for the insistent buzzing sound that broke us apart as keenly as though a bot fly had arrived on the scene.

'Dax?' I asked sympathetically, as Mac dragged the phone from his pocket and stared at the screen. 'Telling us to—'

'Turn our fucking cameras back on, yes.' Mac gave me an apologetic grin and slapped his camera until the light winked its blue eye at my face.

'He's going to have a *lot* of editing to do.' I raised my eyebrows at Mac, who took the opportunity to lean in and give me another swift kiss.

''Til later, then,' he half-whispered.

The whisper ran down my nerve endings and into my underwear. 'Yes,' I whispered back, thanking every god that might be watching that I had time for a decent wash and enough clean clothes to change into. It might be a fake date, but there was enough potential in us to melt the nylon of our tents into a crispy mass, and if potential turned into actual, I didn't want to disgrace myself in saggy knickers and a sports bra that had practically worn a groove into my rib cage.

'Team meeting,' Ruth said, as we wandered back into camp. She, Kanga and Sebastian were sitting around the firepit. Kanga was sitting on the ground on a blanket, probably trying to get 'closer to nature' in preparation for her *Springwatch* role while the other two sat on opposite sides.

'Kanga has raised the issue, again, of our wrapping up this charade and heading back home.' Sebastian cupped his hands around a mug and seemed to be trying to avoid looking at Ruth. She wasn't doing too badly, all things considered. Her eyes would occasionally travel up to gaze at Sebastian, but she was mostly staring at the fire, clearly fighting her crush for all she was worth.

Mac groaned. 'Not *again*. I thought we'd agreed to sit it out?'

'But now I've got my presenting role, I don't need the extra exposure,' Kanga said, smugly. 'And I thought others may feel the same.'

We all looked at each other.

'I've achieved my objective too, I think.' Sebastian shifted in his chair. 'I think, if everyone agrees, that I've managed to gain a little more humility and understanding.'

Now we were all looking at Ruth. 'I'm not sure...' She caught my eye, and I could see her silently pleading with me. She was torn between wanting to stay close to Sebastian and at the same time wanting to be a long way away from these new-found feelings, and I hoped she wasn't looking to me to make the decision for her.

'Well, I want to stay.' I plonked myself firmly down on one of the chairs that had kept its structural integrity, leaving Mac with nothing but the spontaneous stool. 'I want to see this to the end. It's only another ten days, after all.' I didn't want to have to go through this all *again*.

Mac flicked me the quickest of glances. 'And I vote to stay too.'

Kanga and I met one another's eyes and shared a momentary glance of shared secrets that weren't for public consumption. We had to trust one another here. After a second, she snorted. 'Well, of course you do. You're still trying to get into Izzy's knickers, aren't you?'

'Oh, I say!' Sebastian pulled a face. 'That's hardly fair!'

'It's true, though.' Unconcerned, she pulled the sleeves of her jacket tightly around her wrists. 'So, Sebastian and I want to leave, Izzy and Mac...' she made a little moue of distaste, '...vote to stay, because *obviously*. So that gives you the casting vote.' She turned suddenly intense eyes on Ruth. 'And I don't think you *really* want to stay, do you?'

Ruth gave me another 'help me' look.

'I mean, Sebastian isn't going to fall in love with you, no matter how much you moon after him,' Kanga went on smoothly. 'So you may as well admit defeat and go home.'

There was a collective intake of breath that pulled the flames in all directions, then silence.

Ruth went pale, then very, very red. She got to her feet with a slow dignity that I could only admire, and said, 'I don't think you know anything about anything, Kanga. I vote to stay.' Then, with the poise of someone twice her age, she stalked away from us, to her tent, and zipped herself in. Only the glowing scarlet of her cheeks gave away the fact that Kanga had been right.

'That was unnecessary.' I turned on Kanga, who shrugged.

'She said she came on this expedition to help her grow up. Mollycoddling her won't do that,' she said.

'But humiliating her will?' I'd not really decided how I felt about Kanga. I'd alternated between feeling irritated by her chore avoidance and her obviousness in front of the cameras, and a slight pity that she felt she had to conceal her true background. But right now, with the eyes of the team now on me and hearing the background stifled sobs from Ruth's tent, I *hated* her. 'Were you never secretly in love with someone? Didn't you ever have a crush on a pop star or a teacher?'

What I wanted to say, of course, was, how dare you call Ruth out on trying to hide a crush when you are hiding your entire upbringing and pretending to be someone posh when you aren't anything of the sort? But

I daren't. She'd blow my secrets up in front of everyone and, despite all my pep talking to myself, that sense of shame still hung over me. I bit my lip.

The men were staring. Sebastian was looking at the ground, a bit pink around the ears. Mac just sat.

'It's pathetic, that's all.' Kanga stood up. 'Really pathetic. As though Sebastian would ever reciprocate – with someone who's barely out of school. We should all stop tiptoeing around and be honest here.'

I remembered that Sebastian had turned Kanga down on our first night here, and wondered if that was what really lay behind her words. Was she afraid that he *might* start something with Ruth, making her look like the desperate reject?

I met her eye again. We both knew that this could blow up. I could see that half-triumphant look on her face, that knowledge that I couldn't throw anything at her without her throwing something right back. Was this what mutually assured destruction looked like?

'I think you ought to stop talking now,' I said, through clenched teeth. 'None of this is Ruth's fault. Sebastian has behaved perfectly decently, and you are trying to make us so fed up that we will all agree with you and get Dax to take us off the moor. You may have achieved *your* objective, Kanga, but some of us want to stay on!'

Kanga walked up to me. She put her face very close to mine, close enough that I could see the tiny tracery of very fine wrinkles in the corners of her eyes. 'Oh, yes?' She almost hissed at me. 'Well, don't forget I know why you're really here, Izzy. I know what you're running away from that makes you so desperate to live in a tent and pee in a bucket to earn a few grand.'

Then she straightened her back and stalked off. Not to her tent, because that would have meant following Ruth's route, instead she walked off onto the moor behind the camp. I suspected she'd try to look picturesque on top of the boulders, in case any of our cameras followed her.

Mac blew out a long breath. 'I think we voted to stay.'

'Looks like it. Ah, well.' Sebastian held his hands out towards the flaring firepit. 'I'll have a word with Ruth in a moment. I mean—' He glanced at me, but I wasn't going to say anything to anyone. 'I knew she was, er, *attracted* to me, but I would never do anything to jeopardise my marriage. Besides, Ruth is so young.'

'I know she said she wanted to grow up,' I said. 'But this is a bit of a crash-course. Poor Ruth. Now everyone knows, and, let's face it, crushes are best kept private.' I was talking quickly, hoping that Sebastian wouldn't ask about what Kanga had said. Mac was giving me little side-glances as though he wanted to say something about it, but I couldn't talk about it. Not here. Not now.

'There's some disturbance down the valley.' Unnoticed for such a big bloke, Junior had come into the camp, striding jauntily down from the track. 'Like something big has been laying up. Crushed bracken, that kinda thing.'

With an alacrity born of relief, we all turned to him. 'Something that wasn't there before?' I asked.

'Yeah. It's like a lair. Overlooks this place, on the far side, over there.' He pointed at the opposite side of the dale, where the hill rose blue-black with shadow and was still slightly gilded with frost. The sun didn't reach that side of the valley until it was almost setting. 'Looks like we're under observation or somethin'.'

'But you didn't see anything?'

Junior stared at Sebastian. 'Well, yeah. I saw crushed bracken.'

'I mean, no actual *animal*?'

'Got ma camera on.' Junior tapped his shoulder-cam, rather smugly. 'If there'd been anything, I'd have got us that evidence.'

I pulled a face. 'I'm not sure I like the idea that something has been watching us. *Why* is it watching?'

Junior shrugged. 'Could be that it feels threatened?'

'Or it's planning to attack,' Mac put in dryly.

'It's a dog, not a SWAT team.' I shivered and pulled my chair a little closer to the fire. Kanga's sudden assault had made my skin chill into little pricks of gooseflesh which hadn't subsided yet, and the thought that a big animal might be watching and waiting wasn't helping.

'Yeah. Big predator animals, they stalk. They don't sit and wait for you to go to bed,' Junior said. 'They pick you off, one at a time when you leave camp. They don't do forward planning, they're opportunistic.'

We all sat, obviously entrenched in our own, individual visions of a creeping beast, waiting in the undergrowth to snatch and mangle us when we left the safety of others.

'But dogs don't hunt people down, do they?' I thought of all the dogs I knew. Big, dignified Golden Retrievers, hyperactive beagles and small, intense terriers. Not one of them could I imagine having the desire to hunt down humans, unless they thought we were carrying a particularly alluring squeaky toy. 'And we all agree that what we've been seeing is a big loose dog. So maybe it's been lying in the sun up there and it's purely accidental that it happens to be opposite our site?'

Junior shrugged. 'That's most likely what's happening,' he said slowly. 'But, y'know, if we're trying to make this TV thing run to the wire, we need to find some reason to stay out here. Us chasing about after shadows isn't going to make great television, but us investigating every clue we find might.'

'He's got a point.' Sebastian stood up. 'We really should look into anything. We have been guilty of being rather less than proactive here, haven't we?'

I didn't like the idea of being proactive, when proactive seemed to mean dashing about on the moor and poking anything likely with a big stick to see if it attacked us.

'I mean,' Sebastian went on, 'we're all talking about what we're getting out of the experience, but we aren't really thinking much about poor Dax and what *he* is getting from *us*.'

Mac pulled a face. 'It might not look great from this side, but Dax is going to cut the film to ribbons and intercut with all the other teams. I reckon he can make six people living out here and never seeing anything more than shadows into "must watch TV".'

It was the first time I'd heard Mac say anything complimentary about his brother. The argument-fight-rapprochement must have worked better than I'd thought.

'He's a complete dick, of course,' Mac went on, and the little pink lights of hope for a smooth sibling relationship from here on winked out in my head. 'But he does know what he's doing when it comes to making programmes.'

'Look, I'm going to talk to Ruth.' Sebastian did a wobbly sort of walk, where his intent didn't seem strong enough to carry him forward. 'Clear the air, hopefully make her feel better. Try to undo whatever damage Kanga has done.'

'Kanga did do us a favour, though,' I half-whispered to Mac, my words covered by the sound of the sucking mud as Sebastian walked off towards Ruth's tent. 'If Ruth had voted to leave, we'd be packing right now.'

'Hm.' Mac looked down at me and smiled. He kept his eyes fixed on mine to such an extent that I began to worry, until he made the tiniest motion towards Junior, whose camera was winking away in our direction, and I realised that we were being filmed 'enjoying an intimate moment'. Otherwise known as 'setting up the scene for us to share a tent later'.

I really wasn't built for these obfuscations and misdirections. I would rather have been having a flirtatious dinner and a few drinks, knowing that we would likely be going to bed afterwards, without all the pretence. But then, I did want to use the phone, so I had to put up with it. I stared back into Mac's eyes, and tried to plaster a look of adoration onto my face.

'It's all right, you can stop looking constipated, he's gone,' Mac said.

'That was my best worshipping expression,' I said indignantly.

'Wow. Okay, I'll bear that in mind for later.' He grinned broadly at me.

'I'm sorry, but I've never had to display conspicuous intent before.'

Mac looked thoughtful. 'When all this is over,' he said, slowly, 'I am going to expunge the word "tent" from my vocabulary, in all contexts.'

'You really mean it? You're going to stop travelling?'

He shrugged. 'Like I said before, I think it's time to stop running away and start living a real life. I've been trying so hard to forge my own identity that I seem to have managed to end up with no real identity at all. Even bloody Dax has got a boyfriend and a crew. All I have is a professional level knowledge of bivvy bags and the ability to buy dry rations in twenty languages. It's not a lot to show for thirty years, is it?' He looked at the toes of his boots, the ends of his curls flopping in a bedraggled way around his chin.

'It's more than I've got,' I said, trying not to sound too bitter. Then I firmed up my chin and shook my head slightly. 'But I'm going to work on that as soon as we get out of here.'

Mac reached out and took my hand. Given that we'd been talking about sex and had had that hot kiss, it probably wasn't surprising that the touch of his fingers should have felt as intimate and sexual as it did. When he looped them through mine and half-whispered, 'We are both going to get something real out of this fiasco, aren't we?' I could do nothing but nod.

15

Night came. It came early too, with clouded skies and sharp rain that swept through the valley as we ate, sudden and swift and carrying the intent of winter on its edges.

Mac and I had kept up the – well, it wasn't a pretence. But we'd probably imbued it with slightly more lingering glances and lip licking than any seduction outside a porn film. I couldn't help feeling a bit ridiculous and over the top, especially when the others kept catching sight of us and smiling indulgent little smiles, like parents whose toddlers have just mastered the use of a knife and fork. I didn't want it to be like this. I wanted our first night together – and I realised that I was now thinking of being with Mac as a definite, rather than something that might possibly happen at some time in the future – to be sweet and gentle. I didn't want it to be something with an audience. Not that the entire viewing public would be looking in on us, but I didn't put it past Dax to make something of it. But then I needed the excuse to be in Mac's tent, alone, with the phone. And, after all, we weren't actually *going* to have sex. We were only pretending. Weren't we?

We waited until Kanga, and a slightly-shyer-than-before Ruth, who seemed to have taken Sebastian's down-to-earth talking-to very well, had gone to their tents. Then, in full and plausible view of Junior and Sebast-

ian's cameras, and with our cameras firmly turned off, Mac took my hand
and tugged me towards his tent, trying for just-on-camera pretend-
subtlety.

'God, this feels awkward,' I muttered to him as we tried to look jauntily sexy, crossing the camp. 'I feel like the heroine in one of those horrible
old-fashioned romance books, you know the kind, where she's being
seduced by a billionaire but she's an innocent virgin and doesn't know
what's happening to her.'

Mac gave me a rather pained look. 'I'm not a billionaire, and this is
hardly seduction.'

'I'm not an innocent virgin either, but it's the *feel* of the thing,' I
retorted.

'Everyone is going to be so busy imagining us "feeling things" that
hopefully everyone will be too distracted to even think about the phone.'

We sat down in the tent. I scuffed an amount of Mac's sleeping bag
under me, and he perched on his rucksack, which sat empty and deflated
like a disappointed football, in one corner.

'So,' he said cheerfully, 'we'd better give them a few minutes to talk
about us, I suppose.'

'We don't have to make exaggerated moaning noises or anything, do
we?' I felt nervous and I had no idea why. It wasn't as if we were going to
do anything, and it was Mac, hardly a stranger. I'd spent more time in his
company than I had with my ex, if you considered that Mac and I were
around each other more or less every waking hour, and the ex had liked
gym-going and road cycling rather more than was concomitant with a
relationship.

'I suppose we can if we want.' Mac shuffled as though he were uncomfortable. 'But let's not bother. Look, the phone is here. We'll give it about
half an hour, for the sake of my ego, and then I'll creep off to the loo and
you can – well, do what you need to.'

I'd felt so sure when we'd kissed. The kiss had been sweet and familiar
yet full of potential and had made me feel things that I hadn't even
thought about for a long time. Yet now I felt embarrassed and awkward,
as though I'd talked myself into something I didn't want.

'We could play cards.' Mac was looking at my face. 'A couple of hands of pontoon for buttons ought to be a decent stand-in for sex.'

'I'm not even going to think about that. But yes.' A red-hot flush of gratitude rolled over me. He wasn't going to insist. Well, of course he wasn't. This was Mac. Mac, who had felt so bad about not being able to help his girlfriend that he'd studied exactly how not to make a woman feel pressurised. Who understood how my life had been. 'Cards. Yes.'

'I know.' Mac groped about underneath a pile of stuff and came up with the little box of cards which had already seen a fair amount of action around the campfire of an evening. 'I'll show you how to play Drubbins. Dax and I used to play this...'

Drubbins turned out to be the card game equivalent of 'Mornington Crescent'. Mac basically made up the rules as we went along and, by the time he'd told me that I'd lost a 'curly play' because my ten of spades had more straight lines in it than his eight of clubs, we were both weak with laughter and leaning against one another so as not to fall over.

'That's not fair!' I gasped. 'I lost the last two points because I was holding the cards "upside down"!'

'Well, you were.' Mac dealt another hand. 'Now, let's see if you can win this one. Hearts are high, ace to three are exempt, double ten doesn't count and if you sneeze, you are automatically disqualified.'

'You're making this up.' I was suddenly aware of how warm he felt, there against my shoulder. I'd been so used to him wearing layers and layers of clothing, that to feel the scratch and snag of his woollen jumper against my fleece was almost like feeling his naked skin against mine.

'Of course I am. But you're laughing and it's good to see you laughing again. When we were dancing and laughing the other night, I looked at you in the firelight and I thought, "This is a woman I could fall in love with."'

The laughter was gone, as suddenly as if it had been pulled back into my throat. The cards lay between us. Hearts on top.

'You're very attractive, you know,' Mac went on, conversationally, as though he was still talking about the cards. 'Under all the camp grime and stuff. But I didn't want to tell you, because I thought you might have heard all that from Paul and I didn't want you to associate anything I may say or do with that creep.'

The previous amusement was sitting under my lungs now. It squeezed at my heart with its weight.

'I'm really sorry about what I said when we first started all this, about you being too cheerful and everything.' Mac was very carefully laying the cards out, not looking at me but concentrating on them as though he were dealing a Tarot deck to read our future. 'Because actually I'm amazed that you can smile at all, with what happened.'

Now he looked up. The side of his face was lit by the torch that sat on a box, illuminating our card playing area, and it made his eyes look very big and dark. My mouth had gone oddly dry.

'And before I say or do anything else, I'm going to go out for a little while. Take a breath of air, maybe a walk around camp.' There was a sudden gleam of humour in his eyes and a twitch of his mouth under the stubble. 'So, you know. Don't touch anything while I'm gone.' He flicked his head towards the phone, which was innocently lying on charge, on top of the battery pack. 'Because I think you may need some space.'

I still hadn't said anything. After he'd gone, shuffling through the tent flap like an inelegant butterfly exiting a cocoon, I sat still for a few moments, letting the laughter bubble down towards my heart. He didn't want me to associate him with anything that Paul had said. He was being so careful, so protective of my feelings.

I wanted to meet the people he'd talked to about how to process his girlfriend's rape, and kiss every one of them. Although I'd like a good wash and a change of clothes first, obviously.

Mac thought I was attractive. This, what I was beginning to feel, could be real. The laughs I'd swallowed down came twisting back up my throat and exploded in a sort of choked giggle. I'd thought he was feeling sorry for me. But he really, genuinely, liked me.

I couldn't process all that now. All of it, the confusion of feelings, the potential that was making my hands prick with sweat and my blood feel weak, needed to be secondary right at this minute. I had things to do, the whole reason I was here in this tent, probably making the rest of the camp think that I was laughing myself silly at Mac's attempts at lovemaking. The phone.

I picked it up and didn't dare give myself time to think, or to weigh up the sense of doing any of this because I knew I would chicken out if I did. I dialled the familiar number, and waited. Mum wouldn't recognise the number, but she would answer. She was a nurse, used to neighbours calling to ask her to check on little Tyler's bruised foot, or whether their dad ought to go to hospital with those strange chest pains he was having. She would answer.

Whether she would talk to me was another matter.

'Hello?' Brisk, no-nonsense. She was probably not long home, still in her work persona.

'Hello, Mum.'

A cold, long silence. Both of us breathing down the phone, neither of us hanging up. Well, this was good. Wasn't it?

Then a catch. A little hitch in her breath. 'Izzy? Where are you?'

I looked around me. At Mac's belongings packed tidily into the tent. Then I thought beyond, of the long moors spread along the skyline, still as corpses in the night. The lonely wind coming down the valley like the words of the dead. The beast that hunted through the dark. 'It would take too long to explain.'

'You...' That catch again. As though she was having to force her words over razor blades. 'You're all right, though?'

All right. Was I *all right*? Then I realised I had a gang of five behind me. Well, four, if I assumed that Kanga didn't care whether I lived or died. Mac, he probably counted for more than one. 'I'm fine, Mum.'

A pause. Heartbeats. Then we both started talking at once.

'I honestly and truly never touched Paul, I would never, and besides, he's an utter creep and a liar!'

'I was so, so stupid, Izzy, I can't believe I fell for it at my age! Then, when you'd gone, people started talking, and Jackie said he'd been flirting with her, and Margot's daughter, you know, that one with the hair, *she* said he'd been trying to get her to go up the allotment with him. And others, there were others, and I'm so sorry I didn't believe you!'

We ran out of words. The silence whistled. 'Will... will you come home?' Mum sounded as though she thought I'd slap her.

Home. All my equipment was there. My little room. With the door that hadn't kept him out. *And she'd believed him.*

'Not for a while.' The words sounded colder than I'd meant them to. Or *had* I intended that steely chill? 'I mean, I will, one day. We need to talk about this properly.'

Mum made a noise. A cross between a sob and agreement. It sounded as though she'd gone beyond words.

I thought of Mac. His offer of a place to stay. I could use the £3,000 from being on this ridiculous show to pay my way in a new life. Glasgow.

'I'll pick up my kit, all my stuff, and we'll talk. But I won't come home to live, Mum.' The words I wanted to say ran underneath the actual statement. *You move men in that make me unsafe. You believe them over me.* All right, it had only been the one man, so probably a bit over the top, but my emotions were a touch hyperbolic tonight.

'No.' A soft acceptance. 'No. I can understand that.'

No, you can't, I wanted to shout. How could you? You can only see what he was doing in hindsight, and that's no good to me. I wanted you there, at the time, throwing yourself in front of my bedroom door, shouting and protecting me. You're my *mother*, for god's sake.

But then I stopped. Thought of Mac, whose parents hadn't exactly been optimal. Kanga, being raised to believe she had to lose her background and pretend to be posh to succeed and Ruth's narrow, religious upbringing. I didn't know anything about Sebastian's childhood, but right now, I would willingly have believed that he'd been forced to scrub his family home clean with a toothbrush every night. Parents. They did what they could. There was no manual, no list of instructions. Mum had thought Paul was a good man. She'd thought I was safe.

We needed to deal with the fact of her believing Paul over me, of course, but we'd get to that in time.

'I've got somewhere to go,' I said, my voice stronger now. A little bit less weighted with the unsaid and buoyed with certainty. 'I'll be fine. Once I'm back from – where I am now, I'll come and collect my stuff. But I think we need some space.' Before I can talk to you about this, the unwanted appendix hung in the air, unsaid.

'Of course. I never meant...' That soft choke again. I could picture her face, still surprisingly young-looking at fifty-eight, topped with the no-nonsense practical haircut above her uniform. Blue eyes, like mine, crinkled and lined from years of staring suspiciously at doctors and smiling at patients. She always closed her eyes when she cried.

I wondered whether she'd cried about me leaving. Whether she *really* missed me or missed having someone around to cook for.

'I have to go, Mum.'

'But where *are* you?' The practicality of my location was easier to talk about, I could tell from her voice.

'At this minute, in a tent in the middle of nowhere, hunting an animal that doesn't exist.'

'Oh.' She didn't sound surprised. 'Well. Be careful, then.'

The words were so familiar, so much my practical mother, that I felt a weight of wet heat rise behind my eyes and a momentary longing to flee home, throw myself on her shoulder and be hugged into extinction. But then I remembered: Paul. Her seeming blindness to what was going on.

'Careful doesn't really help, though, does it?' I sounded sharper than I meant to, and heard her indrawn breath of reaction, so my subsequent words were softer. I didn't want to hurt her. I really didn't. I wanted her to *understand*, that was all, and if that came with a certain amount of pain then that was up to her. 'I mean, against an imaginary beast. I'm fine, Mum. Really.' I thought of Mac. *You're really attractive, you know.* Of his dark curls escaping under his stupid hat. The laughter. 'Everything is going to be all right.' These words were firm, but with hope, with promise, rather than reproach.

'I hope so.' It could have meant anything. But the spin she gave those words made me hope that it really could. That this, all this, the stuff with Paul, her not listening to me and not even asking for my version of events, the truth as I saw it – it could be all right.

Besides, I thought as I pressed the button to disconnect the call, it sounded as though Paul was firmly in the past and she'd eventually seen through him. It had taken other people to make her see, but she'd got there. I wondered how that had felt for her. Having the realisation that her daughter had been in the right, and that she had let me go out into that night with nothing but a Sainsbury's carrier bag of clothes, for a man who had been a liar and a creep.

Another furious flush of anger heated my skin, as it rose with that image of Paul's smirk. I could only hope that Mum had poured petrol over his clothes, slashed his tyres and taken a Stanley knife to all his treasured LPs, before she kicked him out.

'Knock knock.'

'Who's there?' I answered, with only half my mind on the tent, my position, all this. The rest of me was back in that little terraced house in York, sprawled on the sofa watching endless repeats of *The IT Crowd* while Mum ironed her uniform and the dinner bubbled and filled the kitchen with steam.

'Er. Sorry. I haven't got a joke to follow up with.' Mac slid his head through a sliver of opening. 'Have you done? How did it go? Are you all right?'

'I'm not sure.' I put the phone down. 'She's split up with Paul because everyone *else* told her he was a creep. She seems apologetic.' I wondered why I didn't feel more triumphant. 'But I won't go back other than to collect my stuff.'

Mac crawled further into the tent. 'So you really will come to Glasgow with me?'

I smiled. 'If you promise to be neither a creep nor a pervert, then yes. I may as well start over again in Glasgow as anywhere else.'

'I presume most creeps and perverts don't actually have the insight to realise that they *are* being creeps and perverts.' Mac sat inside the entrance, looking at me. The torch illuminated random parts of his body, a knee, the arch of his chin, a tumble of curls, making him look like a jigsaw that had yet to be assembled.

'You were right, though,' I went on. 'I did need to talk to Mum. I feel better now, even though we haven't really sorted anything out.'

Mac nodded. At least, I think that was what he was doing, his chin went out of the light and his hair bobbed. 'You were right about me talking to Dax, and we haven't quite got to the bottom of that, so it's payback.' I saw the light gleam in his eyes as he looked at me. 'But you feel you achieved something?'

'I don't know,' I said again. The emotion was beginning to roll in now, like the tide of an unruly sea, sweeping in waves over my heart. 'She misses me. She wants me safe.'

'Things may never be the same again.' A cautiously extended hand touched mine. 'But you will be fine.'

His caution broke me. The tears came, clogging my eyes and breaking my breath into ragged sobs. Mac put his arms around me and enclosed me in an anorak-heavy embrace. He didn't speak, just hugged me tightly until the worst was over and I had gasped myself to a sniffy, snotty standstill.

'Sorry.' I wiped a hand over my face. Thankfully the torchlight was still aimed downwards, at the scattered cards and discarded phone. 'It's been a bit of a – well, anti-climax, really.'

Mac kept me held against him and I didn't push myself back. I felt less alone with him here, that's what it was. He understood and knowing that I didn't need to explain myself or go over what Mum had said was surprisingly comforting.

He didn't burst into platitudes either, just sat in the doorway to the tent, with the torch illuminating his knees and the side of his face, and held me close. 'I'm glad you're not trying to do Total Cheerleader any more,' he said quietly. 'Living with that would have become wearing after a while.'

I nudged myself away from him and wiped my eyes with the back of my hand. 'And I'm glad you're not as miserable as you were at the beginning,' I said, through a smile. 'You were such a grumpy git that I would happily have fed you to any passing beasts.'

Half his return grin was illuminated by the torch beam. 'We were the ones with least expectation of all this, weren't we?' He pushed his hair away from his face with the back of a wrist. 'And yet, I would argue, we are the ones to have gained the most.'

I'd opened my mouth to agree when there was a scream. Not a surprised 'there's an earwig in my sleeping bag' scream, but an elongated shriek of terror. It broke up, then came again, and suddenly everything beyond our tent was moving lights and shouting.

Mac and I emerged into pandemonium. Ruth was still screaming, hands pulling her cheeks down so that her eyes showed white in the snatches of torch beam. There were heavy sounds; ripping and the noise of plastic boxes being thrown around. Junior was yelling something I couldn't hear, Kanga and Sebastian were shining their torches beyond the camp, into the darkness.

Where something moved. Something big and sleek, keeping out of the range of the torchlight. It had torn through the fabric of a tent, scattering pegs and ropes and equipment across the flat part of the site away from the fire and was now a presence and sounds over by the food store.

Ruth still screamed into the night.

'Get under cover!' Junior yelled.

'What cover? There isn't any!' I shouted back.

'It's gone through Ruth's tent like tissue paper.' Sebastian stood in front of us, turning his torch to try to get a fix on whatever was running riot through the camp. 'We're not safe. We need a secure location.'

'What about the Portaloo?'

He stared at me. Kanga knocked into him from behind and then crashed up against me. She'd got a still shrieking Ruth by the arm. 'It's going to eat us all,' she hissed in a low, desperate voice. 'It's going to pick us off one by one.'

'The Portaloo is a rigid structure and the door locks.' I grabbed bits of everyone's clothing and dragged them with me. 'Get in there and we'll be safe.'

'Good thinking.' Mac and Sebastian formed a sort of corral with their bodies and hustled us all up towards the patch of gorse where the Portaloo stood in isolation, concealed behind the spiny shrubby growth, which looked sinister and snatchy in the light from half a dozen running torches.

Behind us, Junior was rotating in a panic of action tempered with caution. 'Ah need the gun!' he kept shouting, whilst doing nothing about getting it. I wasn't even sure who had the key today.

Shadows flickered. Something big ran behind the food store, lights on fur that gleamed patchily as torches shone towards it, but it moved too fast to get enough light to fix a proper image. There was something more terrible about it being half-seen than I was sure there would have been if we'd been able to see it properly. I couldn't even tell how big it was, little jigsaw-scatters of body, tail, a glimpse of limb, all moving, moving in a chaos of action, to the background noise of Ruth's high scream, Junior's yelling, a tussle of bodies trying to get to the Portaloo. Somewhere along the route, Junior pushed past me and ran off out into the dark, but none of us had the breath or brain space to remark on his going.

Eventually we were all inside, with the door locked. Only Junior was still out there in the dark with the beast, which meant five of us were occupying the space meant to be taken by one person, and it involved quite a bit of juggling. Ruth and Kanga were sitting perched on opposite sides of the seat. I was jammed in one corner, Mac in the other, with one foot up on the spare bit of seat between Kanga's knees to enable him to fit. Sebastian occupied the doorway, his back flat up against the door and his thighs rammed against Kanga. We looked like a panicked Guinness Book of Records attempt.

Because we'd all been in bed, or, in the case of Mac and I, *supposedly* in bed, none of us had our big jackets on. No jackets, and no cameras, so all this was going unrecorded and if the cat didn't get us, Dax was going to kill us for the loss of high-stakes TV.

'Stupid! Stupid!' Sebastian kept repeating, smacking his fist against the frame of the building, which caused it to rock in its plastic-shrouded foundation. 'We took our eye off the ball, that's what we did! Forgot what we were here for!'

'It's not your fault.' Ruth had stopped screaming but there was the tight hysteria of fear in her voice.

'But there's something out there! We should be there, getting film of it, getting a body. Something definite, something to show for all this. We don't even have our cameras!'

Mac and I made eye contact in the dark smelliness, lit only by the emergency battery-powered light in the ceiling. 'We agreed, we couldn't shoot it,' Mac said, his voice impressively steady.

'Self-defence.' Sebastian ran his hands through his hair. 'Good lord, we've left Junior out there to face it alone.'

'It came through my tent.' Ruth's voice was shaky. 'I'd turned out my light and I was lying down to go to sleep and it tore its way in.'

'But it didn't touch you?' I asked.

'No. I don't even know if it saw me. All I saw of it were these eyes and then it was panicking, I think, tangled up in the tent, then it sort of burst free and headed for the food store.'

We all stood, silent, in the smelly dark of the Portaloo. The flickering emergency light illuminated only the closest features with its eerie green glow, giving cheeks a ghostly pallor and eyes a spark as though life had been breathed into the inanimate. We were all pressed so tightly against one another that I could feel the fast, scared breathing of everyone else. The metal and plastic frame against which I was leaning suddenly felt flimsy and inconsequential. 'Are we safe, do you think?'

Sebastian gave a short laugh, but said nothing. We were all listening. There was a distant sound of banging, as though the creature was still tearing its way through the food store and then the sudden rapping at the Portaloo door that made us all jump so hard that we practically knocked the building over.

'It's me. I need in.' Junior was on the threshold. 'It's dangerous out here.'

'It's not exactly fabulous in here either.' Kanga leaned over and opened the door a crack and Junior forced his way inside, having to insert himself past Sebastian and between Mac and Kanga in order to fit. I got pushed further back against the wall, with Ruth almost in my coat with me. 'Ow.'

More silence. Or as much silence as you could get with six people rammed together in a Portaloo – arms and legs banged against the sides as we breathed, there was a constant stream of half-suppressed muttering and exclamations of pain and the rustle of various collections of clothing making contact. The smell was making my eyes water too.

'Just don't anyone need the toilet,' Mac said eventually.

'Don't worry, I think terror has dried up all my bodily functions.' Sebastian kept his voice low. 'Is it still out there, do you think?'

We all held our breath. The faint barging, banging and tearing noises were continuing.

'I think so.'

Ruth gave another slight sob. 'This is *awful*,' she said.

Sebastian put his hand on her shoulder and she threw him a grateful look, which bore a lot less soppiness than her recent interactions with him.

'I shoulda shot it,' Junior said, head down. 'That's what I'm here for.'

'Well, I've got the key here.' Kanga fished out the little key, which was on a string around her neck. 'So crack on.'

'But the gun is in the food box,' I said. 'Where that creature is currently running riot.'

Kanga shrugged. 'You want the money,' she said. 'If we bring it in, we get a quarter of a million pounds each. It's out there, all you have to do is get the gun.'

Silence descended again as we all weighed up the potential of the money, and put it against the possible death of one of our number.

'It's why I'm here,' Junior eventually muttered.

'Have you shot any Bigfoot yet?'

A particularly loud crash came from somewhere in the camp. It sounded as though the beast, whatever it was, had knocked over the meat storage.

'There were sausages in there,' Sebastian observed.

'I don't think there are any more.' I looked at Mac. 'Have you got the phone on you? We may need reinforcements.'

He shook his head. 'Nope. I usually have it in my pocket but—' he stopped, widened his eyes at me and then finished, 'tonight I left it in the tent.'

Brilliant. So it was my fault. My desire to speak to my mother had meant he'd had to leave the phone unattended and my subsequent emotional outburst meant neither of us had thought to pick it back up again.

'Bugger.'

'What the hell *is* it?' Kanga leaned back against the frame and the whole structure swayed, until Sebastian counterbalanced by leaning against the other side. 'It's so dark and it was moving so quickly...' She threw an almost accusatory look at Ruth. 'Did *you* get a proper look?'

The hysteria seemed to be ebbing out of Ruth now. 'No. Like I said, I'd turned the light out when it came through my tent. It's big and it's dark and it moves really quickly, that's all I can tell you.'

'Quarter of a million pounds, though.' Kanga seemed to have gone into a dream state. 'That's a lot of money.'

Nobody said anything.

'I mean – for people without my advantages, obviously.'

Again, silence, except for the distant sound of all our food being gone through.

'I'm homeless.' I had no idea why I said it. Why the life from outside camp, the one I'd kept hidden the whole time we'd been here, suddenly burst out of me. Maybe because I'd spoken to my mother? 'I've been living on the streets and in temporary accommodation because a man got me thrown out of my house.'

Five faces, fragmented and rendered ghastly by the emergency lights, turned towards me.

'You don't need to...' Mac started.

'Yes, I do. Kanga knows, I've already told her, and I've no idea why I didn't tell all the rest of you. I need the money to start again.' I looked at Kanga, who had dropped her gaze now. 'Nothing salacious. Nothing illegal. Just stupid decisions and impulsive walking out.'

Another moment of quiet. Then Ruth said, 'It's nothing to be ashamed of, Izzy.'

Ashamed? Yes, that was why I hadn't talked about it. I'd felt stupid and humiliated. My mother hadn't taken my side, I'd let a man get the better of me. Here I was, a twenty-first century woman, and I'd *let it happen*. I couldn't reply to Ruth. I wanted to say, 'I know,' but did I? Really? It happened, and to all sorts of people, and yet I still had this sense of embarrassment that I'd let it happen to me. Why hadn't I gone to Mum the first time Paul got too touchy-feely for my liking? Why hadn't I shouted him down, told him to stop? Read him the riot act and slammed a few doors?

I'd let it happen.

I could feel Mac's eyes on my face and remembered his reaction to his girlfriend's rape. He had started out blaming her and had to educate himself on how internalised self-loathing worked. I was loathing Paul, but still using words like 'blame' and 'guilt' about myself, when I hadn't caused any of it.

It wasn't my fault.

'I know,' I said to Ruth now. 'I do know.' My voice sounded strong. In the dark, Mac's hand brushed mine. 'I had to think it all through. And now I realise that me being honest and open about what happened to me is probably better than keeping quiet. You never know.' I tried to sound bright. 'It might help someone else out there. If I can use this whole experience and the TV exposure to tell everyone that being homeless could happen to anyone, that it's not some shameful secret and that you can fight your way back, then maybe it's been worth it.' I stopped and looked around at the industrial grey metal and felt the fumes giving my sinuses a good kicking. 'Although I wouldn't recommend going on a reality TV show and trying to catch a puma as a way out.'

Kanga was looking at me in a strange way. Although it was hard to tell, under this partial illumination that flickered and gave us all a certain Dr Frankenstein look, she seemed to be thinking hard.

'You've told them all now,' she said. There wasn't the trace of disappointment at the loss of blackmail material that I had been expecting in her voice. Instead, it held a tiny tremble. Surely she didn't think that I'd blurt out her secret, did she?

'Yes. I really don't know why I kept it quiet.' Mac gave my hand a little squeeze. 'But I'm hoping there are ways out.' A tiny feeling of guilt made itself known in the back of my mind, that it was only because of Mac, only because he and I had a putative relationship, that my 'way out' was manifesting, and that if he hadn't been attracted to me and vice versa, I'd *still* have nowhere to go.

'I think you are very brave.' Ruth's voice wobbled a bit. 'I mean, our church works with the homeless and so I've seen how easy it is for people to slide into awful situations. And yet, here you are.'

'I'd like to point out that I'm locked in a Portaloo with five other people whilst an unspecified animal eats all our food,' I said, trying to keep my voice level. 'That's a pretty awful situation.'

She gave a little giggle. 'You know what I mean. You'll probably be famous after this. The magazines are all going to want to know everything about you. Once they find out, of course, I mean, we're not filming any of this, are we?'

A tiny jolt ran through me as the reality sank in. We'd all got so used to the cameras' blinking lights that knowing we were recording everything that happened to us had become different to *knowing we were recording everything that happened to us*. Yet here we were, possibly at the climax of the entire event, every one of us having left our cameras in the tents with our outer jackets. But at least it would give me chance to get my story straight and picturesque, before the others revealed it to the nation. Probably.

'Ruth's right.' Sebastian's voice was very deep, but that could have been the fumes. 'That little confession might make you famous, Izzy. From homeless to – well, whatever you go on to do after this. But I know you'll make a success of it, you've got that mix of pragmatism and sense that made me see how I was fudging up my life and marriage.'

'You talked a lot of sense to me too.' Ruth shuffled her feet somewhere along the base of the toilet. 'You were very kind.'

'You made Dax and I talk,' Mac put in. 'And we've been avoiding doing that since 2018, so, good job.'

'Yeah.' Junior's bass vibrated the walls. 'You don't panic easy either. You're a good woman to have in a crisis, and I'm glad you were on board here.'

There was a cascade of silence as everyone clearly waited for Kanga to give me a testimonial. In the febrile light, I could see her nervous fingers picking at the toilet seat. Her head was down and I could only imagine her turmoil.

'That's very kind of you all,' I spoke before any of the others could prod her. 'I'm glad if anything I said has helped you in any way…'

'Oh, all right!' Kanga tried to stand up haughtily, but there really wasn't room. She kind of rebounded off Mac and wobbled back to her situation on the side of the seat. 'Yes, yes, Izzy, since we all seemed to have formed your fan club here, you were right with what you said when I fell in the river. I *should* be honest about my background.'

She paused. Dramatic effect rolled around her in waves, backed by the sound of more plastic boxes tipping. I wondered if she *really* thought coming clean about her background would help other people, because I suspected that it was more the effect of Sebastian's certainty that I would get famous for coming from homelessness to – well, whatever I came to. Mac's solidity beside me was reassuring.

'I'm not really from money. I live in a flat in Wandsworth with my mum and four brothers and my agent is a friend of my mum's.' She stopped, cleared her throat, and then clearly felt she'd passed the point of no return because the rest of her words flowed out of her on what sounded like a raft of relief. 'We never had any money. I worked on the market but Mum saw this programme on TV about modelling and all, and Tanika's bloke Solly dabbled a bit and he got me in with his mate, taking pictures of—' she cleared her throat again, 'well, lingerie and stuff. And *he* suggested that I get on *Love Island*, but that I ought to pretend to be posh and all, so he got his mate to give me lessons on how to talk and all that crap.' A note of defiance crept into her voice. 'So. Now you know.'

'Wow,' Sebastian said. 'Now you'll be famous for coming from nothing, Kanga.'

'It *weren't* nothing!' Kanga lost the crisp, posh tones. 'We got a lovely flat an' all, and we work hard and I got GCSEs and everything!' Then, in an 'all or nothing' confessional splurge, 'And my name's really Kellise, 'cos Mum saw someone on the telly called that when she was pregnant with me an' she said if I was a girl, that's what she'd call me. So she did. Just Sol thought "Kanga" sounded more like a posh girl that's been to boarding school and all that schizz.'

I felt a sudden rush of affection for Kanga. It was only a small rush, she'd been a complete cow for most of the time out here, but she really did sound proud of her upbringing and it must have been a struggle for her to maintain the clipped accent because her real one was giving all our ears a beating.

'You did the right thing, Kanga,' I said gently. I emphasised her name too, so she'd know that we all thought of her as 'Kanga', the posh girl with all the advantages, rather than 'Kellise from the council estate'.

'Yeah, well.' She sniffed. 'Don't want you taking all the credit for coming from nothing, do I?' But she flashed me a look that held a hint of complicity; a touch of knowing that life wasn't always easy and you could be one person's kindness away from real suffering. One eyelid dropped in a hint of a wink, and then she said, 'Don't want you taking all the glory. *Cosmo* interviews will be far more my thing than yours, you can keep *Good Housekeeping* or whatever.' Then her head came up and her hair whipped across my face as she stared around at us. 'Just, when we comes to tell Dax about this, confessing everythin' and all – can we make it that we talked somewhere other than a toilet?'

I looked down at the stamped earth floor to hide my smile. 'I'll do that,' I said and felt Mac bump my arm again in support, as everyone else murmured an agreement.

'It's gone quiet,' said Junior, who'd had his head pressed against the wall of the Portaloo, whether to listen or because there wasn't room for him to stand upright, I wasn't sure. 'I think it's gone. Or moved off the food, anyhow.'

We all held our breath. Junior was right, the sounds of crashing and plastic boxes being torn into had stopped.

'It could be waiting for us to come out,' Ruth whispered.

'Yeah, it's an animal, not a serial killer.' I tried not to sound as though I were amused by the thought of our camp-buster hiding behind the tents in dark glasses.

'It'll have eaten enough anyway.' Junior sounded definite. 'Once it's fed, it won't be interested in us, even if it is still there.'

I noticed he didn't immediately unlock the door, though.

'We have to get out there.' Mac tried to push his way through, but Kanga and I were in the way. 'I need to get to the phone to call Dax.'

'Will he come? It's the middle of the night?' I asked.

'He will if he knows what's good for him,' Mac replied, tightly. 'We can't stay out here now. Not with something rampaging around.'

'Does that mean this is all over?' Ruth sounded small. 'I mean, I know it came through my tent, but it didn't attack me or anything.'

'We won't get any money for that,' Junior said, in a tone so resigned that it sounded as though it were halfway home already. 'But we *can* prove there's *something* out here.'

'We should have sedated it,' Kanga said. Then, 'What? I'm only saying what we're all thinking. Two. Hundred. And. Fifty. Thousand. Pounds.'

'I'm going out.' Mac high-stepped over Kanga's legs, still jutting from her occupation of half of the toilet seat, hula-moved past me and unlocked the door.

Ruth and I squeaked. 'Nah. He's right. Gotta get out there.' Junior stood at Mac's side. 'Can't stay here all night. Someone's gonna need to pee and there isn't room for us all to turn our backs.'

The door swung open.

Outside the toilet, the moor was illuminated by a moon so full that the light positively burst from it, spilling over the ground in a cold whiteness that echoed the frost now forming on every surface. After the body-heated warmth, the cold felt almost unnatural, and our breath clouded the air.

'Is it still here?' Ruth was clutching at my arm, and I was holding Mac's hand on the other side. Junior, taking tiny steps, advanced towards our erstwhile food store, now so many empty plastic boxes and chilled containers spread angularly across the moorland around the camp.

'Gimme the key,' he hissed at Kanga, who was creeping along in his shadow, clearly prepared to let him take the brunt of any savage attack by a sausage-crazed quadruped.

'You can't shoot it!' Ruth hissed back at him, her grip on my arm tightening. 'We can't put it in a zoo! Remember, we agreed!'

'Being in a zoo means it won't have to come raid people's food supplies. Regular meals, healthcare...' Junior helped Kanga unwind the key from her neck, pulling her hair through and leaving it swinging in his grasp, catching the moonlight like a talisman from another world. 'It's a kindness. Now, where's the gun?'

'I'm going for the phone,' Mac said quietly. 'We need to get out of here.'

Part of me wanted to dispute the need to leave the moor, to hang in there for the last of the money, but even the desperation for a measure of financial security fell away in the face of possibly being eaten alive in my tent on a subsequent night. I needed to be alive in order to use the money we'd made, and a few extra hundred suddenly didn't seem so important.

Junior was carefully poking through the boxes in search of the gun, Mac had cautiously gone into his tent, which didn't appear to be bulging with sated beast, so was presumably as safe as anywhere else out here. The rest of us stayed in a tight huddle, Sebastian trying to form a protective barrier around Kanga and Ruth, whilst I rotated with anxiety on the periphery, in case something leaped from the shadows at us.

Above, the stars twinkled crystal clear and the moon continued to spotlight the camp, only failing to illuminate some of the more stubbornly shaded areas behind rocks. Every dark patch suddenly held movement as the wind rippled across the moor and rattled the leafless branches of trees. I was so hot with terror that I was surprised I wasn't steaming, and all of us were breathing so fast that I might have been, because it would be impossible to tell.

'Mac?' There was no sign of his reappearance, and the tent was suspiciously still. Junior had unlocked the gun case, with much fumbling and some mild cussing, as the lock was frozen shut, and was now creeping around with the pistol resting on one forearm, looking as though he meant real business. It was chilling in a whole different way to the cold of the night.

Ruth was praying, half under her breath. 'Oh, do stop that!' Kanga snapped.

'I'm asking God to help us out.' Ruth didn't even sound hurt.

'We've got an armed man for that.' Kanga pointed at Junior, who was doing a sort of cross-legged crouch around the back of the camp, with the gun winking in the moonlight. 'And I'll take a pistol over God right at this minute. Little bit more corporeal, less big on the forgiveness.'

Unabashed, Ruth carried on praying. Junior completed his walk around the site. 'All quiet,' he said, letting the gun drop to his side. 'We should secure the perimeter, though.'

We all looked at him. The moonlight glittered. 'And how do you suggest we do that?' Sebastian said finally, in an impressively level tone.

Mac slithered out of his tent. 'Dax is coming,' he said. 'He's going to take us down to the town and drive us back to Leeds tomorrow for debriefing. He wants us to be able to tell him exactly what happened. Obviously we've not got our cameras on, so we're going to have to go into detail.'

'So that's it,' I said, and my voice sounded dull. 'It's over.'

'No £250,000.' Kanga was staring out across the moorland. She shook out her hair. 'I was going to buy my brothers a car each. Oh, well. TV presenting, here I come.'

'This shouldn't be about the money,' said Ruth, with a certainty that she was too young for. 'It really shouldn't. It's a *life*. We couldn't take a wild animal and condemn it to a life behind bars.' Again, that certainty.

'Just watch me,' Kanga replied darkly. 'For a quarter of a million, I'd cage you.'

There was a moment of staring quiet. 'No, you wouldn't,' Ruth said, and she sounded different. There was an adult sureness in her tone. 'You are a good woman, Kanga, and I don't believe you would willingly do anyone harm.'

I was impressed. Kanga had berated her so horribly for her crush on Sebastian that I wouldn't have blamed Ruth for personally throwing Kanga to any creature that might be out here. Ruth had certainly reached her 'growing up' objective out here.

'Ssssh.' Mac turned his head suddenly. 'There's something still there.'

'Where?' Junior went into a crouch, gun raised.

'Over by those rocks.' Mac's voice had become little more than a hiss and he'd gone rigid.

Our huddle tightened. Kanga and Ruth and I jostled together, even closer than we had been in the toilet, almost wrapping ourselves around each other in our panic. The men grouped themselves around us, but there weren't enough of us to form a proper protective enclave so we crouched into a semi-circle of panic and fear.

'Should we go back into the Portaloo?' Ruth muttered.

'It's too far away. The animal could be on us before we got there.'

The moon flickered out from behind the muslin of cloud which had been straining its light and we were all suddenly spotlit in our hunker of fear. And Mac had been right. Over on the rocks at the opposite side of the camp sat *something*. Clear white light gleamed off fur of the deepest black and huge eyes were picked out in amber. Small, blunt ears twitched, but otherwise it was completely still.

It was the biggest cat I had ever seen.

Nothing moved, apart from those ears, ridiculously small atop a wide head. Even my heart had stopped and I could feel my blood coagulating in my veins as fear curdled all my bodily functions. The creature looked on us, lazily, unfearing. What did it have to fear, after all? It looked like a fist wrapped in fur; it could have taken us all on simultaneously and left without a scratch. Plus it was full of all our supplies, it probably couldn't move without waddling.

Junior raised the gun, very, very slowly.

The moment seemed to go on forever. Just the cat, motionless apart from the ears, watching us. Sitting with its paws splayed across the rock, tail laid out behind, for all the world like a huge domestic moggy thinking about whatever it is that cats consider when they stare at humans so unblinkingly.

When it stood up, Ruth gave the tiniest squeak. Moonlight played over a compact, solid body. Shoulders rolled under thick fur, blacker than the night around us, and there was a sense of power and intent that made the air feel as though an electric current had been run through it. As unconcerned by our presence as though we'd been nothing more than weedy saplings, the cat stepped down off the rock, elastic and graceful.

Junior raised the gun to shoulder level. Without a word, Ruth and I moved in front of it, obscuring his firing line, and Kanga put her hand on his wrist. Pushed down slightly until the gun lowered, and Mac removed it from his hand. Behind me, Sebastian gave a noise that sounded like a sob.

Without another glance, the cat paced off into the night, away from the camp. When the final lines of its sleek body had dissipated into the darkness, the almost magical tension that had held the six of us upright vanished and we sprang apart.

Sebastian dropped to the ground, face in his hands. Ruth stared down the route the cat had taken, eyes tracing the heather, while Kanga, fists balled, punched herself in the leg, muttering something about money.

Mac turned to me and I found myself in his arms, our heads close together, and I wasn't sure which of us was crying.

'I think...' I said eventually, pushing myself slightly away from him, 'that one of us should put that damn kettle on. Even giant cats don't eat teabags.'

16

Dax found us still there, a couple of hours later. The shock, or awe, or whatever it was, had largely worn off, but none of us could find it in ourselves to go to our tents. We'd shared something so improbable and astonishing that it had kept us together by the fire on that cold night. None of us had wanted to face remembering it alone. We went over and over what we'd seen, what had happened, until the worst of the shock had been worked through and we were left with fragmentary images of dark fur in moonlight, a sense of power and grace and the pure, unutterable *reality* of something none of us had believed in.

We didn't talk about not shooting it. Even Kanga didn't vocalise what she'd clearly beaten herself up about immediately afterwards. We *couldn't* have shot it. There was simply no way we could have captured something that had shared the grimness of survival on the moors with us and, by the looks of it, was doing a far better job of making it through.

There was a silent kind of acceptance that none of us would have blamed it if it had eaten us all alive.

Sebastian seemed to feel it most of all. He kept shaking his head and saying, 'I *knew* I saw a cat! I *knew* it!' as though he felt vindicated for his suspicions all those months ago. Now he knew he hadn't imagined it, it seemed to give him a new perspective, and he got a bit bossy again when we complained about the lack of sausages. I had to take him to one side and point out that he was being officious, but, to his credit, he apologised immediately and even whinged slightly himself about the fact that the cat had eaten absolutely everything even slightly edible, and all we had to sustain us was three packs of teabags and twenty-four Mars bars.

By the time Dax turned up as dawn was trying to nudge its way through the brittle lines of frost, we were all high on relief, lack of sleep and confectionary.

He was alone, driving the Jeep slowly and carefully across the moor towards us. We hailed him like a band of marooned sailors seeing the first sail on the horizon, as he manoeuvred the vehicle into camp and stopped, looking a bit stunned at the sight of the wreckage. Ruth's torn tent flapped in a new breeze, we hadn't bothered to collect up the scattered boxes and bags, some of which had been slashed into ribbons, and we were grouped around the fire as wide-eyed as a bunch of amphetamine addicts at a music festival.

We all started talking at once, following him around as he examined the mess our camp had become, each one of us trying to get our perspective across, although Kanga was, predictably, mostly trying to ascertain whether any of this would be enough 'proof' to get us the big prize.

'Sorry, no.' Dax answered her query first. 'Like I said before, we need actual, physical proof. You could have been mistaken in what you all saw, too easy to misread perspectives.'

'*Misread perspectives?*' Kanga enunciated every consonant with evident horror. 'How? It was a fucking enormous *cat*, sitting right there!' She pointed at the rock the cat had sat on to watch us. 'How were we supposed to get perspective, snuggle up next to it saying, "Look at the size of these teeth removing my arm?"'

Dax shrugged. He looked shellshocked too, as though our stunned incredulity was infectious. 'The finance department set the rules,' he said. 'Film of a cat, with people in shot for perspective, or other proof. Shame you'd all taken your cameras off, I did *tell* you to keep them on at all times.' Then, springing back, with his eyebrows indicating his pleasure, 'Bloody amazing result, though. You actually saw something, and it's coming across wonderfully. Well done, guys!'

We huddled, muttering mutinously about how much evidence would be good enough, and how one of us should have arranged to get attacked, for proof. None of us, not one, ever mentioned the fact that we hadn't shot it.

'We had to fetch the Highland contingent back. Weather closed in and they were afraid of exposure,' Dax went on, now completely cheerful. 'The Cannock Chase boys are still out, though. We couldn't find them when we went over to film, we're worried they've gone feral.' He twined his fingers in a hand-wringing motion. 'Oh, this is *so* great!'

'Not even £50,000 great, though,' I said. I'd hoped that our sighting would have been enough. Even allowed myself to believe it. Dax's shaken head and muttering about there always being the possibility of it being a large domestic cat misidentified had sent my ebullience back down where it belonged. But realism had reasserted, I'd got a small amount of money, I'd sort of reconciled with my mother and I had somewhere to go. *And Mac*, the ebullience had whispered before it retired completely, and I'd had to smile to myself.

'Well, no. But...' Dax took me by the elbow and led me away from the others, who were arguing lightly but with a tone of relief that it was over, and Mac was rifling through the Jeep to see if there were any peanuts. 'You know that sample you found?'

'Sample?' I asked blankly. 'Of what?'

'*You* know.' Dax looked like his brother suddenly. A bit cheeky, a bit cautious. 'The... scat.'

I had forgotten about that. The huge lump of poo I'd picked up from near the Portaloo. Even *I* had half-suspected that it was overflow from the waste system, but, back then, we'd still been about evidence rather than endurance.

'Mmmm?'

'I wasn't going to say anything until the end. Wanted to keep it as a "big reveal", you see, when we got you into the studio to do the final wrap up filming.' Dax took a deep breath. 'But I'm going to tell you now, and *please* try to look surprised when we film.' He looked pleadingly at me.

My heart had started to bump against my ribs. 'What, Dax?'

'London Zoo didn't know what it was. There's DNA in there, definitely big cat, but they can't say what kind. Best guess is a kind of interbreeding or something, they did explain but I wasn't really listening, they're going to email me the paperwork and stuff, but anyhow. The companies who have been sponsoring all this are happy to call it proof. You all get the £50,000. Well done.'

When he'd gone off to listen to the others giving their fourth or fifth version of what had happened out here whilst packing their belongings, I collapsed onto a boulder and sat for a moment, staring out over the moorland.

Mac joined me after a few minutes. 'Hey.' He sat next to me.

'Did Dax tell you?'

'Course he did. We've kind of agreed not to keep stuff from each other from now on. It's how Mum and Dad were managing us, stopping us from communicating by stirring up bad feeling. So he had to tell me. Anyway, I threatened to tell Junior his deepest secrets if he didn't.' Mac gave me a wicked smile. 'He still sleeps with his teddy, you know. When he's not got a better offer.'

'You think he and Junior will stick together after all this?' I couldn't help but smile.

'They're hoping so. Dax is working on getting Junior presenting another show. One with a touch more organisation and a touch less anarchy.' Mac put an arm around me, carefully but casually. 'And what about us? Will we stick together, do you think?'

I felt the relief of having money wash through me. That £50,000 was enough. It would set me up with my equipment, let me get my business running again. It would give me security, back-up, the knowledge that I could be with Mac, but that I had choices. 'Well, we can only give it our best shot, can't we?' I leaned into his arm.

'There's something else.' Mac wasn't looking at me now, almost as though he were afraid of my reaction; his eyes were combing the grey stretch of hills that rose and fell like panting breath ahead of us. 'Dax wants to spring it on you, but I don't think that's fair.'

'Mac?'

I must have sounded anxious, because his eyes met mine now. Calm eyes. Caring. It made me nod inwardly to myself in the knowledge that I could do a lot worse than Mac.

'Dax is going to use his production company to start making the sort of programmes he wants to film and quit all this "commercial television" stuff.' Mac stopped, as though that had been the sum total of what he'd wanted to say.

'Nice. But how does that affect me? Us?' I was still scanning that part-bearded, ragged face with the huge brown eyes. It was so familiar now that I could hardly remember a time when I'd not been looking at it. It felt as though Mac and I had known one another forever, but a month in a tent on a freezing moor with the threat of being eaten will do that to time. Stephen Hawking could have used us as a control group.

'He wants to make programmes to help people. He's already got backers, apparently, and they're nothing to do with Mum and Dad, so he means business. And...' Mac took a deep breath. 'They want you to become an Agony Aunt. Just a little slot to start with, maybe filming once a week, a kind of "head to head" with someone who's got a problem. Dax says that the sponsoring companies have been watching the footage and they're so impressed with your level headedness, they think you're the right person to help other people.' He gave me a little grin. 'You could be famous.'

'I can't. Kanga would hunt me down and kill me.'

'Yeah, our hunting skills aren't exactly top notch, though, are they? You could probably change your hairstyle and put on a daft accent and get away scot-free.' Mac was looking down now, at his boots. Hair flopped and curled and jiggled around his cheeks, largely obscuring his face. 'Would you do it?'

Would I? No, that wasn't the right question. *Could I?* That was more like it. What did I know about helping people, after all?

'And what would it mean for us, if you did?' Mac carried on staring at the ground. The black, peaty mud carried the marks of our panicked stampede of the night before, and, in the back of my mind, I was impressed that I could still tell all our footprints apart. 'It could mean a whole new life for you. TV exposure, a new career. I've seen what that does to people, don't forget.'

'Does it cause them to detonate on impact?' I asked. There was a bubble of something – hope, affection, amusement – deep in my chest, inflating until it forced a little laugh out of my throat.

'What?' Mac looked up now, confusion rampant. 'No, of course not.'

'Shame.' I glanced towards Kanga, who was indicating, with forceful gestures, the place where the cat had sat to watch us. Dax was listening and, I noted, had one arm around Junior, who wasn't objecting. 'Never mind. It's not going to give me a total personality transplant or anything?'

Mac had begun a little smile himself now. 'No. You'll still be the annoying cheerleader type. It might even make you worse, in fact.'

'So then.' I hunched myself a little closer to him. Close enough to put a hand up to his cheek and feel the softness of beard forming amid the scrape of stubble. Close enough to watch the conjoined steam of our breathing rise between us. 'It won't do anything but give me options. I'll have money and I'll have choices.'

Our heads moved and our breath coiled into one single entity as our mouths met in a soft kiss. 'And I think I'll choose you.'

ACKNOWLEDGMENTS

Firstly, Callum, who requested that I use his name in a book, having used his brother, Ryan's in a former novel, and not wanting to cause sibling strife... Also, my daughter Fern, who 'saw something' driving on a late and lonely road home one night and planted the seed of the idea and Richard Watson, who said I should write a book about Bigfoot (sorry, couldn't fit one into the UK) for lending me the books and DVDs.

MORE FROM JANE LOVERING

We hope you enjoyed reading *There's No Place Like Home*. If you did, please leave a review.

If you'd like to gift a copy, this book is also available as an ebook, digital audio download and audiobook CD.

Sign up to Jane Lovering's mailing list for news, competitions and updates on future books.

https://bit.ly/JaneLoveringNewsletter

Explore more funny and warm-hearted reads from Jane Lovering.

 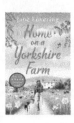   

ABOUT THE AUTHOR

Jane Lovering is the bestselling and award-winning romantic comedy writer who won the RNA Novel of the Year Award in 2012 with *Please Don't Stop the Music*. She lives in Yorkshire and has a cat and a bonkers terrier, as well as five children who have now left home.

Visit Jane's website: www.janelovering.co.uk

Follow Jane on social media:

    f facebook.com/Jane-Lovering-Author-106404969412833
    🐦 twitter.com/janelovering
    BB bookbub.com/authors/jane-lovering

Boldwood

Boldwood Books is an award-winning fiction publishing company seeking out the best stories from around the world.

Find out more at www.boldwoodbooks.com

Join our reader community for brilliant books, competitions and offers!

Follow us
@BoldwoodBooks
@BookandTonic

Sign up to our weekly deals newsletter

https://bit.ly/BoldwoodBNewsletter